The Tragically True Adventures of Kit Donovan

Patricia Bailey

Albert Whitman & Company
Chicago, Illinois

For John, who believed

Library of Congress Cataloging-in-Publication
data is on file with the publisher.

Text copyright © 2017 by Patricia Bailey
Cover artwork copyright © 2017 by Jon Lau
Published in 2017 by Albert Whitman & Company
ISBN 978-0-8075-8143-8

Printed in the United States of America
10 9 8 7 6 5 4 3 2 1 LB 22 21 20 19 18 17

Design by Jordan Kost

For more information about Albert Whitman & Company,
visit our website at www.albertwhitman.com.

Chapter One

I killed my mother. Twice, if I am to be completely honest—though she only died the one time. And since honesty was one of the things I promised her as she lay on her deathbed, I reckon honest I must be.

I made a lot of promises.

I promised I would study diligently so as not to grow "dull and stupid in this savage place." I promised that I would read—though the only books I have are her worn Bible and a copy of Mr. Mark Twain's *The Adventures of Huckleberry Finn*. And, since I am being truthful here, I must confess that the Twain book isn't even mine. I found it in Old Joe Smiley's stable when I was hiding from Leslie Granger and the passel of girls who follow her around complimenting her hair ribbons and treating her like some sort of queen. I also promised that I wouldn't hide in the stable anymore. That I would say *please* and *thank you* and *ma'am* and *sir* religiously, that I would brush my hair without complaint and take a bath every Saturday—whether I needed it or not.

I promised all of it. And I really did mean to abide by it. I would have promised her anything, even marriage to Old Joe Smiley himself, if I thought it would make a difference.

But my promises didn't matter one lick. Promises to the dying never do.

I only hope that redemption does.

Redemption brings me to the corner of Main Street and Ramsey Avenue on the day of my mother's funeral (April 3, 1905—a date I am sure will be seared into my memory), wearing a sign that reads *Mother Killer*. On my left, a bewhiskered man tied to a post slumps drunkenly, a hastily scribbled paper bearing the words *Wife Beeter* pinned to his chest. On my right, an urchin of a boy dozes, swaying against the rope binding him to the post, his stomach growling loud enough to wake the dead. The moniker *Theef* is written in newsprint on the paper he holds. Neither bothers to acknowledge me with so much as a grunt of greeting when I show up just after dawn, despite my best attempts at establishing some sense of camaraderie among my fellow wicked-doers. Even my "Howdy," is met with a blank stare and, in the boy's case, a snore.

Cretins.

Perhaps the simple fact that I made my sign myself and spelled all the words correctly has something to do with their standoffishness. Or maybe guilty folks don't take kindly to people who sentence themselves to public punishment. Still, you'd think a murderer—and a matricidal one at that—would raise an eyebrow.

In Goldfield, Nevada, I just blend in with the crowd.

Still, I am determined. There must be a way to show the world the role I played in Mother's death. Something that will tell everyone that it wasn't just bad luck or God's plan that took Mother from the earth. An action that will expose the guilt that squeezes my heart and seizes my breath when the cabin is quiet and I am alone with my thoughts and my shame.

Public humiliation seems like a good place to start.

In less than an hour, the heft of the board I painted my sign on and the roughness of the rope I used to secure it to my person have rubbed a raw and bloody spot on my neck. By the second hour, the blood seeps into the ends of my braids, making them stick to my face whenever I shake my head to displace an overly exuberant fly or dislodge the pomegranate seeds being spit at me by Evan Granger and Stewie Hines, two impossible boys from school who possess neither good manners nor good looks—but have more than enough money between them to buy not one, not two, but three pomegranates, and more than enough time to spend the morning spitting the seeds at me. And, as I am still being honest, I use a goodly portion of that hour praying they get the trots from their indulgence. God forgive me.

I spend the third hour of my punishment imagining how Jesus must have felt on the cross. The staring eyes of passersby. The nettle-like sting of raw skin. And I feel nearly holy until I remember that I am not Jesus, all brown-eyed innocence and forgiveness. I am me—Kit Donovan—green-eyed Responsibility Shirker and Mother Killer. Oh, and Book Thief. I can't forget that, though it does pale in comparison to my other deeds.

Not that I killed Mother on purpose. Even I am not that wicked. But I did kill her. First, by bringing the influenza into the cabin. Then, by failing to bring the doctor.

The influenza wasn't entirely my fault. Some of the blame lies with Miss Sheldon, who insists on weekly spelling bees and encourages the likes of Jenny DeMillo to come to school even though she is riddled with lice and vermin and what all from living in the horrid tent hotel with her father and the scores of miners who pass through Goldfield determined to strike it rich. I suppose some of the blame rests with the miners themselves, though most belongs to the town—a place that promised "riches beyond imagining" and has delivered nothing but cold and want, and in Mother's case, a cruel and ugly death.

Of course, none of that would have mattered if I had not crawled out of bed with a stuffed-up nose, then whined and complained until Mother relented and let me stay home from school to drink hot ginger tea and loll around on my cot for an entire day. Oh, and as a bonus, miss the dreaded spelling bee. The next day, my nose was clear, and I was spelling bee–free for at least a week. So off to school I went.

But Mother fell ill while I was away—and not the "recline on your cot and play hooky" kind of ill. Real ill. Fever and chills and not recognizing the people you love ill. The day after that, she died, carried away on the wings of a sickness even the old Shoshone women had no remedy for, while I stood outside the Northern Saloon, too mesmerized by dancing girls' laughter and gunfighters' curses to find the doctor I was sent there to fetch.

I am four hours into my punishment when Papa finds me. As much as I wish he would yell or curse or even cry, he doesn't. He simply picks me up—board and all—and carries me the half mile to the cemetery where the preacher is nearly finished with his "mysterious ways" blather.

I focus all my attention on the undertaker, a sweaty old man with greasy hair, clearly itching to cover Mother in dirt so he can get back to the whiskey bottle he keeps patting in his pocket. He should hide his transgressions better, if you ask me. Anyone with eyes can see the cap of the bottle peeking out of his shabby suit. As if his bulbous red nose wasn't proof enough of his weakness.

Mother hated drunkenness.

She hated it almost as much as she hated bad singing. Which is what comes next—courtesy of the Ladies' Aid Society.

Sometime during the singing, Papa must realize that I am twelve years old—much too old and too heavy for even a strong man like him to tote around. He sets me down when the first shovelful of dirt flumps onto the coffin. As soon as my bare feet hit the ground, I run, but it's all for naught, really. I will never get that sound out of my head.

The thing Mother hated most of all was dirt.

I race toward the center of town, cutting through vacant lots and skirting chicken coops, horse droppings, and workers loafing on their lunch break. The men lean against the storefronts they are building, blocking the makeshift sidewalks with legs and arms and shirtless torsos. I jump over their booted legs and skip around discarded sandwich wrappers and beer bottles.

"Where's the fire, kid?" one of the men asks as my foot clips his upraised knee. I don't apologize, and I don't slow down.

I just run.

I run despite Mr. Henderson's rooster, Henry, chasing me down Miners Avenue, pecking at my shins and flapping his wings. I run even faster when men from the telegraph office come out to watch the scene. I keep running until Mrs. Henderson herself steps out of the doorway of the Presbyterian church, blocking my path.

She snatches Henry up by his feet. "Danged kids," she yells, grabbing me by the arm with one hand while she holds the flapping rooster in the other. "Quit teasing my rooster, or I'll wring your scrawny neck."

Henry squawks at the word *neck*, twisting and squirming against Mrs. Henderson's grip. "Don't you peck me," she warns, giving the rooster a shake.

While Mrs. Henderson deals with Henry, I struggle to free myself from her clutches. Mrs. Henderson's hand stays firm around my upper arm. Like Henry, I'm not going anywhere.

"Best be careful, there, Maude," a man says, nodding at the sign still strung around my neck.

"Mother Killer." I watch Mrs. Henderson's lips move as she forms the words. Her eyes go round. "My stars," she stutters.

I stare up at her, hoping to see a flash of anger or even disgust fill her eyes. But all I see is pity.

Stupid, useless, undeserved pity.

The grip on my arm slackens. Before long, she'll be patting my shoulder and saying things like "Poor girl" and "This too will pass." That's the last thing I need. With one big jerk, I wrench free.

"Bwak." Henry flaps and flops. He reaches his neck out and pecks Mrs. Henderson on the leg.

"My stars!" Mrs. Henderson cries. The muscles around her eyes tighten, and her face turns red. There's the anger I was looking for. Only she's not directing it at me, but at Henry, who she flings to the ground in one swift motion. She rubs her palm against her shin. "It's the cook pot for you, you no-good…"

I squat down and pick up the stunned rooster. I smooth his wings and pet his head. "I won't have another death on my conscience," I whisper in what I think must be his ear. "Not today."

Then, with Henry tucked snugly under my arm, I run.

I run by all the places I walked to with Mother when she was alive. The town well. The Ladies' Aid Hall. Exploration Mercantile. Bon Ton's Millinery where she used to look at hats she knew she couldn't afford. I don't stop until I get to the electric streetlight on Crook Avenue.

Mother loved that light. She'd stand beneath it whenever she got the chance. "Progress," she always said. "This place may become a proper town yet."

It's the memory of her face lit by the magic of electricity—tired and wan but still a little bit hopeful—that finally makes me cry. I bury my face in Henry's ruffled neck and bawl all the tears that have been locked up inside me since the day I came home to find her flushed and feverish and too weak to even speak my name. When I'm all cried out, I get up and tuck Henry back under my arm. "There's no redemption in this," I tell him as I fluff his feathers. "No way to make it up or pay it off." The realization settles in my chest as I walk home in the fading light, and I know that this ache is never going to leave me—no matter how hard I try to make it right.

The sun is setting by the time I get to our cabin. I introduce Henry to the two laying hens out back, throw them some feed, and go inside. I am all run out, so I don't struggle when Papa takes the sign from around my neck and tosses it, rope and all, into the

cookstove. I don't complain when he cuts my blood-soaked hair—
even though he's making it short and crooked and too much like
a boy's. I just sit there, still and tired, while he says over and over
again, "It was not your fault."

Finally he kneels in front of me and takes my hands. "You have
to promise never to run off like that again."

I drop my head so I don't have to look him in the eye. He is so
sad and so determined, I have no choice. "Yes, sir," I lie.

What difference will one more broken promise make anyway?

Chapter Two

We moved to Goldfield nearly six months ago this week so Papa could strike it rich in the mines. He has not struck it rich.

Papa said Goldfield was a "paradise of riches" and that gold was so plentiful a man just had to bend over and pick it up. He even showed me a newspaper clipping from the *New York Times* that called the strike "sensational." Another clipping promised "an abundance of wood and water" and "above-average accommodations."

Papa made his share of promises too. A big house in a proper city. Grand dresses and parties and friends with fine names and manners. He promised that it would be different here. That people would be kind and helpful, and that Mother and I would have friends again—like we did back in Baltimore before the fire destroyed our store and our house and nearly all of Mother's good humor.

So far, not one of those promises has come true—not even the one about water, which I can't help but remind Papa whenever I set out, bucket in hand, to trudge the mile and a half to one of the public wells in town. I only wish I still had that news clipping to wave in his face.

It's funny, but Mother was the only one of us who didn't make promises. Instead, she wrote letters to her people back East. In them, she described "the dull dryness of the land, the soulless sound of the wind as it tears through our tent cabin, and the godless people who scurry from mining camp to dance hall." Even the dogs here are mangy and rude, and Mother never failed to note it—as if this detail summed up all that was wrong with this place. She asked her family to pray for us, and on good days—on days when I believe Papa is right that her death wasn't my fault—I wonder if they did. If the fever wasn't just God's way of answering all those prayers.

On bad days, I know better. No one answers prayers out here.

Most days are bad days.

It doesn't take me more than a day to break my first promise to Mother. I take off for the stable during our lunch break at school. I just can't bear to stay in the middle of all that commotion one more minute. My brain longs for quiet, and in the contest between what my head wants and what my heart knows to be right, my head wins. *Sorry, Mother.*

I don't think anyone notices me leave the schoolyard. Heck, I don't think anyone notices me at all. They are all so enthralled by Leslie Granger and her story about some dress her mother ordered her from San Francisco for her sixteenth birthday that sneaking away is easy.

Truth be told, skipping out of school at noon is never not easy. Even when the weather is pleasant, Miss Sheldon stays inside, eating her restaurant-packed lunch at her desk, away from growling bellies and covetous eyes. Only the students are outside, and they huddle around the front of the school tent, watching Leslie and laughing or sighing on cue as she sits on the lone step in front of the school door and holds court.

An especially gifted sigher might be rewarded with a store-bought cookie or a smidge of licorice. So far, Stewie holds the title, but when I hear Jennie sigh like someone punctured a hot-air balloon, I know he's got some competition today. Still, I don't stick around, sliding away from the crowd just as Leslie crows, "Oh, the lace—let me tell you about…" and Jennie releases yet another chest-heaving gush of awe and envy.

If a girl is quick, she can slink around the back of the tent, cut across Mr. Dumphey's side yard (watch out for the pig!), and end up on North Main. From there, she just has to walk with purpose to the stable. I am both quick and purposeful. And, with my newly shorn hair, I am ugly. Ugly helps one blend into the crowd, I've discovered—especially the crowd that fills the dusty streets of Goldfield. I am at the stable in no time at all.

It doesn't take me long to settle into my favorite horse stall. The smell of hay, oats, and fresh horse droppings never fails to set my head right. I take a deep breath and lean against the worn wooden railing. I dig through the straw for a moment, then breathe a sigh of relief. The book is right where I left it. *The Adventures of Huckleberry Finn* quickly replaces the schoolyard jabber in my head. There, comforted by Mr. Mark Twain's words and the muffled snorts of boarded horses, I turn thirteen years old. At exactly 2:37 p.m.—if Mother's story of my birth was accurate.

Practically a full-grown woman.

I gnaw at the skin around my thumbnail and give myself some time to let that thought settle. At first, it seems promising. Longer skirts. Upswept hair. Boys who act like gentlemen, dances, and fancy hats and perfume. Then I remember Mother. She was the one who was always so excited about stylish hair and flowing white dresses and the possibility that some boy would show up with flowers or chocolates and take me to a dance or an ice-cream social. And she was the one who promised that when I turned thirteen, she'd teach me the waltz and the one-step and show me how to glide around a ballroom like a queen.

None of that's going to happen now. I shake my head at the unfairness of it all and look down at my bare feet.

I could get shoes, though. Now that my feet will stop growing so fast, the money won't be wasted. I can get real shoes and show up to school looking like a proper young lady—just as Mother would have wanted—and maybe Leslie and everyone else will be just the littlest bit nicer to me for it.

The thought rouses me. I bury the book under the hay. "A full-grown woman does not hide in the stables," I announce to the spiderwebs and horse droppings. I smooth my skirt and fluff my hair. I plan on walking out with my head held high, but one peek out the door quashes that idea. Instead I slink out the back, avoiding Old Joe Smiley and the double-barreled shotgun he keeps on hand to ward off "trespassers and vagrants."

I will practice being a full-grown woman tomorrow.

* * *

Or not.

After washing and darning socks that are no better than scraps, sweeping the floor, tending the fire, and trying to keep the few pieces of beef we have from shriveling to nothing in a pot of potato-colored water, I am convinced that being a full-grown woman isn't such a grand thing after all. If Mother were here, I'd surely tell her as much.

Of course, if Mother were here, she'd be doing the washing and the mending and the cooking and the fire tending.

Still, she should have told me that being a woman means little more than being expected to do no less than three things at the same time—and make supper to boot. I am certain I would prefer being a man. All Papa has to do is come in from work, ask, "What's for supper?" and spend the evening with his head bent over the newspaper. He doesn't even read it aloud so I can have some entertainment as I toil away.

Some birthday.

I don't see my presents until I go to bed, and since I ended my day in a bit of snit, the sight of them perched on my pillow makes me feel a fair bit ashamed. Two newly sharpened pencils, a tin of butterscotch candy, and a brand-new blue pinafore Mother must have sewn on the sly.

Forgetting all about my guilt—and the fact that I may have muttered "lazy sot" when Papa asked for a refill on his coffee before I turned in—I race over to him in my nightgown, the pinafore clutched to my chest. "Thank you! Thank you!"

He smiles his sad smile. "I wondered when you were going to notice." He runs a thumb over the pinafore's hem. "She wasn't sure it would fit," he says, "but I think it will." We stare at the stitches. They are tight and even. Perfect. Just like her. For just a minute, it feels like she's here with us again—holding us together somehow. "I miss her so…"

Papa clears his throat and stands up. He brushes a quick kiss against the top of my head. "Now off to bed with you. It's late."

I swallow hard and force a smile. He's right. It is late. And it is much later by the time I go to sleep, tossed between the shame of my joy at new things (Pencils! Pinafore!) so soon after Mother's death, my anger at being forced to become a full-grown woman, and the sweet bliss of butterscotch melting on my tongue.

That combination may be why I am so slow to wake this morning. Papa's good moods always passed quickly, but they disappear even faster now that Mother isn't around to coax a smile and a laugh out of him. One thing is for sure—whatever patience and humor Papa may have once had died with Mother. All that's left are impatient sighs, ragged nerves, and a harsh and weary tone. Which is what I hear when I ignore Papa's "Up and at 'em" and grumble from the comfort of my cot, "Life holds no adventure. Stupid school. Why can't I go out looking for gold with you?"

"Kit." Papa sighs. "We've been over this."

"But I could get a job. I could work in the stables. I'm sure Old Joe…"

"Thirteen-year-old girls go to school."

I toss the covers off and climb out of bed. "I already know enough. More than most. I can read and do arithmetic…" I stomp across the room and point to the pamphlet about gold mining Papa tacked to the door when we first moved in. "I could prospect for gold while you're at work. That way we'd—"

"This whole conversation is childish!" He slams the coffeepot down on the table. "Ladies do not prospect for gold. They do not work at the stable or ride burros or roam about on their own."

14

I put my hands on my hips. I feel my face crease into a scowl, but I don't try to stop it, not even caring if it does freeze that way like Mother warned. "Ladies don't get to do anything but cook and clean and go to school. It's not fair!" I fling myself across the room and collapse on my cot. "Why can't ladies have adventures?"

I feel the cot sag as Papa sits next to me, and I press my face into the pillow, refusing to look at him. "You've seen how adventure has served us so far, Kit. Do you really want more of the same?"

The tears in his voice bring tears to my eyes, and I am again reminded of the promises I made to Mother. I slink from my cot and grab my clothes without another word. I ball them up and carry them out to the privy so I can change in private—and cry in peace.

I am half dressed and nearly cried out when I hear the clang of the water truck's bell. I fumble with my shirtwaist and lunge for the door. "Wait! Oh, wait," I cry as I grab the buckets off the porch. I hike up my skirt and run after the truck. "Stop! Just stop, you stupid devil truck," I yell as it turns the corner and disappears from sight. "Damnation!" I fling one of the buckets into the street and burst into tears again.

Papa's waiting on the porch. He hands me a biscuit and a piece of bacon. "You better get a move on, or you'll be late." He nods toward the bucket that's still lying in the street. "Take the buckets and stop by the well on your way home."

I stuff the food in my mouth, then grab a bucket, retrieve the other one from the street, and head off to school. The biscuit and bacon sit heavy in my stomach—settling in right next to my anger and my guilt.

But even guilt doesn't prevent me from walking to school in a pout, nor does it keep me from wondering what my old friends back in Baltimore are up to. Not sweeping floors made of dirt, or toting empty buckets across town to beg water from one of the housewives rich enough to have her own well, of that I am sure.

I miss my friends. I miss sipping lemonade and playing the piano and whispering about Kevin McDaniel and Cindy Howard holding hands on the way to the ice-cream parlor. I try to remember how I had made friends back then. Did I smile more? Or tell jokes? Was I quieter? Kinder? I run a hand over my too-short hair. Maybe I was just more normal looking?

As I approach the schoolyard, I pause to smooth my skirt and arrange my face into a smile. "I'll make a friend today," I whisper to myself as I stash the buckets in some weeds. "Just one friend." Determined, I round the corner to the school.

* * *

"Scag!" Stewie yells.

My smile fades as rocks, sticks, and handfuls of dirt whiz my way. I dart and dodge, but there really is no place to hide. The schoolyard is barren. There is not a tree in sight—another promise broken. *Someone should inform the newspaper.* Boy, do I miss Baltimore and its white oaks.

"Blob!"

"Scrub!"

"Mother Killer!" Another round of rocks and dirt zip by as I lunge out of the way. I sprint to the front of the school and am nearly at the door when another blast, a bigger blast, catches me right across the shoulder blades.

I whirl around to see who would do such a chicken-livered

thing as throw rocks at someone's back. A flash of emerald skirt catches my eye. Leslie Granger. I should have known.

I look at the scattering of rocks at my feet. There are some doozies in there. It's a miracle that blast didn't knock me clean out of my head.

It's a bigger miracle that I throw only one of those baseball-size rocks back.

But what I throw is beautiful. Doc Adkins beautiful.

I watch that rock leave my hand and glide across the playground. For an instant, I forget what I'm doing—I'm so mesmerized by the rock floating through in the air, the perfect speed and arc to hit its target. In fact, I kind of forget what the target is. At least I do until I hear Leslie cry out.

The *oomph* part of the cry is nearly silent, but the wailing part can probably be heard all the way to Old Joe Smiley's stable.

The rest of the kids are on me before I've fully come back to my senses. I'm punched, kicked, and spit on. I hear someone shrieking—high and frantic—and only begin to realize it's me when Miss Sheldon comes out of the school tent.

"What in the world?" she says as kids jump away from me, eyes wide and feigning innocence.

All but Evan Granger, who kicks me hard in the shin before walking away. "That's for throwing a rock at my big sister," he says with a sideways grin at Stewie. As if on cue, Leslie starts crying again.

"But they…" I begin to protest, but my words turn into a yelp when Miss Sheldon grabs me by the ear and twists. "In the corner, now, Miss Donovan." She shoves me inside before turning and ringing the bell. "Let's go, class."

At least my hair is too short for her to drag me by. I face the corner and rub my sore ear and try desperately to count my blessings. I've counted them all—short hair, feet to stand on, not having to sit next to smelly old Brant Dixon—before the class has finished the Pledge of Allegiance.

It's going to be a long day.

By the time school is finally dismissed, my legs are so worn out from standing that I can barely walk. Miss Sheldon either doesn't notice or doesn't care because before I can shuffle from the corner to her desk, she says, "Erasers, Kit."

I shamble back to the chalkboard to grab the erasers. Then, with a great show of limping and leg slapping, I make my way to the door. Once I'm certain that Miss Sheldon is not coming out to watch, I grab the water buckets I stashed outside before the rock throwing started. I manage to sneak two buckets of water from the school well and clean the erasers before Miss Sheldon sticks her head out the door to check on me.

At least I do not have to go begging for water or waiting in line at the town wells this afternoon. I should thank her for the punishment, really. It has saved me quite a walk and a fair bit of humiliation. As a bonus, the schoolyard is empty by the time Miss Sheldon releases me with a wave of her hand and a disdainful, "You really must grow up and become a lady, Katherine. Your behavior is tiresome."

I don't tell her that hers is too.

See, I'm already more of a lady than she thinks.

Chapter Three

I race across town, despite the tired tingles sparking my legs. I stick to side streets, taking special care to avoid Fifth Avenue and the Grangers' house—where I am sure Evan and Stewie are playing in the yard like they usually do. I don't even stop by the San Francisco Bakery to peer in the window and smell the sugar-sweet goodness. I head straight to the cabin, so anxious to get home and get supper started so Papa won't know I had to stay after school that I ignore the bucket banging against my bruised shin and the water sloshing on my bare feet. When I reach our tent cabin, I don't even bother to set the buckets down. I press my shoulder against the door and shove. The cheap latch gives, and I stumble over the threshold certain that I have beaten Papa home.

But I haven't.

Papa is not at work.

Papa is laid out on our table, ashen-faced and shaking, while the crazy old lady who lives in the broken-down cabin behind our tent hovers over him, clucking her tongue and poking at the flesh on his shoulder.

"What happened?" I cry, dropping the water buckets and rushing to hug him. Clara holds up a hand, stopping me before I throw my arms around him, but not before I see Papa wince.

"Water. Finally," she says, distracting me from Papa's pallor. She snatches a bucket from the doorway and pours the water into the kettle on the cookstove. Her pour is hurried and sloppy. Precious drops splash the floor, and I can't help but frown. My arms ache from lugging that water halfway across town. Careless woman. I open my mouth to complain, but Papa's voice brings my attention back to him.

"It's just a scratch, Kit. That's all."

Clara harrumphs. "A scratch that might still take your arm off if infection sets in."

The word *infection* shakes me out of my pout about the water. "What happened?" I ask again.

"A loose beam in the tunnel support." Papa grimaces as he shifts his weight to look at me. "Popped itself free and splintered up my arm."

Splintered up is an understatement. Sharp knives of wood are embedded in his shoulder, and it is all I can do to stay indoors while Clara plucks them out with tweezers heated white-hot. Papa talks himself through the makeshift surgery while I shield my eyes and take long, slow breaths—trying desperately not to pass out from the trauma of it all.

"It happened quicker than a thought," he muses as he looks down at the smudged bandage Clara wraps around his arm. "The ceiling gave a creak and then…whoosh. I was covered in dirt and wood. Damned lucky the whole place didn't come down on me."

Clara mutters a curse. "I lost my husband in ninety-six when one of the mines out in Colorado gave way. Killed my Malcolm and seven other men." She shakes her head like she's shooing a fly, not a memory. "It's a dangerous business," she says, sipping the whiskey she brought over for doctoring. "And them greedy bastards don't give a damn who gets hurt so long as their gold gets out."

I want to ask who she means by "greedy bastards," but by the time I figure out how to ask the question without using the words *damn* or *bastards*, Papa is taking a swig from Crazy Clara's bottle and settling back onto his bed.

Clara pats me on the shoulder. "I'll come check on him tomorrow. You don't be bothering him now. He needs his rest."

"I'm sure I can handle it." I move to Papa's bed and rearrange his blanket, tugging at the end so that it covers his feet. Pleased with the effect, I reach for his pillow. "I'll just fluff this a bit, then I'll get supper…"

"Ouch, Kit! Watch what you're doing," Papa hollers.

Clara hustles over and rechecks the bandage I somehow dislodged in my eagerness to make him more comfortable. "You'll do just fine, dear," she says, catching my arm and walking me over to the door. She pauses and regards me seriously for a long moment. "Only remember every movement is going to hurt like the devil— at least for a little while."

She lets herself out while I stew about her treating me like some sort of child instead of a proper grown woman who has seen a thing or two in this life—even if she's seen most of it with her hands covering her eyes.

"I really can manage," I whisper to myself, as I set about preparing supper. I imagine myself wiping Papa's brow and changing his bandages like a real nurse. It's not like before—not like when Mother was sick. I'm not a child anymore. I'll show that Clara—and I'll show Papa that I'm plenty old enough to take care of folks properly. Besides, what's more ladylike than helping others? I'm sure Mother would agree.

* * *

I spend the next two days living the life of a servant. Papa is the worst patient imaginable. *Demanding* doesn't even begin to describe it. "Fetch my boots." "Get the eggs." "Is that the water truck going by?" "Run, Kit!" "Be careful of my arm."

That last one really gets to me. I only accidentally bumped his arm because he woke me from a much-needed nap with his cry about the water truck. One would think someone getting such outstanding care from a round-the-clock nurse would be appreciative, humble even.

One would be wrong.

I am nearly happy the next morning when I am released from caregiving to return to school. Bless the whiskey and Crazy Clara, Papa is on the mend.

Or he is simply worn out by my *not-so-stellar-nursing* and *ever-rolling eyes*, words I heard him utter to Clara just yesterday. I am choosing not to take them to heart, because the injury has clearly unhinged his sense of propriety. Mother would certainly have reminded him that we never talk to strangers in such a familiar way.

In either case, his "Back to work for me; back to school for you" makes me smile for the first time in days. I am free. Even if freedom means Miss Sheldon and the Grangers. And, because I am in such a fine mood, I decide to approach my first day back to school with a clean slate and a renewed determination to please Miss Sheldon and make a friend.

I enjoy my newly won freedom a bit much, I must admit, and spend a fair amount of time on my way to school peeking in store windows and pausing to pet a stray cat or two. I get to the school tent after Miss Sheldon has rung the bell and have to stand awkwardly to the side as the class recites first the Pledge of Allegiance and then this week's poem (Emily Dickinson's "There's a Certain Slant of Light"). Finally, the students sit, heads bent over their arithmetic. I march right up to Miss Sheldon to tell her of Papa's accident and how I have been caring for him.

"He nearly lost his arm," I explain. "And I had to cook and clean and change the dressing."

Miss Sheldon doesn't say anything. I figure she is so troubled by the news that she needs a moment, so I pause in my telling to let her recover. When she doesn't look at me, I know I have figured wrong.

"A mining accident is no excuse for missing two days of school." She clears her throat and waits. The sudden silence fills the room, causing the rest of the class to look up from their books. Once they are all watching, she continues. "It is your duty to get an education, Katherine Donovan. You owe it to your poor dead mother and the good people of Goldfield who pay my salary so you won't grow up slovenly and ignorant and drain society of its goodwill and coffers."

Whatever that means.

Miss Sheldon raises her eyebrows and taps her ruler on the desk. I know the meaning of that. I am dismissed.

I return to my seat without uttering so much as a "Yes, ma'am." I don't even bother to open a book or raise my hand or stand and recite the entire morning. I put my head down on my desk and scribble the word *coffers* over and over onto the scratched wood until my pencil lead breaks. Then I just sit and fume.

I used to like Miss Sheldon. I thought she was pretty and charming and right smart for a southern woman and a blond to boot. But now, I'm not so sure.

Finally, the clock on her desk shows twelve, and Miss Sheldon takes off her glasses. "Lunchtime," she announces. Before I can lift my head from my desk, Miss Sheldon sets a cloth and a bucket beside my chair. "Cleaning time for you, Katherine. Get some water, then start scrubbing these desks. I want them gleaming by the time lunch break is over."

Gleaming was on last week's spelling list. *Gleaming* was the word I went down on in the spelling bee.

G-l-e-a-m-i-n-g.

I'm no imbecile. I can spell. There's just no way on earth I'm going to stand up next to Leslie or Stewie in my cast-off clothes and spell a bunch of words no one here knows the meaning of.

I made that mistake once. When I first arrived in Goldfield. I stood up, proud as could be, and out-spelled the lot of them— all the little kids and then the older ones, one by one, until the only people left were me and the two oldest students—Stewie and Leslie. I took Stewie out easily with *scurrilous*, biting back a smile when he stumbled over the *r*'s. Then I bested Leslie on *acrimonious*.

I should have known from the way Leslie cut her eyes at me when she took her seat that I had made an enemy. But sometimes I'm a little slow to pick up on such things. It wasn't until I sat on the front step to eat my lunch while basking in the glory of spelling-bee victory—a victory that had me beating kids an entire four years older than me, mind you—that I'd realized I'd made a mortal mistake. This girl was more than just rich and pretty. This girl was in charge.

Leslie had nodded to the others and stood with her hands on her hips as they dragged me off the step and across the schoolyard. I lay in the dirt, trying to make some sense out of what was happening, while she picked through my lunch. "Feed this to Dumphey's pig," she said, shoving my biscuit and apple into Jenny DeMillo's outstretched hands.

A flicker of longing crossed Jenny's wan face. She pressed the biscuit to her thin lips, then turned and ran behind the school tent. She returned and stood at the base of the step.

Leslie turned Jenny's face back and forth, then checked each palm. "You didn't eat any, did you?"

"No!" Jenny shook her head so hard her braid bounced against her cheeks. "Not a bite. Swear to God."

I could hear her stomach growl clear across the schoolyard.

Leslie patted an empty space on the step next to her, and Jenny squeezed into it, smiling wide.

I got up and walked over to the Dumpheys' side yard. The pig was chomping on my apple. The biscuit lay in the mud, soggy and brown. Jenny didn't lie. Not a single bite was missing. I watched the pig finish my apple and vowed that I wouldn't stand up and spell a single word correctly again, no matter how many spelling bees Miss Sheldon arranged. I'd go out in the first round—bungling the first baby word I was given. And I have.

But Miss Sheldon couldn't know that. Could she?

Still, I don't complain. The punishment is fair, and even I know it. It is wrong to write on the desk—no matter how unjust Miss Sheldon is. As I scrub away at the pencil markings, my anger fades. I start to think that it could be worse. At least Miss Sheldon didn't embarrass me in front of the class while I was ruining my desktop. I dip my cloth into the bucket and scrub harder.

But when I see her at her desk, sharing a bakery-bought chocolate turnover with Leslie Granger and laughing, I scowl and wring the cloth until it squeaks. Miss Sheldon is nothing but a low-down climber trying to get into the good graces of wealthy mine owners like the Grangers. She doesn't give a lick about me or my "poor dead mother."

That realization gives me an idea. An idea that may end with me hiding in Old Joe Smiley's stable, sure, but an idea too wonderful to ignore.

* * *

"Katherine, we will hear your essay now."

I grab the essay entitled "Our Heroic Founding Fathers" from my desk. It is neatly written and full of wonderful insights about standing up to tyranny and living honorably. Before I changed it, it would have earned me an A, I am certain. It truly was that good.

Mother would have been proud.

I carry the revised essay to the front of the room, taking the orator's place behind Miss Sheldon's shabbily built lectern. I stare out at the class. I clear my throat and try to erase the image of Mother's disapproving face from my mind. Finally, I begin.

"If the good people of Goldfield can't come up with a better school than a dirty old tent and a better teacher than a slow-talking old maid from Georgia who says *cud'n* instead of *cousin* and *hep* instead of *help*, then they have bigger troubles than me."

Miss Sheldon gasps so loudly I'm surprised the walls of the school tent don't fold in. The students sit round-eyed and gape-mouthed. I pause for a moment to take in the scene. I can feel a smile tickle the edges of my lips, but I contain it. Then I continue.

"As Thomas Jefferson wrote, 'All men'—and I think by men, he meant women too—'are created...'"

I stop. Miss Sheldon's gasp has turned into a sob. A series of sobs, really. And then a high-pitched squeal. "Katherine Donovan! You will..."

I don't hear the rest. I am ashamed to say it, but I run. Straight out the door and across Mr. Dumphey's side yard. I don't stop running until I make it to Old Joe Smiley's stable. I dive into the stall that I have begun to think of as my own and try to catch my breath.

I am still doubled over, breathing hard, when Old Joe himself spots me.

"Get out of that stall, girl. You ain't got no business in there."

I hold up a hand, desperately hoping he won't unload his shotgun on me. When I finally catch my breath, I explain what just happened.

Joe's bushy eyebrows go up as I relate my tale. "I had to run. Once she stopped crying, she'd have whipped me for sure."

"I reckon you're right about that." Joe scratches his chin, then spits a stream of tobacco juice over the stall door, splattering the hay and barely missing my foot. "Keep an eye on that mare," he says, pointing to the bay in the stall I am hiding in. "She gets a mite antsy from time to time."

So I stay. I read *The Adventures of Huckleberry Finn*, and when the mare gets the fidgets, I read it right out loud to her. Something about Huck's story settles us both down as calm as can be. I guess sometimes it's just nice to hear about a person who's in a worse fix than you are.

I get so caught up in the story that I don't even hear the school bell mark the end of the day's lessons. The sun is nearly set when I wipe my eyes and put the book away. I pat the mare on the flank as a good-bye, then I run for all I'm worth, hoping I beat Papa home.

I don't.

"You'll apologize first thing," Papa says when I walk in the door.

I should have taken Miss Sheldon's whipping. Papa's slowly shaking head and refusal to look me in the eye are much worse. My stomach clenches. I think back on what I said and feel my skin flush hot.

"Yes, sir. I'll go early, before school even starts."

"No." Papa's voice drops so low I have to lean forward to hear him. "You'll apologize to her in front of the class. And you'll apologize to them for ruining the lesson and disrupting their learning."

Apologize in front of everyone? I picture Leslie Granger's smug smile. Evan's smirk. The whole class staring at me, laughing at me.

I shake my head, slowly at first, then rapidly—desperately—as the enormity of what Papa expects takes root. "I won't do it!" I cry. "Not in a million years. I won't. You can't make me."

Papa doesn't say a word. He rubs at a stain on his shirtsleeve, not even bothering to look my direction.

My yelling cascades into bawling. Ugly, loud bawling. "Can't you just whip me?" I sniffle. "You can whip me every day for a week. You can make me fetch water or haul dung or…" I cast around, desperate for a chore, for anything I can offer that will get me out of humiliating myself in front of everyone tomorrow.

Papa shakes his head. "You will apologize."

My heartbeat pounds in my ears. "It's not fair," I cry. "This is all your fault! You're the one who brought us to this stupid place. You're the one who said it would be so great." I gulp. "If Mother were here, she'd…"

Papa's eyes flash at the mention of Mother, but his voice remains calm. "You'll apologize."

"Maybe you're the one who should apologize," I mutter. I stalk around the room, feeling like a bear on a too-short leash. "Maybe you should apologize for being such an utter failure."

Papa opens his mouth to speak, then closes it with a snap. He takes a deep breath and lets it out slowly as he stares down at the floor. "I'm going to pretend I didn't hear that."

A lump forms in my throat. I try to catch his eye, but he keeps staring at the floor. "Fine. I'll apologize," I say, trying to keep my voice heavy and even. "I guess I'll die of embarrassment, and you'll have to sweep the cabin and make the fire and chase the water truck yourself. That'll show you." Another sob escapes me, and I have no choice but to hurl myself on my cot and collapse under the weight of my tears—only now I'm not sure if I'm crying about having to apologize or if I'm crying about the awful things I said to Papa.

Chapter Four

The morning comes far too quickly. I sulk over my breakfast, too sick with dread about having to apologize in front of everyone and shame over what I said to Papa to eat a bite.

"Chin up," Papa says as I leave for school. "A good, honest apology never hurt anyone."

"We'll see about that," I mutter, not bothering to say good-bye.

I slink into the schoolyard just as Miss Sheldon rings the bell, trying to ignore the churning in my stomach as I make my way to the door.

I walk up the aisle and stand next to my desk. I close my eyes, shutting out the glances my classmates cast my way as we recite the Pledge of Allegiance. I keep my head down and mumble through the recitation of this week's poem. As the class triumphantly shouts the final "Excelsior!" and takes their seats, I silently wish I were dead in the snow like Longfellow's traveler, instead of standing here alone, waiting for Miss Sheldon to recognize me.

Miss Sheldon methodically makes her way to the board and oh-so-slowly writes out today's date. She turns around, chalk still in hand. "Yes, Katherine?" she asks, lowering her glasses and settling her stern blue eyes on me.

The class titters. Students shift in their seats. I hear Evan's laugh and see Leslie whisper something to Jenny DeMillo.

I take a deep breath and begin. "I want to apologize for what I said yesterday. It was mean and wrong." My words come out in a rush so that *mean* and *wrong* sound like one word. *Meananwron.* I take another breath, close my eyes, and press on. "And I want to apologize to the class for..." What was it that Papa said? "For messing up the lesson."

The silence nearly kills me. I open my eyes to Leslie and Jenny sticking their tongues out at me.

"I'm sorry," I say, but I doubt Miss Sheldon can hear it over the class's laughter. Thankfully, she doesn't ask me to repeat it.

"Take your seat, Katherine," Miss Sheldon says before turning back to the board. "Class, arithmetic."

The laughter subsides as the first group of students goes up to the chalkboard to complete today's problems. I grasp the back of my chair and breathe a sigh of relief.

I did it.

And I didn't die.

By lunch break, I'm actually feeling pretty good about things. I did well in arithmetic and even remembered how to diagram a particularly curly sentence full of prepositions and dangling something or others during grammar. I'm feeling so good that I decide to stay for the whole day. No running off to the stable for me. I spread my lunch out on the ground next to the makeshift baseball field and eat. I'm toying with a biscuit and watching some of the younger kids toss a ball back and forth when Evan and Stewie sidle up next to me.

"S…s…s…orry," they stammer in unison. Stewie pitches his voice high but keeps it loud so that everyone in the schoolyard can hear. Evan is too taken by the giggles to continue, so Stewie asks, "Did your daddy make you apologize?" He makes a sad-eyed pouty face and pretends to rub his eyes like he's crying. "Poor, sad Kit ca…"

My good feelings wither and something inside me snaps. I jump to my feet and punch him in the gut before he can finish the sentence. Whatever he was about to say is lost in the whoosh of air he expels as he bends over, clutching his stomach and gasping for breath.

"S…s…s…orry," I singsong as I gather up my lunch. I'm already through the Dumpheys' side yard when I hear Miss Sheldon ring the bell.

I race to the stables, intent on getting to my stall and back into Mr. Twain's story so I can forget all about Stewie and Miss Sheldon and the Grangers. I slow down a little when I get close to the bay mare's stall, so I don't startle her. But before I can reach it, I trip and end up facedown in straw and dirt and horse droppings.

I force myself to a sitting position and shake straw from my hair. A Shoshone boy reclines against the wall, reading *The Adventures of Huckleberry Finn*, his long legs stretched out in front of him. No wonder I tripped.

"That's my book," I say and wipe what I hope is mud from my cheek.

The boy looks at me and blinks his bright-green eyes. He stares the way you do when you've been reading something hard and aren't exactly sure where you are yet. Finally, he comes to his senses.

"This here book?" he says all innocent-like. "Why, I've been reading it for the better part of a week now, and I didn't see no girl's name in it."

He's got me there. There isn't a *Kit* or *Katherine* or even a *Katie* written anywhere in that book. There is an *LM* on the inside cover, though, and I have to admit, I never did bother to ask around after him.

"Are you *LM*?" I fidget with my skirt, scared of the answer. "I was just reading the book. I didn't ever take it from the stable. I wasn't trying to steal it or nothing."

The boy laughs and sticks out his hand, proud as you please. "I'm Arnie."

His laugh makes me laugh. It turns out Arnie is nearly as far into the book as I am and just as antsy to see if Huck will help Jim to freedom or turn him in to the slavers.

I think he'll help, friends being friends and all, but Arnie is convinced that Huck will turn Jim in and collect the reward "…'cause that's mostly how folks are."

I consider his words and what he might know. He's older—old enough to be out of school surely, though I wonder if they even let Shoshone kids go to school here. He may even be as old as seventeen. I study his face, his clothes. Everything looks worn. Neat and clean, but frazzled around the edges. Everything but his eyes, which are bright and sparkling and serious too. Like he's taking everything in and forming an opinion on the spot. There's a good chance he might be right about Huck Finn.

I sure do hope he's wrong, though.

"Toss ya for it," he says, holding up the book and digging into his pocket for a coin. "Winner gets to read it today. Loser gets it tomorrow."

"I'll take heads."

The coin lands in Arnie's hand showing its tail, so he will get to know what happens to Huck before I do. Normally losing like that would bother me, but there's something about the way Arnie smiles—and the fact that he doesn't gloat about his good luck—that makes me almost happy.

"I'll leave it here in the stall. You can pick it up tomorrow, then put it back the next morning," Arnie says, settling in against the now-fidgeting mare. "If it's here in the stable most of the time, it's not quite stealing," he explains. "Ol' LM can come and claim it anytime."

I guess I agree, though I doubt Mother would. Semantics, she'd call it. Mother hated semantics.

Papa's not a fan of semantics himself, so I don't fudge my story too much when he asks how my apology went. I tell the truth, mostly, and only skip the part where I punched Stewie in the stomach. I may as well admit to the running off; he's sure to hear it from Miss Sheldon sooner or later. "The kids were teasing me something awful," I explain. "So I hid in the stables. I was just afraid I'd do something or say something and get in trouble all over again."

Papa puffs his breath out of his mouth and shakes his head. He walks over to the chest where he keeps Mother's things and takes out her Bible. "Sit here and read this. There's bound to be something in there that speaks to staying in school and behaving like a lady."

"But what about supper?" I ask. "I haven't finished cooking the beans."

"I'll do it. You just read." He shakes his head again.

So I read, and when the beans are done, I read and eat beans. I keep reading while Papa washes the dishes and reads the paper and takes a trip to the privy. Finally he declares, "Bedtime."

I put down the Bible, hoping he doesn't ask me what I've learned because I didn't find anything about school or ladies or even stealing books. Just a long list of begats and something about a silver cup in a sack. But Papa doesn't ask. He just waits for me to call "ready" when I'm settled into my cot, then he blows out the candle, and I'm left in the darkness with nothing but the wind and the lines from a foreign-sounding book for comfort. I try not to think about Arnie, who gets to read all about Huck Finn and the raft and whatever adventures he's getting into next.

Some people have all the luck.

Boys, mostly.

But even that doesn't make me as mad as it usually would, nor does it keep me from remembering Arnie's smile or the way he waved and said, "See ya later," when it was time for me to leave. Could I have made a friend? The thought leaves me giddy, and it's all I can do not to shake Papa awake and tell him all about it.

Maybe my luck is changing after all.

Chapter Five

Maybe it has nothing to do with luck. Maybe it's simply choice. Mother used to say that each day you get to choose who you will serve. Of course, she was mostly talking about serving God—and she usually brought it up when I was doing something she considered unladylike or particularly lazy.

Still, this week has been different. Easier somehow. Not that anything has changed. Kids still chase me around the schoolyard and throw rocks at me when Miss Sheldon isn't looking. Stewie and Evan tease me about my hair and my clothes, and Leslie still sticks her tongue out at me every chance she gets. But somehow it doesn't bother me nearly as much as it used to. Even Miss Sheldon's exasperated sighs aren't making an impact. Instead, I spend my days in school thinking of Arnie and Huck Finn and feeling special—like I have a secret treasure that no one else can touch.

Which may explain how I've managed to stay in school for nearly one whole week. Well, four days, really, but it's still a feat worth celebrating. No running away at lunchtime. No hiding all day in the stables. I even complimented Miss Sheldon on her reading of John Keats's "Ode to a Nightingale." And I didn't laugh—at least not out loud—when Leslie Granger was knocked out of this week's spelling bee by the word *etiquette.*

I figure such stellar behavior deserves a reward, which is why I've convinced Papa to give me some money to go by Larson's Department Store for their Big Slaughter Sale. Papa needs a new pair of work boots and some socks, because I am tired of trying to find enough fabric in the ones he has to hold a darning needle.

Of course, most of the good merchandise is gone by the time I get there—dang Miss Sheldon and her never-ending lectures—and I am left to wrangle with Mr. Larson himself over the price of three pairs of mismatched socks and a not-too-worn pair of used work boots.

"Two bits for three pair," I say, holding up the socks. I like dealing in bits since it sounds nothing like dollars and cents—both of which are too scarce to talk much about.

Mr. Larson nods about the socks but refuses to budge on the boots, so I am stuck paying full price. I slowly count out the twenty-five cents for the socks and the $2.25 for the boots. To tell the truth, I would willingly pay twice that amount and be happy to do it if it meant I could put away my darning needle for a spell and stop swiping cardboard to seal up the holes in Papa's boots.

I count out the change. Two dollars left. I smile, eager to show Papa what a good shopper I am and how careful I can be with his money.

That is, until I see the hat on my way out the door. Dusty brown and broad brimmed, with a rounded crown. Clearly it's a man's hat, but when I try it on, it fits. I pull the brim low over my eyes and step out on the sidewalk to test its effectiveness. Then I go back inside to find a mirror.

It doesn't look half bad. It will keep the sun out of my eyes whenever Papa pushes me out of the tent to find dung for the cook fire or to fetch water from the truck. It will also serve double duty, being a bit of a disguise on the days I want to hide from my schoolmates or blend in with the crowd. Who's to say that's not worth $1.90? Not me, and not Mr. Larson, who is so happy with my purchases that he tosses in a small bag of jelly beans and bids me good day.

I don't start to regret my extravagance until I get home and put all of the change—a lone dime—on the table. It looks so small sitting there, and my purchases look so trifling sitting next to it. Papa doesn't say a word. He just frowns at the mismatched socks and turns the boots over in his hand, feeling the leather and searching the soles for weaknesses. He doesn't even acknowledge my hat. Nor does he listen when I list its many uses.

Instead, he hands me a letter, scoops up the dime, and says, "I'm going to a meeting tonight. You ought not wait up."

With an attitude like that, why would I? But even Papa can't tear down my good mood, and I just smile sweetly. "Have a good time."

Once he's gone, I put the hat back on my head—no sense not getting all the use I can out of it, now that it's bought and paid for—and turn the letter over in my hands. It is addressed to Papa, but I know instantly why he didn't open it. It's from Mother's sister, my aunt Minerva. Papa never cared much for Aunt Minerva. I guess he doesn't care much for Aunt Minerva's letters either—and now that Mother is dead, he doesn't have to pretend that he does.

My feelings about Aunt Minerva are a bit more complicated.

Mother always held her up to me as the shining example of lady-like behavior—and before Papa got a factory job and we moved to Philadelphia and I actually met her in person, I imagined her to be some sort of princess. Pretty and helpful and proud in all the right ways. And she is all those things, but she is also bossy and short-tempered and the biggest tattletale I've ever met. Not that Mother noticed those things. Mother simply loved her, and she never missed a chance to say how I reminded her of Aunt Minerva. That I was smart and outspoken and even pretty sometimes, and that if I was extra good, I might grow up to be a fine lady too.

I open the letter carefully, slitting the envelope with a knife and sliding the stationery out slowly so I don't tear the delicate paper. It takes me a few minutes to get used to Aunt Minerva's fancy hand-writing, what with all those extra loops and swirls she uses, but once I manage it, I read quickly, eager for the world of parties and dresses and hairstyles that she always wrote to Mother about. But no descriptions of fine meals or fancy linens fill this letter. There are only anger and blame and what would be, if Aunt Minerva weren't such a fine lady, the strongest cussin' you can imagine.

Harsh words, underlined and circled and marked darker than the rest, express in detail Aunt Minerva's gross dislike for Papa—for his lazy ways and for the poverty that led to Mother's death. She doesn't exactly call him a murderer, but she does say that her "dear departed parents will not rest in their graves until the one responsible for their darling child's untimely death is brought to justice."

That sounds like murder to me.

My vision clouds. I crumple the paper in my hand and get up

from the table. Part of me wants to lash out—to find something to break or hurt. But then I remember the other day. Didn't I blame Papa for Mother's death too? Isn't that what I meant when I told him that everything was his fault? Maybe I really am like Aunt Minerva—and not in just the nice ways.

I sit back down. I straighten out the paper, smoothing it against the table. I imagine Aunt Minerva wrote this letter after sitting in her plush company drawing room, sipping weak, sugar-sweetened tea, and talking with her friends about how it's better to be old and alone than "cleaved to the breast of a man of Papa's ilk."

Of course, any way I imagine her, she looks the same. Exactly like the portrait hanging in her sitting room. Her hair is done in a complicated upsweep; her immaculate white dress is neat and trim; even her shoes are shiny and tightly laced. Nothing is out of place. "No matter the state of her emotions, a lady must always remain cool and collected." That's what she'd tell me when I came in spitting mad at one of the neighbor children or the brigade of the bullying old bats that attended her society parties and loved to boss and badger and pick at my hair, my wardrobe, and my manners.

No wonder Papa didn't want to read her letter. I wish there was a way that I could unread it and get it out of my head. The best I can do is tear the pages in half and take them to the privy. I do my business, using part of Aunt Minerva's letter to clean up. Then I toss the remaining pieces on the privy's paper pile.

Papa may as well have his say too.

* * *

It turns out everyone wants Papa to have his say. Mr. Westchester of the *Goldfield Times* newspaper is coming over today to interview

Papa about the mining accident. He's writing an article about the conditions of the mine and thinks Papa's injury might be important to his story. I think Papa is reluctant to say his piece, though. He flits around the cabin, stacking up newspapers and tidying the bedding. He snaps at me to sweep the floor, then snaps again for me to stop. "You're just stirring up the dust," he says, snatching the broom out of my hands and shoving it into the corner.

I'm tempted to ask just how he would suggest I sweep a dirt floor without making more dust, but one look at his flapping hands and red face closes my mouth. I pull my stool over to the window and try to disappear into *Huckleberry Finn* while Papa paces.

Mr. Westchester is right on time and all business. He declines the coffee Papa offers and gets straight to work asking questions and scribbling in the little notebook he pulls out of his breast pocket.

Papa doesn't say much, though. He answers Mr. Westchester's questions quickly: Name? "Samuel Donovan." Age? "Thirty-six." Employed by? "Hiram Granger, owner of the Goliath Mine." Union Affiliation? "Yes, but not active."

Finally he tells Mr. Westchester about the accident, but he doesn't say anything about Clara tweezing out the sharp shards of beam or how his arm was too swollen to use or how it still hurts him. He just says that it was a "minor injury" and talks about how he hopes that the workers and the mine owners can come to terms on a system that is "safe and good and prosperous for everyone."

Mr. Westchester writes all of it down, taking special care with the last part. He reads it back to Papa. "That right?" he asks.

Papa rubs his bad arm and nods.

"Anything else you want to say?" Mr. Westchester presses.

Papa shakes his head.

Mr. Westchester shrugs. "That's it then. Watch for the piece in the paper. It should run early next week." He closes his notebook and places it and his pencil back in his pocket. He shakes Papa's hand, a tight smile on his face.

He smiles the same tight smile at me and leaves. I watch him walk, shoulders hunched, to his horse and mount. He moves slowly, like a man much older than he is.

I think Mr. Westchester was looking for a more fiery quote—something like Patrick Henry's "Give me liberty or give me death" or even Huck Finn's "All right, then, I'll go to hell." Something that would get people talking and launch a real revolution between the workers and the mine owners. Something that would keep the paper in stories and give the readers heroes and villains and gossip and scandal.

I say as much to Papa.

Papa runs a hand across his eyes. He looks tired and nearly as old as Mr. Westchester looked when he got on his horse. "I am not the man to start a revolution, Kit. Not if you'd like to continue to have a roof over your head and food in your belly."

I do like both of those things, scant as they are, so I don't ask any more questions. But I wonder, don't people who start revolutions like those things as well?

Chapter Six

Papa comes out of his sulk about Mr. Westchester's visit late in the afternoon. "Put on a clean dress," he tells me. "I've got a surprise for you."

I hustle into my pinafore and a clean blouse. I pour water from the bucket and splash it on my head, trying to get my hair to lie down flat for once. When I meet Papa outside, I see that he has changed into his blue dress shirt and has slicked back his hair in a fashion not terribly different from mine. I scowl and rub a hand over my head, mussing my hair. Better to look like a yucca plant than some sort of dandy.

We're nearly to Fifth Avenue before I hear the music. A grin busts out on Papa's face. His eyes twinkle as he looks down at me. "How do you feel about monkeys?" he asks with a wink.

Monkeys! I race toward the music, tugging his hand.

"Wait up." He laughs. "They're not going anywhere." He hefts me on his shoulders as we press against the gathering crowd. I stare over the heads to the makeshift stage. It's a circus! Monkeys leap and turn somersaults, while more monkeys stand on the backs of goats, riding them like cowboys ride wild stallions in the Wild West shows back East. On another part of the stage, dogs perform tricks, jump though hoops, and howl along with a man playing the piano like some sort of motley music troupe.

"Welcome to Cozad's Dog, Pony, Monkey, and Goat Circus," a man in a fancy dress coat and bright-red pants booms to the crowd. "Let us entertain you!" At that, one of the monkeys does a terrific flip in the air and lands on the back of one of the ponies. The crowd gasps, then laughs as the monkey tips his tiny hat at us. "We have the best acrobats in town," the man says, pointing to the animals on the stage, "and free pony rides for the kids."

We clap and laugh at the animals' antics. Sometimes Papa's shoulders shake so hard that I have to grab him by the ear for fear of being flung off. "They're every bit as good as people," Papa says after the final skit that pitted the dogs against the monkeys in a pie-throwing fight.

The woman next to us nods. "Sure are," she agrees. "We should get them to set up shop here. This town sure could use some entertainment that doesn't involve drink."

"Or singing by the Ladies' Aid Society," I chime in.

The lady frowns and turns away in a huff. Papa laughs, then lifts me off his shoulders and sets me on the ground. "Let's get a better look at those ponies." He leads me to the end of the block where three hundred ponies are milling around a vacant lot. Little kids clutch the ponies' manes and ride them in a circle, yelling with glee or crying and begging to be let off. Papa and I ignore the ruckus and find one of the older ponies grazing by himself near the fence. I reach out a hand to pet him. He rests his forehead against the fence and whinnies as I scratch him between the eyes.

"He likes you." Papa smiles at me. "He must know…"

"Donovan." The man's voice comes from behind us, big and loud enough to make me jump. The pony jerks his head up, snorts, and gallops across the field.

"Hey, you scared…" I turn to face the man. Papa grabs my hand and gives it a tug. I shut up and gawk. The man is large, not as tall as Papa, but wider. Heavier. He stands with his legs spread out beneath him like he's trying to take up as much space as possible. His hands hug his hips. A gold ring sparkles on his left pinkie.

"Mr. Granger." Papa nods and turns to the girl standing next to the man. "And this must be your daughter, Leslie."

I tear my eyes from the sweaty-faced man and stare at Leslie. She looks fresh. Bright-eyed and pressed like she just stepped out of the house. Not at all like someone who has stood in the street watching an animal show all afternoon.

"Don't address my daughter," Mr. Granger growls, pushing Leslie behind him. I try to catch her eye, but she stares over my head, biting her lip and fighting back tears. Granger steps forward. Papa's grip on my hand loosens, but he doesn't let go. He shifts his weight so most of his body is in front of me.

Granger leans close to Papa. He raises a meaty hand and points a fat finger at Papa's face. "I hear you've been talking."

Papa holds up a hand and takes a step back. "Whoa, now. I don't know what you think I said…"

Granger works his jaw. His mouth curls into a sneer. "You shouldn't have said anything at all."

"I just answered his questions." Papa shakes his head. "I told him about the beam coming down. That my arm was hurt. That's it."

Granger spits, then wipes his mouth with the back of his hand.

"You better hope that's all they print."

The color rises in Papa's cheeks. "Look, I don't want any trouble." Papa's voice is low and hard—harder than I've ever heard it.

"I guess we'll have to see about that," the man says, dragging out the words. He balls his hands into fists. "Let's go," he growls, lurching away from us. Leslie scrambles after him, head low, hurrying to keep up, but staying just a little bit out of his reach.

I tighten my grip on Papa's hand. "Let's go home," I whisper. My voice is shaky and so are my legs as I follow Papa through the crowds. It isn't long before we can no longer hear the music or the thrum of the crowd, and all that's left is the crunch of our footsteps on the dirt and a deafening silence where words and laughter should have been.

* * *

The very next day, Papa's friend Tom stops by for a visit. He and his little brother, Jesse, have struck it rich! No more working another man's mine for them. The good news is enough to break up the worried frown that's taken over Papa's face since our run-in with Mr. Granger.

Tom drinks our coffee and eats our bread like a man possessed. I cannot help but stare. *Sorry, Mother.* His hair is scraggly and crusted with dirt; his clothes are stiff with sweat and God knows what all; and his beard is wild and foul. He says he's been working on their Baby Sister claim day and night for weeks now, with scarcely time to eat or sleep, and I believe him. The dried food in his beard looks like it's been there awhile.

Men are disgusting creatures.

Papa doesn't seem to mind Tom's filth, though. They stay up

late into the night, long after I've settled into my cot for the evening. I listen to their stories of big strikes and dry holes and stock tickets worth less than the paper they are printed on.

Tom says he gets the assayer's report on the gold they found tomorrow. "If it's good, we'll borrow some money and start digging the shafts." His voice trembles with excitement. "This time next year, we'll be richer than Croesus."

I close my eyes. My eyelids dance with visions of bright-gold specks. If only Papa would do something, maybe we could be rich too. Then we could build a fine house and have our own well and clean clothes and even a dog. If only he would act. Buy a mine. Discover a claim. Something so that he could make his promise to Mother come true—even if it's too late for her to see it.

Papa doesn't seem to be thinking about his own riches, though. He just keeps talking to Tom about how happy he is for him and how solid his plans are for working the mine. "You'll be your own man," Papa says wistfully. "No answering to a boss. No worrying about keeping a job or struggling and sacrificing to keep a roof over your family." Papa shakes his head, then smiles. "You've done it, man. You've really done it." They talk like this for hours. First spinning plans for production, then appreciating the simple good fortune of it all. Finally, Papa bids Tom good night.

I listen as Tom stumbles around the room and lays his bedroll out under the table. I watch his feet move from beneath the blanket Papa hung to separate my cot from the rest of the cabin. ("A full-grown woman needs her privacy," he informed me the night he hung it.) Some privacy. Tom snores all night long and mutters and mumbles right out loud about gold strikes and claim jumpers and a fine suit of clothes. I have to wonder if Jesse isn't a little bit relieved to be shut of him for a couple of nights. I know I will be glad when he leaves. I doubt my staying up all hours of the night because of some rangy miner is something Mother would be very happy about. Perhaps I will mention it to Papa tomorrow. And perhaps I'll urge him to go out prospecting for a mine of his own.

I am too tired to say anything to Papa in the morning. I am even too tired to fight with Leslie Granger at school, despite her making fun of my pinafore, which I scalded while trying to light the cook fire this morning in my staggering half-asleep state. Part of the hem is now scorched and raggedy and so far from new that when I look at it, I want to cry. Dang that smelly Tom and his endless snoring.

I am still tired when school lets out, but instead of going straight home, where I am sure Tom is yammering on about the assayer's report, I detour down First Street, peering in windows and trying to decide how to get Papa to start searching for a claim of his own. I'm staring through the glass at the Ladies' Aid Hall, watching the women set up tables and frown at one another, when I hear what sounds like firecrackers.

Only it's not firecrackers.

It's gunshots!

I jerk around. A man barrels down the street on his horse. Two men race after him on foot, pistols in hand. The man and his horse jump onto the sidewalk just in front of where I am standing. He grabs a rifle from his scabbard and takes cover behind his mount. "Get outta here," he hisses at me.

My breath catches in my chest. Bullets thwack against the

wooden sidewalk. A woman screams. I cast about for a place to hide. The Ladies' Aid Hall is no good—the entrance is all the way around the corner—and everything else seems farther still. I stand there, frozen in space, until the man shoves me into the street.

"Run!" he snarls, raising the gun to his shoulder.

The crack of the rifle propels me forward. I run across the street, dodging back and forth like a jackrabbit, panting and praying, "Please, please, please," under my breath. I duck into an office just as a bullet thumps into the window frame. The bell on the door rings when I slam it shut.

I pause for a minute, trying to get my bearings. A short man crouches under the bookkeeper's desk, while three more men push themselves into corners and hunker behind chairs. I squeeze myself into a narrow space behind one of the safes, hoping against hope that the hard steel will save me from a stray bullet. I gasp when a tall, skinny man grabs me by the collar and hauls me out. He shoves me hard into the center of the room and slides into the space behind the safe himself.

I dart around the room, but all the hiding places are taken. Finally, I fling myself to the floor, certain I am about to be killed or overtaken by tears and mad enough to not really care either way. To my surprise, instead of dying or crying, I commence to swearing—and swearing loud. I run through every curse word I know and am starting over from the beginning when the shooting stops.

For a long moment, the only sounds that can be heard are the men's rapid breathing and my voice, screeching "pigface" at the top of my lungs.

It is not my most ladylike moment.

The men slowly make their way out from under desks and from behind chairs. They back out of corners and from behind the safe. They stare at me—wide-eyed and twitchy-tailed—while my swearing fades away.

I sit up. I am certain Mother is not smiling down at me from heaven.

"How in the world did you get in here?" the short man asks.

"How do you think?" I say through a sudden onslaught of hiccups.

"Why didn't you crawl under something?"

I point to the tall man who won't meet my eyes. "He took my hiding place."

The men look at the tall man in disbelief. Then they all burst out laughing. "Leave it to old Jack," one of the men says, slapping the tall, thin man on the back. "Sacrifice a girl to save your hide." He shakes his head, but he can't stop the smile spreading across his face.

"You have to forgive him," he tells me as he reaches out a hand to help me off the floor. "Old Diamondfield Jack here probably figured they were coming for him."

Diamondfield Jack reaches in his vest pocket and pulls out a bag of chocolate drops. He presses the bag into my hand. Then he grabs his hat and saunters out the door. I can hear the glass of the broken front window crunch under his boots as he walks down the sidewalk. The man who told me to run slumps against the Ladies' Aid Hall. Drops of blood splatter the sidewalk.

My knees buckle, and I stumble. "Is he dead?"

"You shouldn't see this, little miss," the short man says, catching me by the arm before I fall. He places his hand over my eyes and leads me to a chair.

I shake my head, trying to clear the fuzziness out of it. I fumble with the bag of chocolates and frown. I feel weird: hot and cold, excited and exhausted—all at the same time. I mash a hand down on my knee to quell the shaking.

"You're not going to faint now, are you?" one of the men asks. He sets a short glass of brown liquid on the desk next to me.

"No," I mumble as I put one of the chocolate drops in my mouth. Then another. Gradually, the image of the man slumped across the street fades and I can once again focus on what's happening in the room. I finish the candy while the men sweep up the broken window. Once the sweet chocolate taste has faded from my tongue, I take a drink from the glass.

"Good Lord!" I sputter, spewing the liquid out in a stream. My eyes tear up, and I am rendered speechless—engulfed by a full-body coughing fit that bends me over at the waist and racks my very soul.

The short man rushes over to me. "What the hell are you giving her whiskey for?" he asks, taking the glass from my hand. "You trying to kill her?"

"I thought it'd calm her down." The other man looks at me and shrugs.

I cough, hiccup, and gasp all at once. The short man fetches me some water, which I drink in one big gulp.

"I'm okay," I say, waving my hands around my face. "It was just…hot."

"I bet." The short man shakes his head. I peer out the window again. The man is gone. A woman comes out of the Ladies' Aid Hall with a bucket and begins washing the blood from the sidewalk.

I close my eyes and say a little prayer for the dead man's soul. Then I thank the men for their hospitality. The short man smiles, showing his dimples. He reaches in his pocket and takes out a small piece of lead. "A souvenir," he says, handing me the bullet.

I roll it around in my hand. It feels both heavy and light at the same time. I recall the rifleman's hissing voice, the sweet tang of sweat rising from his horse's flanks, the *thwack* of the bullets striking the sidewalk, the long jackrabbit run across the street. The bullet is a fine keepsake. "Thank you," I whisper.

I walk home on trembling legs, going over the events of the last hour in my head and trying to put them in order so that when I tell Papa, it will all make sense. I'm not sure whether I am excited or scared. Whether I will talk about how brave I was or climb in his lap and cry like a baby.

Once I reach the cabin, Papa doesn't give me a chance to speak. He's too excited. His eyes sparkle as he tells me the news of Tom's assayer report. His gold is worth $175 per ton, which, according to Papa, makes it one of the finest strikes in the camp and worth a huge loan from the bank. "It's big, Kit. The claim is right next to the Goliath mine, and Granger's already trying to buy them out."

"No way we're selling," Tom says, puffing on a fat cigar and leaning back in his chair. He's cleaned up some. His hair is less scraggly, and his food-catching beard appears to be brushed and crumb-free. A shave would have been nice too, but "a gentleman isn't made in a day," as Mother would say. At least he no longer stinks, which makes being in the same room with him almost pleasant. Well, it would be pleasant without the cigar.

Mother hated people who smoked. She hated people who smoked indoors worst of all.

I tend to agree with her on that—especially today. I've had a hard enough time breathing this afternoon.

"Tom brought you a fine sandwich from the Louvre Restaurant for your dinner, Kit," Papa says, pointing to the table. "And a surprise for dessert. He and I are going out to celebrate."

I smile my thanks at Tom and feel a smidge guilty for wishing he was gone and I had Papa all to myself. I keep my thoughts to myself, though I hug Papa good-bye a little harder than usual, an act that surprises him into a stammer.

"I—I—I almost forgot. This came for you today," he says, handing me an envelope. He pats me on the head before closing the door.

I turn the letter over in my hands. I can tell by the handwriting—it's from Aunt Minerva. Only this time it's addressed to me, Miss Katherine Donovan of Goldfield, NV. All thoughts of the gunfight and the fine meal fade from my mind.

Why is Aunt Minerva writing to me?

I pace about the cabin, the envelope in hand.

I take it to the table and prop it up against Papa's lantern.

I stare at the envelope, analyzing every dot and swirl of Aunt Minerva's writing while I eat my sandwich (roast beef with fresh onions, tomatoes, and lettuce on soft bakery bread). I fiddle with the letter while I finish off the fancy strawberry cake that is my treat. Once I'm full, I take a knife off the table and slit the envelope open. I pull out the letter. The paper is heavy. Tan and rough.

I run my fingers over it, then almost unfold it before it dawns on me. This just might be Aunt Minerva's way of blaming me for not caring for Mother properly. For letting her die in this godforsaken place with no real doctor to tend to her or proper man of God to give her comfort.

My stomach churns. I see myself standing outside the Northern Saloon the night Papa sent me for the doctor. I felt the same way I felt walking home tonight—scared and excited at the same time. Scared for Mother who was sick with fever. But excited to be out so late at night. Excited to be in front of the saloon with fancy women and hard-eyed men shouting and laughing and dancing up and down the sidewalk.

I'm sure I looked for the doctor, but the women wore such fine dresses and the men such big hats, and everyone moved around so gaily that it was hard to get a good look at anyone. I stayed there a while, staring and listening and even asking people if they knew where the doctor was. No one knew. And I was too afraid to go inside and search for myself.

So I went home. Alone. And Mother died.

I push the letter back in the envelope. I take a deep breath and tear it into long, thin strips. Then I take the paper to the privy and dump it in the hole.

I don't need to read Aunt Minerva's words.

I have more than enough to feel guilty about.

The night is long. The wind whips through the tent, and even though I wrap myself up tight in two blankets, there's something about its lonely howl that chills me down to the bone. Papa doesn't come home until late. I think about telling him about the gun-fight, about throwing away Aunt Minerva's letters, about Arnie and Huck Finn, and how sorry I am about skipping school and talking back and all the things I've done wrong since Mother's death.

But when I hear his bed creak and his boots thump on the dirt floor, I know he's not going to peek behind the blanket wall to check on me.

I tuck the bullet under my pillow and don't say anything at all.

Chapter Seven

No wonder it was so cold last night. It snowed! I am so glad neither the bullets nor the whiskey killed me yesterday. I wrap my arms around myself in a sort of hug. I didn't think I'd ever see snow again—not way out here in the Nevada desert.

I race through my breakfast, then pull on Papa's old work boots and clomp to school, admiring the newly whitened landscape. What a perfect morning. There is no prettier sight than that of a Joshua tree covered in snow, I decide then and there. Not that they are really a tree. Not like an oak or a maple or even an elm. But they are right pretty for such a scraggly bush. I must remember this when I start missing Baltimore so much.

I jog up to the school just as Miss Sheldon rings the bell. I'm cold and flushed, but so happy that I even offer her a "good morning," before taking my seat.

By noon, all that lovely snow has turned into rain, and my mood is no longer cheerful. Water seeps in the canvas roof of the school *drip-drip-dripping* onto students' heads and plunking in puddles on our desks. Even the walls of the tent leak, and almost immediately the whole place smells of old canvas, musty wool, and wet dog—though the shaggiest thing in sight isn't a dog at all, but

Brant Dixon's bushy hair. By the time Miss Sheldon releases us for the day, my desk is covered by a small lake; I am chilled through from being rained on all day; and the streets have turned into a muddy bog.

I slog down the road, happy that I wore Papa's boots, even if they are way too big and look like clown shoes on my slender feet. I flop down North Main Street, too wet and tired to bother avoiding puddles.

When I reach Ramsey Avenue, I notice a circle of men gathered outside the Texas Saloon, slapping each other on the back and jeering at someone. I look around for the target of their fun and see a Pierce Arrow motorcar stuck in the mud in front of the saloon. A tiny man with a handlebar mustache stands beside it, kicking the front tire and shouting some of the finest curse words I have ever had the pleasure to hear.

I only wish I had come across such an exhibition before yesterday's gunfight. Think of the cussing I could have done then.

The tiny man's cursing is so passionate that I stand with the saloon men and watch, not worrying about my damp hair or my soaked feet. Eventually, the spectacular swearing stops. The man slaps his hand down on the hood of the car, like the automobile is a mule refusing to budge, then turns and walks away.

"Get a horse," someone yells as the mustachioed man disappears around the corner. Then the men file back into the saloon, and I am left to continue my trudge home.

I squint at the people I pass on the muddy road. No one says hello. Most don't even look at me as they plod through the rain and the muck. I wonder if anyone would help me if I got stuck in the mud. If someone would stop and pull me out, or if they'd all just gather in a circle and point and laugh at my misfortune.

If I had any money to wager, I'd bet on them laughing.

The thought makes me so sad that I keep my head down and plunge through the puddles, one slippery step at a time. By the time I reach the cabin, I am so splattered with mud and filth that the scalded hem of my pinafore now looks no better than a stained cleaning rag. Lacking the twenty-five cents for a bucket of water from the truck, I set an old pan outside, hoping to catch enough rainwater to clean my clothes and myself.

Of course, that's precisely the moment it stops raining.

Blasted desert weather.

How I long for a warm bath and a clean set of clothes. And a fire that burns more than it smokes. I curse the cook stove, Papa, and Tom Fisherman, the Shoshone man who found the gold that gave Goldfield, Nevada, its spot on a map. Then I wrap myself up in Mother's old quilt and cry myself to sleep.

Papa's voice startles me awake. "I don't care, Clara. I won't be part of any trouble." I wipe my eyes and peer around the curtain. Crazy Clara is standing at the door, a wrinkled newspaper in her clenched fist.

"Someone needs to stand up." She tosses the paper down on the table in front of Papa, who sits slumped in his chair, a steaming cup of coffee in front of him. "Or you're all going to get covered up down there."

Papa stands, grabs his hat off the table, and walks out the still-open door. Clara frowns at his back. "It's only a matter of time before someone gets killed working Granger's mines," she yells after him.

He doesn't turn around.

Clara sits down at the table. I come out from behind the curtain and sit across from her. She takes a drink of Papa's coffee and says, "One of the mines caved in. Trapped two men under all that dirt and rubble."

"Did they find them?"

Clara nods. "They managed to dig them out in time. But just in time."

I try to imagine what it must have felt like, trapped in the dark, covered in dirt and rocks and what all. I shudder.

"I nearly got shot," I say. "I skip school. I'm rude to Miss Sheldon. I stole a book." I swallow the tears that are beginning to clog my throat. "I've broken just about every promise I made to Mother."

Clara takes another sip of the coffee. Even with her wandering right eye, her gaze is steady, and I realize that she doesn't look crazy at all. She just looks kind.

I close my eyes and put my head down on the table. "Do you think I'm evil, Miss Clara?"

A rough hand settles on my forearm. I lift my head and open my eyes. Her gaze hasn't changed. She studies my face with her soft gray eyes for a long moment. Then she laughs. The sound is full of *s*'s due to her missing front tooth. She pats my arm before taking another drink of coffee.

"You've just got a mind of your own, Kit. That ain't evil, though folks will treat you poorly for it just the same."

* * *

Papa is up early the next morning. So early that I am pretty sure he didn't sleep at all. The newspaper is still on the table, only now it is unfolded. The headline is blurred, but I can still make out two of the words: *Dangerous Mines*. "They printed Mr. Westchester's article?" I ask, leaning over the paper.

"Yep."

"And he really did quote you. See here…" I poke the paper with my finger. "'Mr. Donovan winces as he rubs his arm, saying it's just a "minor injury."'"

"Yep," Papa says.

I keep reading. "He left out the thing about finding a solution though," I say when I reach the end. "He just said something about wanting things to be 'safe and prosperous.'"

"Appears that way." Papa scoops up the paper. He folds it and sets it next to the cookstove.

"Don't you want to keep it?" I reach for the paper, taking out the page that holds the article. I set it on the table and run my hand over it, trying to smooth out the wrinkles.

"You can save it if you want. Tuck it away in your box, though. I don't want it lying around."

I refold the page neatly and stash it in my keepsake box, right between the old cloth doll Mother made me and a peacock feather I found floating in a puddle outside the Northern Saloon. I take a deep breath. A feeling of pride for Papa and for Mr. Westchester wells in my chest. They aren't anything like those men who stood around hooting and hollering when someone needed help. They spoke up. They did something.

Clara barges into the cabin, interrupting my thinking. At least she's not yelling today. Papa offers her a cup of coffee, and they sit at the table talking softly about unions and safety measures and "standing up."

Their hushed words follow me as I walk to school. I cannot stop thinking about Papa and Mr. Westchester and all those revolutionaries who stood up despite the threat to their roofs and their bellies. And I can't help but remember how I stood and laughed yesterday when a man needed help. And how, just a few days earlier, I sat down and ate chocolate while another man lay bleeding in the street.

I scrub a hand over my face. My whole body feels heavy. I stare down at my feet as I walk to school, too ashamed to lift my head. I don't think I've ever stood up for someone else. Not really. Not like Papa or Mr. Westchester or even Huck Finn.

I wonder what Huck Finn would do in this situation. Would he tell Mr. Westchester the truth of Papa's accident, or would he simply keep his mouth shut and his head down, even if it meant good people could be hurt?

Chapter Eight

I think on it all day at school. I have plenty of time because Miss Sheldon is out sick, and we are left in the care of the school board chairman who does nothing but read the newspaper and tell us all to sit quietly and practice our figures. By noon, I have decided.

Huck Finn would talk to Mr. Westchester. He would do the brave thing—the thing that everyone else is too mean or too old or too scared to do. And I reckon if Huck Finn can be brave—despite being practically illiterate and a bit of a ragamuffin to boot—so can I.

I manage to stay in school all day. I sketch out Papa's story in my composition book to help me get the facts straight. The school board man dismisses us an hour early, and not even the goody-goodies like Leslie and Stewie bother to correct the mistake. I skirt by the students shouting and laughing at their good fortune and head straight to Broadway Street.

I find Mr. Westchester at his reporter's desk at the *Goldfield Times*. He is shuffling through papers and muttering to himself when I approach. He recognizes me immediately. "Miss Donovan," he says, clearing a pile of books off the chair in front of his desk. "What brings you to the *Times*?" He takes off his glasses and rubs his eyes with the palms of his hands. "I suppose you have a complaint about the article too."

"No, sir. I—I came to talk about Papa's accident." I drag my finger through the dust on the armrest of the chair. "I think there's more to say."

Mr. Westchester puts his glasses back on. He squints at me through the round frames. "You want to talk...on the record?"

"I guess so."

Mr. Westchester looks around the room. I follow his gaze, curious. Stacks of newspaper clutter up desks and lay scattered across part of the floor. Tin cups and plates of half-eaten food rest on a table set up against the far wall. A mouse peeks his head out from under one of the paper piles and twitches his whiskers at me. A tired-looking boy slumps over some sort of machine, picking up blocks and putting them down again, while an old man with a grizzled beard leans back in his chair, snoring softly.

No wonder newspapers get the facts wrong all the time. I don't think I've ever seen a more disorganized place. I can only imagine what Mother would say.

While I'm contemplating the mess and Mother's response to it, a Shoshone woman emerges from the back room wielding a broom and humming to herself. She taps the broom in front of the mouse, which skitters away, nails clicking against the hardwood floor. I recognize her. She was part of a group of women who brought herbs to the cabin when Mother was sick. She showed me how to make tea with them and helped me spoon drops of it into Mother's chapped mouth. My stomach lurches at the memory. I turn to go, certain this is all a mistake, when the woman smiles.

Her eyes are kind, and I see recognition in her gaze. My scowl turns into a smile, and I wave. "Hi."

"Hello," she says. "You doing all right?"

Mr. Westchester looks at me and frowns. "I think it's best if we do this interview elsewhere," he says. He grabs his coat off his chair. He puts his finger to his lips in a shush motion and tiptoes out of the office.

I shrug my shoulders and wave a quick good-bye to the woman. Then I follow Mr. Westchester out the door.

He leads me down the street and to the back porch of the Brown Palace Hotel. He sits on a step, takes out his notepad, and raises an eyebrow at me.

"It's time someone stood up," I say. "Like Huck Finn or Thomas Paine."

Mr. Westchester's lips twitch into a sort of smile.

"I don't think Papa told the whole story."

Mr. Westchester nods.

I tell him all I know. It all comes out in a gush, and I don't know how much sense I make, but Mr. Westchester listens, writing it all down in his little notebook, same as he did when he came to talk to Papa. He doesn't interrupt or ask me questions. He just lets me talk.

I tell him all about Papa's injured arm and how he thought the "whole place was going to collapse" on him. I tell him about the long hours Papa works, and how he comes home too tired to even eat some nights. I tell him how we have little money and scant food and no new clothes ever despite Papa working so hard. Finally I tell him how Papa's arm still isn't quite right.

"It pains him even now—especially in the early morning. Some days he can't even bend it at the elbow. It just stays stick straight." I hold my own arm out in front of me, elbow locked, to demonstrate.

"What do you think needs to be done?" Mr. Westchester asks.

The question gives me pause. I didn't expect Mr. Westchester to ask me my opinion. I ponder for a moment, considering everything I've heard Papa and Clara and even Mother talk about since we arrived in Goldfield. I feel a little mixed up inside. Nerves and pride and hope that this will make a difference get tangled in my mouth, and I have to swallow hard before I can speak. "I guess I think that the men ought to stand up. They ought to tell Mr. Granger to fix the mines, or they'll stop working until they are safe. Until they know the beams are strong and secure and the whole thing won't come crashing down on their heads."

Mr. Westchester scribbles it down. I stand beside him, trying to read what he's written, but his chicken scratch is too difficult to decipher.

He says it back to me, word for word. "Anything else?"

I bite my lip and consider. "Well, I guess I don't like the way they keep the animals—you know, the mules and the burros who help haul the ore. I don't like the way they make them stay down there in the tunnels their whole life. Papa told me about it. How all that time in the dark makes them blind. It's cruel."

Mr. Westchester writes this down too, which makes me feel good. Throwing in a word for the animals can't hurt. It's surely what Huck Finn would have done.

Mr. Westchester shakes my hand. "Thank you, Miss Donovan."

"Will the article be out next week?" I ask, remembering what he told Papa last time.

Mr. Westchester taps his pencil against his lips. A smile lights his eyes. "Sooner, I think. Maybe as soon as tomorrow morning."

I suppress the desire to jump up and down with excitement and hold out a sweaty palm for Mr. Westchester to shake. "Tomorrow," I say. "Wonderful." I hop off the porch and walk home, nodding and smiling at every person I pass. I can't wait until Papa and Clara see tomorrow's paper. They'll really have something to talk about then. And so will I. I imagine Miss Sheldon calling me to the front of the class to explain my views on mine safety. Maybe the story will spread. I picture myself talking to President Roosevelt about how it's everyone's job to stand up and speak out about injustice— even injustice to burros. I don't even try to bite back my smile. I finally did the right thing—and it sure feels good, even if no one knows it yet.

* * *

The newspaper is spread across the table when I get home from school the next day. The front page blares *Special Edition* in big, bold letters. Below that, in large type, it says: *It's Time to Strike!* Smaller headlines, like *Mines Unsafe, Union Organizes,* and *Mine Worker's Family Exclaims, "Enough!"* scatter the page.

"Mine Worker's Family." That's me! My pulse buzzes in my ears as I skim the article, looking for my name.

The article tells how Papa was "gravely injured" in an avoidable mining accident, and how it was high time for the workers to "reclaim what is rightfully theirs." Mr. Westchester goes on to say how the workers are being "exploited" (whatever that means) by the owners and leasers, and that such injustice will not stand.

And there's my name! Mr. Westchester even quoted me, ("Kit Donovan—the waiflike daughter of the injured man") saying that the workers should "stop work until the mines are safe and the men are treated justly and not like burros." That's not quite what I meant when I mentioned the burros, but it sure sounds fiery.

I must say, I appear every bit the revolutionary. Patrick Henry and Huck Finn would be proud.

I take a deep breath and stand a bit straighter. Mother always said that you could tell a person's character by the strength of their posture. I am certain Patrick Henry did not slouch.

Papa comes in just as I finish reading the entire piece for a second time. I hold the newspaper up to him. "Did you see?" I ask, pointing at the part where my name is mentioned. "Front page too."

Papa nods. He rubs the muscles around his jaw. "It's nearly time for supper, isn't it?"

My smile turns into a scowl. "I guess so."

"Well?"

I get up from the table and head over to the crate that holds our food supplies. Supper. I may have fixed everything, and all he cares about is supper! The blood rushes to my face as I rummage through the box, pulling random items out and setting them on the table. "Are crackers and cheese and sardines okay?" I fold my arms across my chest and glare at him.

"Fine." He takes his hat off and hangs it on the hook near the door.

I set two plates on the table and pour him a cup of coffee. "Can I take it with me tomorrow?" I ask, pointing to the paper. "To show Miss Sheldon and the other kids?" I can't wait to see Leslie's face when she sees my name in print. I bet she's never been quoted in an actual newspaper.

Papa shrugs and shakes his head. "I guess," he says through pinched lips. He sits down at the table and runs his hands through his hair.

"Is something wrong, Papa?"

He raises his head and looks at me. His eyes flash. He slams his fist against the table. "Damn it," he mutters at the tabletop. He rubs his forehead and shakes his head again. "I thought you'd have better sense than to pull something like this." He picks up the newspaper and crumples it in his hand. "You shouldn't speak of things you know nothing about."

I search his face, trying to figure out what's made him so angry. "I was just…"

"Sticking your nose in where it doesn't belong." His voice is low and strained.

I feel my face go red. I was only trying to help. To keep him from getting killed down there in the darkness. "But Clara said that someone had to…"

He smacks his fist on the table again. "I don't give a damn what Clara said!"

I take a step back. Tears fill my eyes. I can't remember the last time Papa yelled. "But, I thought…"

He takes a deep breath and lets it out slowly. He unclenches his fist and lays his hands on the table. His voice goes flat. "Don't you see, Katherine? What you think doesn't matter one lick in all this." He sighs again. "And what you thought has done nothing but stir up a nest of trouble. Trouble that will not be easy to make right."

"But I…"

Papa just looks at me with his sad eyes and shakes his head.

I lower my head to avoid his eyes. Part of me wishes he'd hit the table again. Or swear. Or something. Anything. But he doesn't. He doesn't say another word to me the rest of the night.

Sometimes silence is the worst type of yelling.

Chapter Nine

The newspaper is still on the table in the morning. I flatten out the creases, then fold it carefully and stick it inside my lunch pail before Papa comes in from using the privy. I carry it to school and am pleased to see Miss Sheldon is back and as healthy as can be—with neither hollow eyes nor a lingering cough to show that she had been ill at all. Praise God, I guess, because even though I don't particularly like her, I do not want her to die.

I wait until the entire class is bent over their readers before I go up to her desk. "I'm glad you are better," I say.

She looks up with wary eyes. "Yes, Katherine?"

I unfold the newspaper. "I thought you might like to see this." I point to the headline. "They quoted me."

Miss Sheldon's eyes sweep over the newsprint. She snatches the paper from my hand and deposits it directly into the trash can next to her desk. "We have no time for such claptrap. Back to your seat."

I shuffle back a step and stare at Miss Sheldon. A flash of anger tingles throughout my body, and my hand twitches for the trash can. "Why?" I yelp. "You…" But I have no more words, and even if I did, Miss Sheldon wouldn't hear them.

"Shut your mouth. You're catching flies," she says before turning her attention back to her lesson book.

I snap my mouth closed so hard my teeth click. My brain reels with questions and protests and a few extra-bad curse words. I stand there silently fuming for a long minute before slowly walking back to my desk.

The class titters as I sit down. They titter again when I refuse to stand for recitation. They don't stop tittering until Miss Sheldon grabs me by the elbow, hauls me up to her desk, and strikes the knuckles of my right hand three times with a ruler. "Nose to the wall, Katherine," Miss Sheldon says.

"You are...claptrap," I say, biting back the curse words that fight their way out of my mouth. "You and this stupid school—you're all claptrap."

Miss Sheldon hauls me back to her desk. The class doesn't make a sound as she strikes me three more times. Whack. Whack. Whack. I don't say anything when she sets the ruler down, and Miss Sheldon doesn't say anything when instead of heading to the corner to face the wall, I stride down the aisle and out the door.

I manage to still the shaking that has taken over my body until I've gotten out of the schoolyard. Then I move slowly. My body feels broken, and it hurts to breathe. I don't know who I'm madder at—Miss Sheldon for treating me so roughly or myself for thinking she'd be at all interested in what I've done. *Stupid...stupid...stupid...* The word echoes in my head as I stagger down the street. *Stupid, stupid girl.*

Papa all but called me that when he saw the article. And Miss Sheldon couldn't even be bothered to read it. Hot tears fill my eyes. Maybe the whole thing was a mistake. Maybe standing up is something other people do.

When I finally reach the stable, I stagger into the bay horse's stall and slide into the corner. The horse rests her head on my shoulder as I try to read, but my red and swollen hand hurts too much to hold the book. I press my sore knuckles against my mouth, roll over on my side, and cry myself to sleep.

* * *

Shouting and yelling men startle me awake. I jump up and look around. Fire? I don't smell smoke, and the mare is calm. She flicks her tail at me—to show her annoyance at my sudden movement, I am sure—but her eyes are dark and steady. Most likely a bar fight.

I run my hand through the horse's mane and lean my head against her neck, smelling her sweet scent and letting my pounding heart find its regular beat. I squint into the night. How long was I asleep? A full moon shines down, cutting through the darkness. It's well past sundown. Papa will be furious.

I walk out the huge front doors of the stable and into the street. The yelling is louder now. The voices are sharper. A crowd of men gathers in front of the Miners' Union Hall. People line the sidewalks on both sides of the street, watching.

I spot Mr. Westchester standing outside the Texas Saloon and push my way through. I cram myself into the space next to him. "What's going on?"

"Union meeting." He takes off his glasses and rubs the lenses on his shirt. "Looks like something's got them a bit riled up." He winks at me.

The newspaper article. My stomach tightens. "Papa."

I scan the crowd for him. I think I see him slouched against the Union Hall building, his hat pulled low over his eyes. He looks like he's trying to fade into the wall, like he'd rather be anywhere than where he is—stuck in the middle of that group of men.

"Here comes Mr. Granger!" a man yells.

Mr. Westchester settles his glasses back on his nose and peers down the street. "And Mr. Hines," he says, scrunching up his nose like he smells something bad. He points at the heavy man walking next to Mr. Granger. "Local union organizer," Mr. Westchester snorts. "More like local union apostate."

"What?"

"Turncoat. Local union turncoat."

"Oh."

Mr. Granger and Mr. Hines stop in the street in front of the Miners' Union Hall. A few men shout, "Hoorah," but most grow quiet, watchful. Mr. Hines says something to the crowd. I am too far away to hear the words, but I can see several men step aside and make way for them. Once they reach the sidewalk in front of the hall, what's left of the shouting fades to a murmur. Almost immediately, the crowd breaks up. Men wander down the street, voices low. Several duck into the saloons that line Main Street. Others head for the Louvre Restaurant.

"I guess that's the end of that," Mr. Westchester says.

The breath I am holding comes out in a whoosh. I want to say *Good.* I want to say *At least no one got hurt.* Instead I ask, "What do you mean?"

He waves a hand at the scene. "No one wants to cross the big boss man." He laughs a sharp and ugly laugh and turns to go back into the Texas Saloon. The crack of a gunshot stops him.

We both whirl around and stare across the street.

The men remaining in front of the Miner's Union Hall scatter. Mr. Granger staggers into the street, clutching a smoking pistol. "Self-defense. It was self-defense," he shouts. He points his free hand toward the building. "That agitator threatened me!"

Mr. Hines stands beside the body of a man slumped in the mud next to the sidewalk. He holds up a hunting knife, shouting, "A knife. He had a knife. He'd have killed you for sure, Mr. Granger!" He waves the knife in his hand like he's stabbing the sky. "He'd have killed all of us."

Whispers fill the air around me. "Who was it?" "Who's the agitator?"

Someone bumps my arm. "Did you see?" The woman plucks at my sleeve. Her hair is falling loose from its fancy updo, and her eyes are wild—wide and rolling. "Did you see who it was?"

I don't answer. I can't. All the noise and all the sights fade. The only thing I can see is the light of the moon glinting off the blade of the knife Mr. Hines grips in his hand. A knife I recognize as surely as I'd recognize my own face. Papa's knife. And there, slumped in the mud in the streets of Goldfield, is Papa, dark blood pooling onto the ground in front of him.

Chapter Ten

I pull myself free from the woman and run across the street. I kneel in front of Papa. Smoke rises from his tattered shirt. His entire chest is wet with blood. His head is thrown back, and his mouth gapes in an unspoken "oh." His eyes are wide open and empty. "Papa?"

I lay a hand on his sticky chest, patting at the smoldering fabric of the shirt. The blue one. Mother's favorite. I search the faces of the men nearest me. "A doctor?" I ask. "Will someone get a doctor?"

"No use," one of the men says. He scratches his head and spits. "The undertaker will be here shortly, I imagine."

"And the sheriff," a voice from the sidewalk adds.

"Don't mess with that body!" Mr. Hines yells from where he stands next to Mr. Granger. "It's evidence."

Evidence. I look again at Papa's face. The wide *o* of his mouth. The expressionless eyes. I fight the urge to run back to the stables. To bury myself in hay and horse sweat until all of this is finished.

I close my eyes and will my lungs to breathe for what feels like forever, but must be only a second or two. I drop onto my bottom, settling in next to Papa in the mud. I take his hand in mine and wait. "See, Papa, I can keep my promises." I brush his hair across his forehead with my free hand. "I can keep my promises just fine."

Sheriff Earp shows up before the undertaker. He rests his rifle on the sidewalk, takes off his wide-brimmed hat, and kneels down next to me and Papa. He places the tips of his fingers on the side of Papa's neck. Slowly, he reaches over and covers Papa's eyes with his palm. When he removes his hand, Papa's eyes are no longer staring. They are closed. Gone.

I cover my eyes with my hands.

"Sorry, girl." Sheriff Earp rests his large hand on my head for the briefest of seconds, then stands and addresses the crowd. "I will take each of your statements one at a time." He positions his hat back on his head and picks up his rifle. "Granger. I'll start with you."

"It was self-defense," a voice shouts out from the crowd. "No question about it."

"Man was a known agitator!" another voice shouts.

The crowd buzzes around us.

Sheriff Earp nods. "Granger?"

Mr. Granger walks toward Sheriff Earp, the pistol still clenched in his hand. Together they walk down Main Street. Mr. Westchester runs behind, fumbling with his notebook. I watch their backs fade as they turn onto Elliott Avenue and disappear out of sight.

"This your kin, girlie?"

I look up to see the watery eyes and red-veined nose of the undertaker. The same man in the same sweat-stained suit who managed Mother's burial just a month ago. I gag at the sight of him, and the small amount of lunch left in my stomach erupts out of my mouth, splattering the ground and my bare feet.

The man wrinkles his nose and backs away. "He yours?" he asks again.

I nod and rub the back of my hand across my mouth. "He's my pa."

"We'll get him ready for the ground."

My body begins to shake. First my knees, then my wrists and hands. The ground is cold against my feet, and I shiver, remembering Mother's funeral. The deep dark of the hole. The scratch of the shovels. The flump of the dirt hitting Mother's coffin. I grasp Papa's hand and scoot closer to him, shielding him with my body. I stare up the undertaker and shake my head a determined no.

The undertaker sniffs and reaches into his pocket. He pulls out a bottle, takes a swig, corks it, and stashes it back in his coat. "It's warming right up now that it's nearly June. We can't be wasting no time."

I clutch Papa's hand tighter and shake my head. I can't let him go. I can't let them put him away in the ground. I reach up and touch his cheek. It's rough. Whisker stubbly, and I squinch my eyes and try to pretend that his face is warm and that Papa's just resting, and that we're both at home and not on the street, and he's not bloody and slack and cool to the touch. But pretend is just like promises. It doesn't do any good. He's gone. And the loss of him fills the air all around me, tugging at my breath and making it impossible to speak. I pull my hand away from his face and grab his hand once more.

"Got a preacher?"

I shake my head again. Papa was never one for church.

"That'll make it easier. Saturday then. Eight o'clock."

I think I nod.

"You gotta let go of his hand, girlie, so Jake there can lift him."

I clasp my hand tighter around Papa's. I won't. I can't. But Jake doesn't seem bothered by my hand. He grabs Papa from behind, hooking his arms underneath Papa's limp ones and jerks his body forward so that Papa's hand practically leaps out of mine. I rub my empty palm against my chest as Jake drags him to the wagon parked in the street. Jake jumps into the wagon bed and pulls Papa up after him. I watch Papa's boots disappear, then I hear his head slap against the wooden wagon bottom. The sound makes me gag again.

The undertaker jumps back, eyeing my warily. But I don't throw up this time. I stand, take one more look at the wagon that's carrying Papa away, and I run.

God forgive me, I run.

I tear through the crowd that remains. I crash into a man who waves his cane at me, but I pay him no mind. I simply plow through, displacing hats and knocking over ladies. I think I hear Arnie cry out, "Kit! Wait, Kit," but I don't bother to look. I just run. Run from the blood, the stares, the thrum of voices, low and accusatory.

I run through town, the chant of *Sorry Papa, Sorry Papa, Sorry Papa* filling my head and helping my feet keep pace. I run by all the places I ran when Mother was buried, and then I run out of town, past the Catholic church and all the way to the school tent. Still I don't stop. I run, despite the pain in my side and the raggedness of my breath. I cut across lots and jump over sagebrush and scatter field mice and jackrabbits until I reach the gate to the cemetery. Then I stop. Slowly I make my way to Mother's grave—surprised at how easy it is to find even though I have not been back since that awful day in April.

The moonlight shimmers on a small grave marker, making it look almost pretty. Papa put up her headstone. I pass my hand over the carved words: *Sarah Donovan d–1905*. We ordered it from Sears, Roebuck, and Company the week after Mother died. I had wanted it to say something lovely like *Beloved Wife and Mother* or *Rests in Angels' Arms*, but Papa said they charge by the letter, so we can't get too fancy.

Sarah Donovan d–1905. Nothing fancy about that.

"I'm sorry, Mother," I whisper. I lie down next to the grave and rest my head on the crook of my arm. "I killed you, and now I've killed Papa." I choke on the tears filling my throat. "I'm sor…" I can't get the word out. All that come are tears and a wail that sounds more animal than human.

* * *

Somehow I make it back to the cabin before dawn. I flop down on Papa's cot and bury my face in his pillow. It smells like him. A mix of soap and sweat and something faintly peppery. I close my eyes and inhale with all my might. I pull his blanket up over my shoulder and roll over to face the wall of the tent. I stare into the darkness.

I must have fallen asleep because I wake with a start. Clara has me by the shoulder and is shaking me. "Grab anything worth a damn," she says, pulling me to my feet. "Let's go!"

I jerk away. "What the heck?"

Clara doesn't bother to answer, nor does she give me time to ask any more questions. She scoops the blankets from Papa's cot and wraps books and papers and Papa's old handgun into a bundle. "Is there anything else you want?" Her eyes are cold and steady.

"No." I clutch Papa's pillow against my chest and follow her to the door. "Wait!" I go to my own cot and pull my keepsake box out from underneath. I stuff my hat on my head, scoop the bullet from beneath my pillow, grab my skirt from the drying line, and follow her out the door, too stunned to think of anything else to take.

Clara leads me and our three chickens to her cabin, a rickety old shack made of loose boards and tar paper. She places the bundle on the floor and points me to a room in the back. "You can put your stuff in there." She watches while I set my box on the cot. I take another sniff of Papa's pillow, then set it on the cot too. I take a deep breath. The whole place smells of leather oil and dust. I look around the cramped room. Then I turn to Clara. "What's going on?"

"Make some coffee," she says. "I'm going to get these chickens settled and fed. I'll be right back."

I want to protest, to make her sit and explain, but she's gone before I can speak. So I work. I find the beans and the grinder on a shelf beside the stove. Once I've run them through the grinder, I scoop them into the little muslin bag attached to the top of Clara's coffeepot. Then I pour water into a pot and set it on the stove to boil. I search through her mess for a couple of clean tin cups and a place on the table to set them. My mind races with questions. Was I wrong when I thought she was kind? Is she really crazy after all? Have I been kidnapped? Shanghaied? Does she even know what happened last night?

"Papa's dead," I say when Clara returns to the cabin.

She settles her wiry body into a chair. She picks up the coffee cup and turns it in her hands. "I know." She shakes her head slowly. "I know."

Clara sits quiet like that, stooped over and shaking her head, until the water boils and the coffee is finished. I pour her a cup. I watch as she lifts it, letting the steam from the water drift up into her wrinkled face. She closes her eyes and takes a sip. Then she looks at me.

Her look is steady. Dogged even. I fidget under her gaze. Finally, I pour myself a cup of coffee—my first ever since Papa never let me drink any. Mother always said I was too young to start. I snort back a laugh.

I wonder what she'd say today.

Clara pushes a sack of sugar toward me. "A little sweet eases the bite."

I shake my head. "Black will be fine." I drink, not bothering to cool it with my breath. It's hot and bitter and burns a little when it hits my stomach. "Perfect."

Clara nods.

"Why'd you come fetch me?" I ask after I've finished my coffee.

"They'll come root through the cabin 'fore long. Looking for evidence."

"Evidence?" I'd have imagined Papa's dead body would be all the evidence anyone would need.

"Something to prove he was an agitator. That he had it in for Granger. Papers. Books. Whatever they can find to prove your papa was a troublemaker."

I set the coffee cup down hard on the table. What gives them the right? The thought of people going through our stuff—through things Mother touched—makes the blood rush to my ears. My hand curls into a fist. "Who's 'they'?"

"Granger's men. That Hines fellow most likely. All those chicken-livered cowards who stood around last night yelling, 'Self-defense.'"

"You were there?"

"I was at Exploration Mercantile when I heard the gunshot. I didn't know it was your pa until later." She looks at me again. Her eyes soften. "You saw it happen?"

I nod. "I was in front of the Texas Saloon." My hands start to shake. I fumble for the coffee cup.

"Dear God."

"I sat with him till the undertaker came. Funeral's set for Saturday morning."

"Oh, Kit." Clara reaches her hand out across the table.

I don't take it. If she touches me, I know I'll cry, and if I start, I'll never stop.

"If I'd have known it was him, I'd have rushed right over." Tears roll out of her eyes, and she doesn't even bother to wipe them away. "You shouldn't have had to handle all of that alone."

I pour another cup of coffee. "I need to see the undertaker today, I reckon, and settle up with him, somehow." I pause for a moment. What am I going to do if I can't afford the undertaker? Panic surges through my body and settles in my chest. I take a deep breath as Mother's calm voice fills my head. "You'll cross the bridge when you come to it." I clutch the edge of the table and continue. "I'm going to talk to Sheriff Earp too."

"They already declared it self-defense. I heard one of the deputies announce it over at the Northern Saloon myself." Clara shakes her head. "All those men swore up and down on their mother's graves that dear old Mr. Granger was in fear for his life."

"You know Papa wouldn't hurt anyone." I keep my voice low and calm even though all I really want to do is scream and cry and rail against the unfairness of it all. "Papa wasn't one to make trouble." I can hear his voice in my head even now. "I'm not the man to start a revolution…"

Clara interrupts my remembering. "Of course I know that. But with the rumors swirling around about unionization and…"

"Mr. Westchester's newspaper article." The words make my stomach turn.

Clara nods.

I swallow hard and force myself to face facts. I caused this. Good intentions or not, my big mouth is as much to blame for Papa's death as Granger and his gun. "Papa said this would be a hard thing to make right." I meet Clara's steady gaze with my own, then clear my throat and stand. "I guess I'll need to think on that once I'm square with the undertaker and…" I can't say the rest. I can't talk about Papa being put down into the ground. It's too hard.

One thing's for sure, it's going to take more than standing in the middle of town with a sign around my neck to answer for this. It's going to take more than promises. More than redemption. It's going to take some good old-fashioned eye-for-an-eye justice.

I'm pretty sure Mother would not approve.

And I'm sorry for that. I really am.

I only hope I'm up to the task.

Chapter Eleven

I take the long way to the undertaker's, avoiding Main Street and the place where Papa was killed. I wonder if his blood is still pooled in the street, or if traffic and the never-ceasing wind have whisked away all evidence of his murder.

The undertaker's office is surprisingly clean and well lit. "His effects," the undertaker murmurs, handing me Papa's watch, a picture of Mother, and his money clip. "It's all there," he says, not even giving me a chance to eye him suspiciously. "I've done my share of dishonorable things, but pilfering from the dead is not among them."

I wrap Papa's watch up in my handkerchief. I cringe at the splash of blood that stains the photograph and place it in the handkerchief too. Then I pull all three bills from Papa's money clip and hand them to the undertaker.

"I take it you want our economy casket," he says, stuffing the bills in his breast pocket. He points with his chin, indicating a sorry, pieced-together pine box.

Rickety and worm-holed barely do it justice. Economy is a kindness, and—as I've just spent the last of Papa's money on it—an utter exaggeration. "It will have to do," I say, cutting my eyes to the floor. I try hard not to look at the other caskets in the room—especially the fine mahogany one with sturdy brass findings and a resting place filled with white satin. Surely the devil and the ground critters will leave that one alone. Still, there is no money for anything more—and yearning for better won't make it so. At least that's what Mother would say. "Will you wrap a blanket around him before you put him in there?"

"Bring one by, and I'll see that it's done." The undertaker's tone drops, and it's clear our business is over. He reaches out his hand to shake, but I don't take it. The scent of fresh pine and the tang of his hair grease already have my head reeling. I am certain his touch will send my stomach right out of my body and onto this newly swept floor. I waggle my fingers in kind of a halfhearted wave.

"Tomorrow morning then," he says, reaching into his suit pocket and taking out his bottle. He raises it in salute before taking a drink.

"Tomorrow morning."

I go to the jailhouse next, but Sheriff Earp is nowhere to be found. "He's got a touch of pneumonia," the deputy says. "On again. Off again. I reckon he's at home sleeping."

"The shooting yesterday?" I ask. "Did Mr. Granger get charged for murder?"

"Nope." The deputy lights a cigarette and very carefully buries the match in the dirt at his feet. "Self-defense. About a million witnesses backed him up. Heck, folks from as far as Tonopah came in this morning to help clear his name."

"No one said anything else?"

"No one that mattered."

"So that's it." I sit on the steps next to the deputy and rest my elbows on my knees. I cradle the sides of my face with my hands. "A man gets shot in the middle of the street, and no one's going to do a danged thing about it?"

The deputy shrugs. "Nothing to do unless someone can prove it weren't self-defense after all." He looks up and down the street, then leans in close and makes his voice nearly a whisper. "'Course if a person were to show some sort of wrongdoing on Granger's part—some double cross or misdeed he tried to hush up that this dead fellow knew about—then we'd have reason to doubt his testimony. Till then"—he smashes the tip of his cigarette on the board sidewalk, extinguishing it, then places the stub in his shirt pocket—"our hands are tied."

I bite my lip and think back on the papers Clara picked up when she dragged me out of the cabin. I wonder if there's something in that pile to prove that Mr. Granger had it in for Papa. I stand abruptly and shake hands with the deputy. "Thanks for your help. I'll be back with some proof."

The deputy smiles. He holds my hand a beat longer than necessary and whispers, "I hope so."

* * *

I stop by our tent cabin on my way back to Clara's, thinking there might be something there that will prove Papa's innocence. If there was, it's gone now. The place has been ransacked. Nearly everything that was inside is now outside. The table lies on its side, turned over in front of the door, two of the legs missing. Our cots have been cut, and strips of white tarpaulin litter the yard. Everything that was left behind is broken—stomped on with heavy boots or ripped apart by knife blades—including the rag rug I made Mother for her last birthday, our one china plate that survived the trip west, and a picture of Mother that must have slipped out of her Bible when Clara and I fled.

I scoop up the picture and rub at the dusty boot print that stretches across the corner of Mother's face, marring her pretty smile. The smudge of grime does not budge. I slip the picture in the handkerchief next to Papa's watch and look around for anything else worth saving. Everything is ruined. Our meager furniture. Our dishes. Even Papa's old work boots. Only slivers and shards of our lives remain.

I make my way to the front door. I peer into the tent to see if anything was left inside and hear the click of a shotgun barrel being closed behind me.

"Get away from the door," a woman's voice rasps. "This is my cabin now."

I turn to see the double barrels of a shotgun pointed right at me. Behind them stands a woman—skinny and long-limbed and pretty, despite her tangled hair and worn dress. She spits a stream of tobacco juice into the dust and hefts the gun a little higher on her shoulder. "Easy there," she warns as I take a step away from the cabin.

I hold my hands up near my head and walk toward her. Tears inch down my cheeks. "Did you do this?"

She eases her grip on the gun. "Just the table. I needed some firewood."

"And the rest?"

"How I found it." She motions me to put down my hands.

When I do, she lowers the gun, letting it dangle off the crook of her arm. "I reckon folks were looking for the gold that agitator stole."

"Papa didn't steal." I scrub a palm across my cheeks, rubbing off the tears. I stand up straighter and look the woman in the eye. "He didn't steal gold, and he didn't steal people's property like some good-for-nothing squatter."

The woman scowls, and she trains the shotgun on me again. "I don't think you know who I am." She smiles sweetly. "Name's Sophie. Ask around. I'm practically famous. Folks'll tell you ain't nothing or no one going to keep me off land I want." She edges closer to me— near enough I can smell stale sweat and just a hint of ginger perfume. "The cabin's mine," she says again. "Fair and square."

I look back at the tent cabin, remembering the good times we had before Mother got sick, before Papa had given up. Back when they both believed gold would be the answer to everything. The list is short—a special dinner the night we arrived; Mother singing while she washed the clothes; Papa reading the paper in that silly voice that made Mother laugh. I close my eyes on the memories, trying to lock them up in my head. When I open my eyes again, all I see is junk. Ruined belongings and spoiled dreams.

"Take what you want," I say, turning my back on her and her shotgun. "None of it matters to me anymore."

* * *

"A squatter's got the cabin," I tell Clara when I get back to her place.

"I figured it wouldn't take long."

"Says her name's Sophie. Says she's famous."

Clara raises an eyebrow. "Sophie Newsome? I reckon she is. They say she killed a man over in Tonopah who tried to take back his house, though no one's proved it yet. I hear she even braved that big brown bear Logan tied up to protect his lot over on Crook Avenue." She glances out the window and exhales a whistling sigh. "Yep, I'd consider that cabin good and gone if I were you.

"Take a look at this." She hands me the newspaper. The headline blares, "Union Agitator Killed in Street Brawl." I scan the article, remembering Mr. Westchester chasing after Mr. Granger and Sheriff Earp, notebook in hand. Sure enough, there's his name in the byline: M Westchester.

I sigh. I guess he's a lying turncoat too.

The article describes the meeting at the Miners' Union Hall, then goes on to report that the *union agitator was drunk and disorderly and pulled a knife on family man and upstanding citizen Hiram L. Granger after accusing him of running a dangerous mine.* Mr. Granger shot Papa in self-defense, the paper claims, and *further investigation turned up thousands of dollars of stolen ore hidden in the agitator's tent.*

"Stolen gold ore," I say to Clara, handing the paper back to her. "If Papa had been stealing gold, we would not have lived in a tent—especially a tent that did not benefit from a coal oil lamp or the occasional new dress. Of that, I can be sure."

Clara crumbles up the paper and stuffs it into her cookstove. "True. He wasn't one for drink either."

"Or disorder." I smile, though tears drip down my face.

Clara takes my hand, and this time I let her. "Take heart in the fact that you know the truth," she says.

"I will try."

But we both know the story printed in the paper is the story that will be believed. Not that it matters because whether it is true or not, the facts remain: Papa is dead and will soon be buried in the Goldfield cemetery; Mr. Granger is rich and happy in his big stone house on Fifth Avenue; and I am left orphaned in this dirty mining town—though no newspaper in the country would be interested in that bit of information, I am sure.

Chapter Twelve

It is cold at eight o'clock Saturday morning, despite the undertaker's prediction of warming summer weather. Clara accompanies me to the cemetery, and she and I shiver in silence as the undertaker's men ready the ropes to lower Papa into the ground next to Mother.

Tom and Jesse arrive after the casket has been lowered. They remove their jackets and pick up shovels, joining in the work of burying Papa. I'm relieved that someone else showed up, that people who knew him—and maybe loved him—are sending him off. Watching them work helps me ignore the flump of dirt on the sorry casket and the racking pain that fills my chest.

I am too weary to run and too heartsick to pray, as Mother would have liked. Knees wobbling, I grip Clara's hand and try not to imagine how quickly the box and its precious cargo will turn to dust in the ground. Instead, I think of Mr. Granger. I think of justice. And I let the jolt of anger get me through the worst of it.

Finally the thwack of shovels stops, and the burying is done. No one says words over the body, and no other mourners show. It is just the four of us and the undertaker, whose "God's will be done" does little to distract me from the real truth of today.

I am alone.

I shudder. My hand clutches my throat as I imagine myself growing up, getting a job, a husband, a dog. Now no one will be around to see it. No one will be around to help.

I look around the cemetery, then up at the clear blue sky. Everything seems dimmer now. Shadowy. Like most of the beauty and all of the excitement has been drained out of it.

Maybe it's just been drained out of me.

* * *

Tom and Jesse accompany us back to Clara's cabin. Both carry heavy packs, which they stash on Clara's porch before coming inside for coffee and biscuits.

"You leaving?" Clara asks as she passes around the butter and jam.

"We're going to try our luck out in Oregon," Tom says. "They say farming's pretty good out that way. Folks are making a fortune growing apples."

"And there's gold in the rivers, so a man can do a bit of prospecting if he has a mind to," Jesse adds, talking around the biscuit in his mouth.

"But I thought you all struck it rich," I say, remembering Tom's recent visit and the hope in Papa's voice.

"Granger's claiming his gold vein leads into our mine. He says all the gold is his."

Granger again. I grimace and fight the urge to spit. I wonder if we'll ever have a conversation at this table that doesn't include that man's name.

Clara stares into her coffee cup. "Sounds like claim-jumping to me."

I have to agree. "Can't you fight it?"

Tom laughs, the same hard, ugly sound Mr. Westchester made the night Papa was shot. "Can't afford it. All our money's tied up in the mine, and the lawyer says we can't dig till it's sorted out legally." Tom shakes his head, disgust clear on his face. "Legally by Granger's buddy the judge."

"We can't afford to lay idle, and we can't afford to fight," Jesse says, pouring himself another cup of coffee, "so it's time to move on."

"But..." I look around the room. Clara is still inspecting her coffee. I turn to Tom. "But you said you were going to be rich as Croesus. You could stay and fight. It's your gold, after all. Besides, what have you got to lose?"

"Our skins for starters," Jesse sputters.

Tom puts down his biscuit. His eyes are kind, but his voice is firm. "There's no way to beat Granger. He's too powerful. Too connected. You of all people should know that."

I swallow hard. Tears threaten, but I sniff them back and sit quietly while Tom, Jesse, and Clara go back to eating and drinking and talking about Oregon.

Maybe he's right. Maybe there's no way to win. Still, I can't help thinking—maybe the reason no one has ever beaten Mr. Granger is that no one has ever tried. Everyone just turns tail and runs the minute he shows up, Papa included. But how will anything change if no one will stand up to the man?

I'm still thinking on it when Tom and Jesse get ready to leave. Jesse waves good-bye and heads down the road. Tom holds back for a moment. "Your father was a good man, Kit. He tried to help.

Tried to do the right thing. Don't you forget that." Before I can stammer out a thank-you, he grabs his pack off the porch and jogs ahead to catch up with Jesse.

I find my feet and race after him. I don't know why, but hearing someone say something nice about Papa tears at my heart. I catch up to Tom and hug him around the waist. "Thank you," I say through my tears.

Tom doesn't quite hug me back, but he does pat me on the shoulder. "Your father was a good man," he says again. "I'm only sorry I dragged him into this mess."

I wipe my eyes and step back. "What mess?"

"This thing with Granger. He said he'd check out the vein in the mine for us. He was going to see if there really was a streak running toward our claim."

"Papa did that?" My breath catches in my chest.

Tom shrugs. "Don't know if he did or didn't."

"Granger shot him before he could talk to you?"

Tom shrugs. "I really am sorry, Kit. I didn't mean to get your father into trouble. I surely didn't mean to get him killed."

My brain whirrs. This may be just the proof the deputy needs. "Will you write down what you just told me?" I grab his hand and pull him back toward Clara's cabin.

"I don't see how this will help," Tom says, taking the paper and pencil I shove in front of him. He sits down at Clara's table and scribbles out the statement.

"You sign as witness, Clara," I insist.

Clara takes up the pencil. She signs her name slowly, like she's taking great pains to make each letter perfect. It still comes out looking like a six-year-old wrote it. "I read better than I write," she says, avoiding my eyes.

"It doesn't have to be pretty. It just has to convince the sheriff that he needs to look a little closer at Mr. Granger's self-defense plea."

Tom gets up and heads to the door. I hug him one more time. "I'll let you know when Granger's been bested," I tell him. "Then you can come back for your gold."

Tom shakes his head. His eyes are sad. He hefts his pack back on his shoulders and jogs to catch up with his brother. I clutch his statement about Papa in both my hands and watch him go.

Chapter Thirteen

The following Monday, I tell Clara my plan. I will show the document Tom signed to the nice deputy and see if he will reopen the case against Granger. "He said he needs proof. Maybe this is it."

"You can take it to him after school," Clara says.

After school! I feel my face flush with rage. She can't be serious. "You don't expect me to go back there, do you? Not after all of this?"

One look at Clara's face, and I know that it is a silly question. Of course she expects me to go to school.

"Life must go on," she says with a shrug. "And a big part of your life is school. You don't want to be old like me and still scratching out your letters like a child."

She reaches out to pat my shoulder, but I jerk away.

"We cannot let everything go to hell just because your pa is dead. He wouldn't like that."

That makes me mad enough to spit, so I do—a gesture she flatly ignores as she hands me a tin of biscuits and beans. "I'll see you this afternoon. I'll even go with you to talk to the deputy if you'd like."

"I won't go back to that school."

Clara just smiles a tight smile, so I try *can't* and *refuse to* but neither makes an impact. Her smile doesn't waver; neither does the firm look in her gray eyes.

We stand, staring at each other, jaws clenched, an angry silence swirling around us.

Finally Clara sighs. "If'n you don't go to school, Kit, there'll be trouble. Before you know it, some snooty women from the Ladies' Aid Society will show up, take you over to Father Dermondy's, and leave you in the care of the church. Mayhap someone will adopt you, but more than likely they'll just put you to work." She presses her hand to her chest. "In either case, they won't let you stay with a shabby old woman like me."

I take in her bowed spine and quaking shoulders. She does look old and tired—and not at all up to the task of caring for anyone, let alone someone as much trouble as me. I take the lunch pail from her with shaking hands. "Okay."

I don't want to hurt Clara or get her in any sort of trouble, and I don't want to hurt myself. Although Father Dermondy is one of the kindest men in Goldfield, the last thing I need is God-fearing folks reminding me what a heathen I've become since Mother's death. Hard work I can handle. Prayers and wailing about my sinful soul I will not abide.

"Hold your head up," Clara instructs as I head for the door. "Remember, you ain't done no wrong."

* * *

Holding my head up does no good. By the time I've taken my seat, three students have pulled my hair, short though it is, and Stewie and Evan have each kicked me in the shin. Miss Sheldon simply pretends I don't exist.

"You missed me, ma'am," I say when she skips over me during the spelling bee. Granted, I was going to botch the word on purpose. I always do. But it's the principle of the thing.

"*Epiphany*," Miss Sheldon repeats. She doesn't even look at me as Brant spells, "*E…p…i…f…u…n…n…y.*" Neither does anyone else.

I sigh and sink down in my seat. I should have stayed at Clara's. I'm worse than invisible here.

All that changes at lunch break. I am surrounded by students before I can even unpack the tin Clara gave me. Evan Granger takes the lead. "Your old man got what he deserved, threatening my pa like that," he announces as much to the group as to me.

Several others murmur in agreement.

"And now he's stuck in the ground," Jennie DeMillo adds, sticking her tongue out at me. "The grubs crawled in. The grubs crawled out…"

Other voices pick up the chant until Stewie stops them with a wave of his hand. "Your pop caused more trouble for the union than all of the socialist hotheads combined," he informs me. He takes a bite of a chicken leg and chews thoughtfully.

"Threatening Granger was a stupid, selfish move," he continues, spitting pieces of chicken at me as he talks. "Everyone says so. The union usually takes up a collection when one of their men dies, but they met last night and agreed no collection is to be taken for you 'cause your pop turned out to be more traitor than union man and got what was coming to him."

I squeeze my hands into fists, but force myself to keep them at my sides. My chest heaves. "I wouldn't want their dirty money if they begged me to take it on hands and knees," I spit out through clenched teeth.

It's true. I wouldn't. I couldn't care less about it. But the part about them calling Papa a traitor—that part gets me 'cause if anyone is a traitor, it's me. I am the one who talked to Mr. Westchester. I'm the one who told everyone that something needed to be done about Granger's mine. And, truth be told, I am the one who should have been shot for my reckless talk. Not Papa.

"I…Papa was not a traitor," I mumble.

Stewie leans in so close I can smell the chicken grease on his breath. He laughs. "What was that, Kit? I can't hear you."

"Cat got your tongue?" Evan adds.

"The grubs crawled in…"

The kids circle closer. I can see their faces, eyes wide, mouths open. Their words swirl around me, but I can't make them out. It's all just a buzz of pointing fingers and pointed words. I sit cross-legged on the ground with my head down and my hands still balled into fists. Tears prick the backs of my eyes, and I use all of my energy to keep them from falling.

Eventually Miss Sheldon rings the bell. I don't look up until the last person moves from the circle. That's when I see Leslie, sitting alone on the swing, plucking at a string on her sash and staring at me. I stare back for a second, meeting her gaze. For once, she's not laughing or sneering. She looks at me with tearful blue eyes and offers a weak smile. Then she gets up and goes inside. I gaze after her, wondering what she's thinking and why she's crying. I shrug. Who cares? I'm too tired to think about Leslie and her problems. I have my own to worry about.

I spend the rest of the day with my head up and my fists down. I guess I can say that I am finally acting like a lady. Wouldn't Mother be proud? My heart sinks as I wonder about Papa, though. Would he have been proud, or would he have been disappointed that the one time I decide not to fight is the one time I am called on to defend his name?

* * *

I bolt from the school tent as soon as Miss Sheldon releases us. I run all the way through town and to the jail without stopping, then pause on the steps to catch my breath. When I knock on the door, a deputy I don't recognize pokes his head out. "Whaddya want?"

"Is the other deputy here? Nice fellow. Brown eyes."

The deputy's eyes rove up and down my frame. He wrinkles his nose. "What business do you have with Miles?"

I offer up the paper Tom signed. "I have some evidence to show him—about a case."

The deputy fiddles with the toothpick he's got in his mouth. "Miles is gone. Took off for Reno this morning."

"Gone?" I choke.

"And good riddance, I say." The deputy starts to close the door.

"What about Sheriff Earp?"

"Sick."

"Do you…?"

"What case are you rambling on about?" He leans on the doorframe. "Come on. I ain't got all day."

"Mr. Granger shot a man the other day. I think I got some proof that it wasn't self-defense like he said."

The deputy snatches the paper out of my hand. He scans it quickly. A small smile plays across his lips as he hands it back. "This ain't proof, little girl. It's hearsay. We ain't got no truck with hearsay."

My body feels heavy. I look away for a moment, cursing myself for not coming here first thing this morning. I shake my head. "But the other deputy said if there was some question—some reason to look at things again..."

The deputy peers past me, narrowing his eyes on something up the street. He rolls the toothpick around with his tongue. "The other deputy ain't here."

"But..."

"Go home, little girl. That case is closed."

"But..." He slams the door before I can utter another word. "Damn it," I mutter. I kick the door with my foot. *I never should have listened to Clara.*

The deputy peeks through the window and frowns. "Get!" he mouths through the glass.

I scowl at him. I continue scowling as I fold Tom's note up neatly and tuck it in my sleeve. This guy is a bully and a fool. I'll wait until Sheriff Earp is back. He'll do something. He'll have to do something.

I wander back through town, so intent on my thoughts that I am nearly on top of Stewie and Evan before I notice them. I catch myself just in time and duck behind the corner of the Esmeralda Hotel before they spot me.

The boys are in the middle of Main Street, shouting and jeering. For a moment I think they've spotted me after all, and I tense, preparing for the teasing I'm certain is coming. But, for once, it's not me they're after. It's a burro. And they're trying to ride it.

Riding a burro is good sport, usually. The wild ones buck something fierce, and it's great fun trying to stay on while they rollick down the street, snorting and twisting to and fro. Even I have given it a go once or twice. But this burro's buck-and-run is pretty well used up. I frown at the sharp outline of his ribs and the tired slump of his shoulders.

Stewie and Brant corral the poor creature between them while Evan climbs on its back. A crowd of boys gathers. They commence hooting and hollering. Several boys stomp their feet, while Stewie, Evan, and Brant pinch and slap the burro, trying to make the poor thing bolt.

But the burro doesn't run or buck or even show his teeth. All he does is slump—bowed-back and knock-kneed. When the boys slap him on the haunches, he drops down farther, until his trembling knees nearly touch the ground.

He is quite likely the sorriest-looking burro I've ever seen. And, by the way he's cocking his head this way and that, as if he's trying to follow the boys' voices with his long ears instead of his eyes, he is certainly the blindest.

The boys don't seem to notice or mind. They keep slapping him, goading him to react. Stewie walks in front of him, tugging at his ears and yelling "Wa-ha!" right in the poor beast's face.

Still, the burro doesn't move.

But I do.

I march over to Stewie and grab him by the ear, twisting it hard. With the other hand, I grab Evan by the cuff of his pants and pull him off the burro. He lands in the street with a thud and an "Oof."

"Let me go!" Stewie squirms.

I twist a bit harder and turn to the other boys. "If you know what's good for you, you'll get out of here and leave this poor burro alone."

They gawk—first at me, then at Stewie, who's trying to turn in circles around his ear. I reckon it feels like I mean to screw it off. Maybe I do.

"There's five of us." Brant Dixon laughs. "You can't beat all of us."

I shrug and give Stewie's ear another twist. I lean in close so the boys can hear me above Stewie's squalling. "You might ask your buddy here what he thinks." I turn back to Stewie. "Kinda hurts, doesn't it?" I smile. "Wa-ha!"

Brant eyes me warily. "She's gone round the bend," he says, taking a step back. "Let's get out of here." The boys follow without a word.

I turn Stewie loose. He rubs his ear and stares at me, his eyes wide, his chin up. His right hand opens and closes slowly, making a fist, then releasing it.

"Go ahead, take a swing," I taunt. I feel alert, alive, like I could take them all on—and the no-good deputy to boot. It feels good. Right, even. And nothing has felt right in a long while. I smile broader, wilder, and wink at Stewie.

He licks his lips and swallows hard. "You're as crazy as your old dead pa." He unclenches his fist and holds his hand out to Evan, who is still crumpled on the ground. "Let's go. We don't want that stupid old burro anyway."

Evan scrambles to his feet, and the two of them follow the other boys down the street. Once they are a safe distance away, Evan turns and yells, "Kit's gone loony! Kit's gone loony!" The other boys join in, and the lot of them continue the chant as they run down the street toward Evan's house.

My energy fades as their voices disappear, and my knees buckle. I lean against the burro and scratch his grizzled head. He bumps me with his muzzle, his old gray face rubbing against my hand. I look around. Wagons and people stream down the street. An automobile's horn honks. I can't leave the poor thing here to be jostled and shoved and generally mistreated. The thought of him alone and blind on the streets of Goldfield near about makes me cry. I rub my cheek against his face. "I guess you'll come home with me," I whisper in his floppy ear.

Maybe the boys are right. I really have gone loony.

Chapter Fourteen

I am leading the burro to Clara's, thinking up names for him and trying to come up with a way to talk Clara into keeping him, when a motorcar charges up the road behind me. I nearly jump out of my skin in my rush to get out of the way, and I nearly jump out of it again when I see who is behind the wheel. "Arnie!"

"I'd give you a ride, but I don't think your friend will fit," Arnie hollers above the clang of the engine as he comes to a stop beside me.

"How'd you…?"

"Bought it from a man who abandoned it in the street." Arnie grins. "For one hundred dollars and a ride out of town. Not a bad deal, even if I do say so myself." He steps out of the car and starts polishing the hood with his shirtsleeve.

"Little guy with a mustache?" I smile, remembering the cursing man in the rain.

"How'd you know?"

I shrug. "How'd you get a hundred dollars?" Last I saw, Arnie was barely scraping by. I'm pretty sure he was living at Old Joe Smiley's stable.

"A girl at the Northern Saloon grubstaked me. She's letting me pay her back by and by, and Old Joe says I can keep it at the livery long as I want." Arnie barely pauses in his telling to take a breath. Nor does he cease polishing the car while he talks. "With all the folks pouring into Tonopah bound for Goldfield, and no train in sight, I'm going to make loads of money. Who needs a gold mine when you can make a killing off the miners?"

He has a point. "I guess driving a fancy touring car beats wielding a pickax in the dark all to heck."

Arnie grins again. "Even if I do have to fix punctured tires every five miles or so."

It surely beats going to a school where no one, not even the teacher, recognizes your existence unless it is to tease and taunt you. "It sounds like a good trade all around, Arnie, and a right smart business move. I doubt Huck Finn himself could have come up with a slicker plan." I don't add that I am right proud of him, though I am.

"Come with me to Tonopah tomorrow." He gets back in the still-idling car. "Who knows, I may even let you drive."

"Seriously?" I can't believe my luck—or Arnie's generosity. I push the image of Clara's weary face—and the guilt that follows it—from my mind. "Okay."

Arnie nods his head and smiles. "Meet me at the stable at seven?" He fiddles with some levers. "I'm sorry about your pa." His bright eyes regard me seriously for a moment. "I tried to catch you that night, but…" He shrugs.

I look away.

"Anyway, uh, see you tomorrow. Tallyho!"

I glance up. He smiles wide, waves, and takes off with a lurch.

I'm sorry too, I think, as I pet Jasper (it seems like as good a name for a burro as any) and wait for the dust to clear.

Clara is sitting on the porch when Jasper and I walk up to the cabin. "Tie him up next to Sal," she says, as if me showing up with a burro in tow is an everyday event. She disappears into the cabin for a moment, then comes back out with two apples. She slices one up, feeding it to her mule, Sal. The second she gives me.

"Cut it up and feed him," Clara directs while she grabs the burro by the hind leg. She checks each hoof, then moves around to his head. She waves a hand in front his face. When he doesn't respond, she clucks her tongue. "He's near about worthless, I'm afraid. Poor thing's blind as a bat."

I tell her how I found him. "I couldn't help myself," I explain. "I just got hot all over when I saw them boys mistreating him."

"White-hot and rage-filled," Clara murmurs. "Isn't that what the preachers say?"

I nod. "I guess I did act a bit possessed."

Clara laughs. "I bet those boys thought they were looking the devil in the eye when you came tearing after them."

I remember Brant's scared face and Stewie's wide eyes. I think she might be right. "Can we keep him?" I hold my breath and wait.

Clara looks Jasper over. She runs a hand across his back. "I don't see why not. Miserable creature, working in the dark all his life. I reckon he deserves some time in the sun." She turns to me, her face serious. "He'll eat just about anything—including the scrub brush and the laundry if we don't watch out—but you're going to have to water him." She raises an eyebrow. "Understand?"

I do. More buckets for me to haul—or more money for the water truck. Even good deeds are expensive out here. Maybe that's why people shy away from doing the right thing. Maybe it just costs too dang much.

* * *

"Good luck at school today," Clara says, sending me off with another tin of food and a small, hopeful smile.

I turn away from her encouraging face and hustle to the road without even a thank-you. A slight twinge of guilt settles in my chest, but it passes as soon as I reach the stable and see Arnie. He grins and tips his hat with one hand as he holds the passenger door of the motorcar open for me. "It's not a raft, but I think it will do," he says. "Ready for an adventure?"

Boy, am I.

One of the best things about Arnie is that he puts me straight to work—without once bringing up Papa or my being an orphan just like Huck or anything about my "predicament" as Clara calls it— so, for the first time in what seems like forever, I feel like a regular person again. He starts right out showing me how the motorcar works, pointing to each lever and doodad in turn. "Foot brake, hand brake, choke, gas, ignition." He even has me flip the ignition switch on. "Now, I'm going up front to crank it."

He runs to the front of the car and turns a lever. Two cranks, and the engine starts right up. The *putt...putt...roar* of the motor is so sudden and loud that I nearly jump right out the car. I'm leaning over in the passenger seat, holding my chest and laughing, when Arnie slides into the driver's seat. He fiddles with the gas feed and the brake, and in seconds, we're crawling out of the stable and into the street.

"We're driving," I say, hush-voiced.

"Yep." Arnie can't contain his grin. "We'll speed up once we get on the open desert. We might even get her up to fifteen miles per hour." He grins even wider. "Don't want to scare the horses here, though." He waves a hand out the window. "Or the people."

We cruise through town and up Cedar Street, honking the horn as we pass by the schoolyard. I'm a bit sad that no one is outside, but I wave to the empty yard and the tent just the same. "Too bad Leslie and Evan can't see me now. Wouldn't they be jealous?"

Once we're out of town, we stop talking about the car and start talking about Huck Finn. "I told you he wouldn't turn Jim in," I say.

"Yep. I was glad for it. Though it does go against human nature."

"You think folks are naturally evil?" I ask.

Arnie purses his lips and stares out into the desert. "Maybe not evil," he concedes, "but greedy. I reckon folks will do just about anything if there's money involved."

"Even betray a friend?" I pluck at my skirt—remembering Clara's hopeful smile. I don't think I want to hear his answer.

"Especially that."

I was right. It didn't even take money for me to lie to her. Just the hint of adventure. Some friend I am.

I decide to change the subject. "Does Old Joe know you're living at the stable?" I ask. Truthfully, I've been wondering about Arnie's situation. Is he alone too?

Arnie ducks his head in a quick nod. "Yeah. Joe and I got an agreement."

"And your parents?"

Arnie stares out across the horizon. His face goes dark and his eyes harden. He's quiet for so long I have to sit on my hands to keep from poking him.

"Ma's dead," he finally says. "Pneumonia, I think, though it might've been the influenza. Father disappeared right after she passed. Some folks say he died. Others say he cut out, went back East, and didn't want a half-breed kid tagging along."

I cringe at the way he says *half-breed*—deep and tight, likes he's hitting a drum with the words. "And you've been living in the stable ever since?"

Arnie laughs high in his throat. "Nah. Passed around the family first. Ma's sister took me for a while. Then someone's cousin over in Tonopah. My father's uncle a little farther west. Eventually there was no one left. They were all either dead or too sick and old to look after some dumb kid. So I struck out on my own." He sits up straighter and rolls his shoulders back a bit. "Been taking care of myself since I was twelve. Nearly five years now." He runs his hand against the hard steering wheel and smiles. "Not doing too shabby—all things considered."

I nod. I wonder how he did it. How he kept himself fed and clothed and whole for all those years with no help. No Clara, no anyone to give him food and a bed and a listening ear. The thought of Clara stirs the guilt that's rested heavy in my chest since I left this morning. I dart a glance out the windshield, then look back at Arnie. I'm figuring out how to phrase my next question when the car goes all squirrelly and he brings it to a sudden stop.

"Tire puncture," he says, reaching into the backseat and pulling out a box of tools. "Want to learn how to patch a tire?"

His eagerness and the crooked way he grins push all thoughts of dead parents and betrayal out of my head.

"Sure I do."

Arnie talks me through the whole procedure. He shows me how to take the tire off, scuff up the inner tube around the puncture—"so the patch'll stick"—and put the whole thing back together again. By the third puncture, I'm pretty sure I can do the whole show myself.

"Do you think I can drive it?" I ask.

"Can you crank it up?" He leans into the car and shifts some levers around.

I go to the front of the car and spit on my hands, just like I saw Arnie do, then I grab the crank lever. I give it a turn, but nothing happens. I look at Arnie.

"One more time," he yells. "Give it all you got."

I spit on my hands again. This time I crank for all I'm worth. The engine catches and roars to life. Arnie runs over to the passenger side and climbs in.

"Give it a bit of gas, there, and a little brake so we don't go lurching forward like we're being pulled by a wild horse," Arnie advises.

I do as he says. The car creeps forward. "I'm driving!" I squeal.

"Look out for that rock there," he says. He watches as I turn the wheel, managing to steer just to the left of the protruding rock.

"Nice work. Now give it a little more gas, or we'll still be trying to get to Tonopah come nightfall." He leans back in the passenger seat and pulls his hat down over his eyes, like he's taking a nap.

I stare straight ahead, focusing on keeping the motorcar on a clear, rock-free path. Jackrabbits flee as we roar by; occasionally, a bird soars beside us.

"Show-off," I yell out over the door as a crow passes over the top of us, spiraling high in the air, then shooting out in front like we're in some sort of race and he's winning. Laughter bubbles out of me. My skin tingles—from the sun and the dust, sure—but mostly from the lightness that's filled my chest. I don't think I've breathed so freely since Mother died. I feel almost peaceful, gliding along the desert like this. Peaceful and happy and full. I let out another laugh, then wrap my fingers around the horn and squeeze it. *Ah-hoo.*

Arnie pushes the hat off his face and looks around. "You're a natural, Kit. Maybe I'll hire you to drive when business picks up."

I pry my eyes off the horizon to grin at him.

When we get close to Tonopah, Arnie has us switch places. "You'll want more practice before you try navigating through all that traffic," he explains as he takes the wheel.

I look at the buildings filling the horizon in front us and am relieved. I watch as he feeds the gas and brace myself for the car's lurch forward. Only this time, it doesn't come. Instead of forward, the car races backward.

My heart drops. I look at Arnie who's muttering under his breath.

"Transmission's stuck again," he explains, laying a long arm across the seat back and looking over his shoulder. He maneuvers the car around so the back is facing the direction of Tonopah and continues to drive—backward—through the desert.

I stare at the floorboard. "Did I break it?"

"Nah." He takes his hand off the seat and smacks my shoulder. "She's just a mite temperamental from time to time. Drives just fine in reverse, though."

She really does. And so does Arnie. He manages to back the car all the way through Tonopah and to the depot without striking a pedestrian, a horse, or another motorcar while I kneel on the seat, flapping my arms and shouting, "Look out! Look out!" at the folks scrambling to get out of our way.

Before Arnie can set the brake on the car, a motley group of men surrounds us. They crowd the doors so we can't get out and pepper us with questions. "You headed to Goldfield?" "How much for a ride?" "Any new strikes out there?" I shrink back in my seat, overwhelmed by the sudden attention.

Arnie shouts, "Step aside," to the lot of them, causing them to jump back. He scowls at the ones who lay grimy hands on the sideboards of the car.

I sit up again and look around. Most of the men are shabby— miners and get-rich-quickers moving from one boomtown to the next trying to make their fortune. One of the fellows is a railroad man. He claims to be working for the Tonopah and Goldfield Railroad. "Scouting the location for a train depot," he says. "Pretty soon, we'll be running from here to Goldfield once a day." He looks at Arnie pointedly. "May put a dent in your business, son."

"I'll worry about that when the time comes. For now, it's a dollar a ride or you can wait for the stage."

A religious man, hoping to start a church and "save the souls of the men and misplaced females who've succumbed to gold fever," asks for a discount. "Perhaps you could use a prayer," he says, resting his hand on my shoulder.

I slide out from under his grasp. "I'm all set prayer-wise," I say, rolling my eyes at Arnie, who manages to glare at the preacher and laugh at me at the same time.

The last man to ask for a ride is an assayer, eager to set up shop and get to figuring out the value of Goldfield's newest strikes. "My brother's an engineer," he tells me as he slides into the backseat. "He's been doing a little assay work on the side but has gotten too busy to keep up with all of it. He wired last month, saying he needs an assayer he can trust."

"And here you are." I smile, caught up in his enthusiasm.

"Exactly." He returns my smile. "Goldfield or bust."

While we wait for the other men to settle up with Arnie, the assayer shows me his kit of scales and chemicals. "Perhaps you'll bring your finds to me," he says with a wink. "Or send your friends. I'll give you a special rate."

"Maybe I will, once my friends get their mine back from a no-good claim-jumping murderer."

The man's smile fades. He looks at me, his eyes wide and questioning.

I cringe, shocked that I've made such a statement to a stranger. I open my mouth to clarify or apologize or turn the whole thing into a joke, I'm not sure which, but no sound comes out.

We stare at each other for a long moment. His eyes are serious, searching, I suppose, for the truth in my statement. He examines my face the same way I imagine he examines mineral specimens under his magnifying glass—intently, purposefully, separating fool's gold from the real thing.

After what feels like an eternity, he leans forward, resting his forearms on the seat in front of him. "There are ways to tell where a piece of gold originates. A chunk of gold ore holds a lot of information. The secrets aren't always in plain sight, but sometimes a person with a good eye and the right equipment can ferret them out."

I nod, relieved that he doesn't think I'm a liar. I think about what he said. My heart beats faster as I begin to speak. "Can you tell where a vein of gold starts? Say there are two claims side by side. Can you tell if the gold starts on one side of the rock wall or the other?"

"Yes. Often quite accurately, though that's really the job of an engineer."

I consider his words. I could take him to Tom's mine and explain the situation. If he could prove the vein originates on Tom's claim and would be willing to testify to that in court, fighting Granger might be worth the time and money. Excitement bubbles up my chest and into my throat. "I wonder if you'd…"

I stop myself. This man seems kind, but so did Mr. Westchester. There's no way to know if I can trust him—to know for sure he won't turn traitor. "I wonder if you'd…let me see one of those crucible things again."

"Certainly." He rummages through his tools and hands me a small clay cup.

I turn it around in my hands. "So this is where gold is made."

"You could say that. The ore is put in the crucible with some chemicals and thrust into the fire. If there is treasure to be had, that's how it will be revealed."

"Through fire?"

"It's an intense process, to be sure, but the gold survives. Some say it's transformed." He makes a magician's hand motion. "*Poof.*

From humble rock to glorious wealth." He smiles. "Treasures birthed from violence, so to speak."

I roll the cup around in my hand one more time. "And all of it happens in this little cup." I give the crucible one last squeeze before handing it back.

"You keep it," he says, pressing the clay cup into my palm. "Bring it with you when your friends are ready to have their gold assayed. We'll use it. For good luck."

I smile at his kindness. "I'll hold you to that discount too. You never know what will happen in Goldfield."

Because I'm sitting in the front seat next to Arnie, only six men can pile in the car. The preacher has to ride propped up on the back, one hand grasping the folded-down buggy top, the other clinging to his grip. "Guess you get your discount, Preacher," Arnie informs him. "Ride's only seventy-five cents for you, seeing as you don't have a seat and all."

If he's grateful for the one-bit break in price, he doesn't show it. If he'd have been nice about it, I might have felt a little bad for taking up the entirety of the front passenger seat, and if he hadn't been so quick to touch and pray, I might have tried to share it with him. But since he was so rude, tossing the coins at Arnie like he was tossing feed to the chickens, I don't feel the slightest twinge of guilt as I settle in the plush front seat and turn the ignition switch for Arnie.

I doubt Mother would be happy about us making the preacher ride on the back of a car in the middle of all the blowing dust and engine fumes, but I doubt Mother'd be happy about me riding in a motorcar with a boy at all. Since I am already "in for a penny, in for pound" as she would say, I see no use fretting about it. I only wish I had one of those fancy driving scarves to keep the dust off my face and that Papa could see me racing across the desert in such luxury. Then everything would be near about perfect.

Arnie starts up the car and fiddles with the levers. I'm all prepared to do my hand-flapping and yelling routine again as we back our way toward Goldfield, but the car has other ideas. It jerks forward—just as it's supposed to—and runs smooth as taffy as Arnie maneuvers us out of town and into the desert once again.

Once they get past commenting on the barrenness of the land and inquiring about the quality of hotels, saloons, and eating places in Goldfield, the men are a quiet group. Most lean back and pull their hats down over their eyes, shading their faces. Only one of the shabbier-looking men keeps asking questions. "And the gambling? How's the gambling?"

"Same as anywhere, I imagine," Arnie says. "Shell games, poker, faro. The usual."

"And girls?"

Arnie glances sideways at me and rolls his eyes. "Yeah, there's plenty of girls."

I stifle a laugh.

"Good to hear." With that, the man takes out a deck of cards and shuffles through it, muttering numbers and commands like "stay" and "fold" under his breath. Other than that, the only sounds are the wind and the motor as the car putts through the desert air until the first tire puncture ends the calm.

"Everyone out!" Arnie urges. "We have a flat to fix."

"I paid for a ride," the man with the cards grumbles. "Not a work detail."

"Sooner you help, the sooner it's fixed, and the sooner you can meet those girls," Arnie informs him. "Hand me that patch kit."

Four punctures later, we are all a bit tired and grumpy when we finally drive into the outskirts of Goldfield. The sight of the town seems to perk everyone up, though. Perhaps me most of all. I was beginning to fear that the puncture kit would be used up completely, and we'd have to start stuffing the holes with bits of cloth from the hem of my skirt.

Arnie drives to the stable and stops the motorcar out front. "Saloons, hotels, restaurants, stores, and brokerage houses." He sweeps his hand left and right, taking in the entirety of Main Street. "Best of luck to you," he says as the men pile out of the car. Several pause to shake his hand.

The assayer stops to shake mine. "It was a pleasure meeting you..."

"Kit."

"A pleasure, Kit. And if your friends need help with their gold, you can find me at my brother's shop on First Street. Just ask for Peter." He tips his hat toward both me and Arnie, settles his assayer's kit in one hand and his valise in the other, and wanders off down the street.

I watch him go, the words he said about locating gold echoing in my mind.

Once the men scatter, Arnie inches the motorcar into the stable and turns it off. He gets out and grabs a bucket and towel from the tool pile in the corner. He fills the bucket from the horse trough and commences washing off the car. "Appearance is important," he explains as he wipes away the dirt.

I grab a mostly clean towel and help. "That was so much fun."

"Wasn't it?" He grins wide at me. "Making money to drive. You can't beat it."

"You'll really teach me how to drive in town?"

"Sure. Come by whenever you want."

All I can do is smile. It's nice to have a friend, and as much as I want to spend my time driving through the desert, I know that I can't. I pick up the crucible and roll it around in my hand. I have to figure out the details of Tom's claim. And I have to stop Granger. I don't have time to play around any longer.

Chapter Fifteen

My renewed determination doesn't kill my joy as I think about the day, though. I'm still smiling when I get back to Clara's cabin, dusty and reveling in the memory of my adventure.

Clara is not smiling. "I thought we had an agreement." Her gray eyes take in my dust-covered face. "I'm fairly certain you didn't pick up half the dirt in Nevada on your way home from school."

"No, ma'am," I manage. I cast my eyes down, trying to look contrite, but a smile keeps tugging at my lips.

"Well?"

"I was driving, ma'am. I drove with Arnie to Tonopah in his new motorcar."

"Motorcar?" Clara's eyes light up at the word.

"Yes'm. He's running a motor coach—hauling miners and other folks into town."

Clara opens her mouth, then closes it with a snap. She turns back to the cookstove. "You can spend suppertime thinking about your choices—and how you can start making better ones." She lays out one soup bowl and one plate of biscuits. "Mayhap an empty stomach will lead to smarter decisions in the future."

I bite my tongue, stopping myself from pointing out that there would be no supper at all if I hadn't begged that soup bone off Mrs. Nelson and set the whole thing to simmer this morning before I left. It sounds childish and silly even in my head—a fact that brings an even bigger smile to my face. The whole scene reminds me of Papa and all the times I got in a snit with him. Truth be told, Clara's bossiness may actually make me miss him just a little bit less.

Laughter tickles my throat. I never could get away with anything in this dusty excuse for a town when Papa was alive, and I guess Clara is going to make sure that doesn't change. Perhaps I'm not totally alone after all.

As tough as the woman is, she is lousy at punishment. Barely a spoonful of soup goes into her mouth before she asks, "What was it like—skimming over the desert in such comfort?"

I laugh. "You won't believe it." I pour out the whole story. "I even drove, Clara. I set the levers and ran the gas and steered us around big rocks. It was…it was powerful."

Clara stares wistfully over my head. "And the land? How's it all look when you're passing over it so fast?"

"Glorious." I sigh, reaching for a biscuit. "The Joshua trees practically waved as we roared past them. And birds and jackrabbits raced and jumped all around. You could taste the tang of the sage and the creosote bushes in the air. Even the dust smelled different. Cleaner somehow."

"Cleaner." Clara continues to stare over my head, so lost in thought she doesn't even notice when I pull her soup bowl to me and finish it off, along with the last of her biscuits.

No wonder men are such big eaters. Adventure works up an appetite.

Clara walks me to school the next morning. "I'm taking no chances," she says when I complain about the humiliation of it all.

"I truly will go, Clara," I plead. "I know when I'm beat. There's no need to shame me in front of everyone."

She places her hand on my shoulder, stopping me. She squints down at me, concern clear in her gray eyes. "I don't have no intention of shaming you, girl," she says. "Whatever gave you that idea?"

I shrug.

"I don't intend to shame you or embarrass you, but I do intend to see you inside that school tent. I'm responsible for you now. I expect you to realize that and act accordingly." She wrinkles her forehead, pushing her eyebrows together as she waits for a response.

"Okay," I sigh, warmed by her concern, but embarrassed just the same.

"Okay." Clara takes her hand off my shoulder and strides forward again.

I follow, drag-footed and sullen behind her.

Miss Sheldon stands outside the tent when we arrive. She grasps her skirt in both hands, lifting it above her shoes, and bustles over to us. "Katherine, you are in grave trouble," she informs me. Her hand twitches toward my ear. Clearly she wants to grab it and haul me wailing inside, but something makes her hesitate. She looks from me to Clara and back again, then runs her hands along her skirt, smoothing it, and turns on her heel. "Follow me." She glances over her shoulder, demanding Clara's attention. "If you don't mind, ma'am. A meeting of parents and…er…guardians is called for."

I look at Clara and shrug. I don't know what I've done to stir up a meeting. I skipped school, but I've done that before, and Miss Sheldon never crossed the schoolyard or smoothed her skirts about it. Curious, I trudge behind her. Clara follows.

Miss Sheldon opens the door with a flourish and charges up the aisle. I start to follow her but freeze the moment I cross the threshold. Mr. Granger stands next to Miss Sheldon's desk, rummaging idly through some papers. He stops when we enter and stares across the room.

I reach a shaking hand toward Clara, who grasps it in her own. Together we walk the length of the tent.

"Take a seat." Miss Sheldon waves me toward my desk. "You may sit here, Mrs...Miss..." she says to Clara, offering a chair.

"Clara will do, and I prefer to stand."

I hold tight to her hand. I guess I prefer to stand too, despite my shaking knees.

I lick my lips and struggle to return Mr. Granger's stare. When his eyes meet mine, I cringe. I press my clammy hand tighter into Clara's cool one, look at the floor, and wait.

Miss Sheldon sits down at her desk. "Mr. Granger says you attacked Evan in the street the other day."

Crybaby Evan. I should have guessed.

My breath bursts in and out of my chest. I think of things to say. *Evan was mistreating a poor, blind burro. Evan called me names. Evan deserved it.* I open my mouth to speak, but it all sounds so silly in my head. I sneak another look at Mr. Granger. "You murdered my father," I mumble into my chest.

"Excuse me?" Miss Sheldon leans forward.

I raise my head. Sweat beads on my upper lip and drips from my forehead. I free my hand from Clara's grip and sweep it, cold and shaking, across my face. I lick my lips again and meet Mr. Granger's steel-blue eyes. "You murdered my father."

Mr. Granger takes a deep breath and lets it out slowly. "This is what I was afraid of," he says. "I cannot have my children exposed to violence. To attacks on my good name. Evan is afraid to come to school, and Leslie is being…defiant." He mops his forehead with a handkerchief and looks both me and Clara up and down. "I am saddened by this child's…situation. But I cannot have my children in the company of such an unstable element."

Miss Sheldon fumbles with some papers on her desk. "Perhaps the best solution is for Katherine to…to take a break from school for a time." She looks at Clara. "She can return in the fall once things have settled some."

My shoulders roll back. *How dare she…*I struggle to speak, to protest, but I can't get my mouth to cooperate.

Clara's back stiffens. She reaches for my hand. "Kit has as much a right as anyone to schooling."

Mr. Granger takes a step toward us. "If we can't resolve this here, I'm afraid I'm going to have to take it to the sheriff." He looks hard at Clara. "The girl did assault my son. She also stole property from him. Some would consider that robbery—strong-arm robbery at that."

My stomach clenches, and I take a step back. Assault? Robbery? Jasper was not Evan's burro. He was a stray. Wild. You cannot steal something wild. And assault? He stands in the very suit he'd worn when he shot Papa and accuses me of assault? I glare at Mr. Granger. I can't speak.

But Clara can. "Children fight, Mr. Granger. They argue. From what I heard, your son was abusing that animal. Kit stepped in to save it."

I tuck my hand a little deeper into hers and take comfort in its warmth.

Mr. Granger's voice booms through the tent. "That child is a thief and a troublemaker, just like her father. I only hope that, in time, his influence will wear off. For now, though, I must protect my children." He smiles at Miss Sheldon, and his voice resumes its normal volume. "I'm sure you can understand."

"Of course," Miss Sheldon stammers. She takes out her student roster and makes a great show of crossing my name off. "Katherine may return to school in the fall—if she can promise to behave at that time." She writes something on a piece of paper and hands it to Clara. "For now, consider her expelled."

Blood roars in my ears. Expelled! Mother would have been mortified.

"Kit has a right to an education, Miss Sheldon, and it falls on you to teach her." Clara tears Miss Sheldon's paper up, scattering the pieces on the floor. "Of course, an education overseen by a woman so easily swayed by money and influence can't be worth much, can it? I reckon she can learn just as well at home—mayhap even better."

Clara clears her throat and turns to Mr. Granger. "I would think murdering her father in cold blood would be enough revenge for you." She turns her back to Mr. Granger and Miss Sheldon and holds out her hand for me to grab. "Come along, Kit."

Mr. Granger takes another step forward. His face is red, and his lips curl in a scowl. My insides roll. I clench a fist to my middle and lean over, trying to soothe it. *Please, God, no, please.* I close my eyes and will it to stop, but it is too late. My stomach lurches, and I vomit, splashing the shiny tops of Mr. Granger's shoes with the remains of this morning's biscuits and gravy.

Clara grabs my shoulder and steers me around gently. She presses a handkerchief in my hand and leads me out the door. "That's my girl," she says loud enough for Miss Sheldon and Mr. Granger to hear. "I couldn't have said it better myself."

I only wish some of my throw-up would have landed on Miss Sheldon as well. And I hope the next time I confront Granger, I can do it without losing my breakfast.

Chapter Sixteen

I toss and turn on my cot all night—haunted by Mr. Granger's glowering face and torn up with worry for me and Clara and Jasper the burro. What if Mr. Granger goes to the sheriff after all? Will Sheriff Earp arrest me? Will he arrest Clara for helping? What will he do to Jasper?

My fretting leads to worrying about everything else I've done. Stealing *Huck Finn*, trespassing on Old Joe Smiley, killing Mother and Papa despite my best intentions. I try to imagine talking to Pastor Travis with his sharp eyes and thin lips, but I decide he doesn't offer much in the way of absolution. In fact, I think Pastor Travis's counseling might look a lot like Aunt Minerva's letter writing. Dark and angry and full of blame and guilt.

I need something else. Someone else. But the only person left to confess to since Mother's dead is Sheriff Earp.

I cower at the thought, then force myself to get up. I slip out of my nightclothes and into my blouse and pinafore in the dark. I tiptoe past snoring Clara, careful to avoid the creaking floorboard next to the cookstove, and ease the front door open. I sneak out into the darkness. I walk in the cool, watching dawn inch toward the horizon, eclipsing the stars and lighting the day. "It's time to face the music," as Mother would say, and though I doubt she'd think that one confessor is as good as another, truth be told, confessing to Sheriff Earp might be even scarier than begging forgiveness from God himself.

I think of Mr. John Adams writing "Let justice be done though the heavens should fall" back when he was simply a revolutionary—long before he was president. If Mr. Granger is right and I have committed a crime, better the fall come from my own making than from the hand of some tattletale crybaby and his bully of a father. And if the rumors about Sheriff Earp are right, the fall comes mighty swiftly when he's in charge.

I approach the jail and knock quickly before I can change my mind. The deputy who shooed me off last time opens the door. I groan inwardly.

"I came to see Sheriff Earp." I push my shoulders back and look him in the eye.

If he recognizes me, he doesn't let on. "Sheriff's not in yet," he says. He blows his nose in a napkin and uses the scrap of fabric to point me to the steps. "You wait out here. Jail's no place for a girl."

I sit on the steps and wait. By the look of the sun, a whole hour passes before I see Sheriff Earp's bent frame coming up the sidewalk. He looks like he stepped out of a photograph in one of Miss Sheldon's history books. Only his injured left arm mars the image of the old-time gunfighter.

A coughing fit overtakes him when he reaches the jail steps. He sits down next to me, his face red and his breath raspy. "Blasted cold," he says once the coughing subsides.

"Gum camphor helps," I offer. "At least that's what Papa always said."

Sheriff Earp looks at me. His eyes are red and swollen but kind. "Gum camphor, huh? I'll give it a try." He turns his face to the sun, leans back against the step, and closes his eyes. "You picked a nice spot to sit."

"I didn't come to sit in the sun, sir." I cross my arms and turn toward him. "I came to talk to you. To confess a crime."

Sheriff Earp opens his eyes. He groans and sits up stiffly. His gaze is still kind but also harder somehow. Serious. The kind of look that makes it easy to believe all the stories about bar brawls and street fights and gunning men down in corrals way down in Arizona.

I rest my palm on my knee, trying to keep my leg from bouncing up and down. "I stole a burro," I admit in a rush. As soon as I say it, the tightness leaves my chest. My leg stops bouncing. I take a deep breath. "Some boys were messing with him—hurting him—so I took him. Now Mr. Granger's come around saying I'm a thief and that I assaulted his boy and that I can't go to school anymore or he'll turn me in to you for robbery. Strong-arm robbery he called it."

Sheriff Earp snorts. "Strong-arm robbery," he repeats, shaking his head. "And how'd you assault his boy?"

"I pulled him off the burro, and he fell into the street. I near about twisted Stewie Hines's ear off too, but Mr. Granger never mentioned that."

"I see." Sheriff Earp coughs. "Did you steal this burro from Granger's residence or one of his mines?"

I shake my head. "Main Street. Right in front of the Esmeralda Hotel."

Sheriff Earp laughs. "Main Street. I imagine that's proven a bit of an embarrassment for both him and his boy." He turns his face to the sun again and stretches out his legs. "Seeing as no one has come in to file a complaint, and since you were acting in service of another, so to speak, I'd be hard pressed to say a crime has been committed here. You don't have anything else to confess, do you?"

"I stole a rooster once."

Mr. Earp's eyebrows go up.

"He was headed for the cook pot due to some inadvertent misbehavior on my part. I was conscience-bound to save his life. But that was a while ago. More recently, I skipped school, and I sneak into the stable sometimes to read a book that's been left there. I've even taken the book home a few times—though I always bring it back the next day."

"Sounds harmless enough. Old Joe will let us both know if it's a problem. You can count on that." He pushes his hat back off his face a little bit more and closes his eyes once again. "What's your name, girl?"

"Kit. Kit Donovan."

He opens his eyes. "Your father wasn't Samuel Donovan, was he?" His blue eyes are sharp, stern.

I nod. I search his face for signs of pity or contempt. All I see is serious thought. A wave of hope flutters in my belly.

"Hell," he spits. "It's no wonder you're in a lather about Granger. You sure that's all there was to it? An old burro?"

"That's all he said."

"Don't worry yourself then." He pats me on the arm. "Busy

man like Granger ain't got time to fool around with some half-dead burro. Neither does an old lawman like me." He clears his throat. "I am sorry about your pop."

"He wasn't an anarchist, you know. He wouldn't have threatened Granger."

Sheriff Earp nods. "I've wondered about that myself."

"I've got a letter at home that says Papa was helping a man whose claim was being taken over by Mr. Granger. The fellow thinks that's why Granger killed him."

A muscle in Sheriff Earp's jaw tightens. "What do you think?"

"I think it's possible. It's a good claim." Hope jolts through me. I raise my eyebrows as I meet his gaze and bite my lip in anticipation.

"Any proof besides the letter?"

"Not yet."

Sheriff Earp sighs. He closes his eyes again. "The law requires proof." He opens his eyes and stretches. "I've gotta get to work, missy." He stands. "No more messing with the Grangers, okay?"

I shrug, trying to ignore the disappointment seizing my heart. "I don't think I can promise that, sir."

A smile appears below Sheriff Earp's walrus mustache. "That's honest. Can't ask for much more than that."

I start down the steps, but a hand on my shoulder stops me. When I turn around, the sheriff stoops, bending at the waist so that he is looking directly into my eyes. "If you need anything, you come see me."

"Thanks, Sheriff Earp."

He presses his hand tight against my shoulder. "Call me Virgil."

I nod. My stomach flutters as hope settles in once again.

Chapter Seventeen

I head back to Clara's, determined to find something that will convince Sheriff Earp to help me. The telegraph boy stops me as I near the cabin. "A woman back at that tent cabin said a girl lives around here somewhere. You her?"

"I might be."

"Katherine Donovan?"

I nod. The boy thrusts the telegram into my hand. He shifts from one foot to the other.

"You sure it's for me? No one's ever sent me a telegram before."

"Your name's right there, plain as day."

I look down at the paper. He's right. It says: *Miss Katherine Donovan. Goldfield, NV.* I read it again, slowly. Dread spreads through my body with each word.

The boy clears his throat and twists his hat in his hands.

I look up from the telegram. "Oh. I don't have any money for a tip. Sorry."

He shrugs. "Good luck," he says, stuffing the hat back on his head. He jogs away before I can say thank you.

I take a deep breath, staring at the big Western Union logo at the top. I'm not sure what some of the numbers mean, but the words below them are clear enough.

Arrive Saturday. Prepare yourself. Minerva Davis.

I flinch at the name and raise a hand to my face like I've been struck. I don't think dropping this in the privy will make much of a difference. Aunt Minerva never was one for making long speeches when a short one would do, and I guess when she's paying by the word, she gets downright terse. Still, those four words say it all— Aunt Minerva arrives tomorrow, and I am confident she will waste no time packing me up, acquiring a train ticket, and hauling me off to Philadelphia with her.

Aunt Minerva. Living with Aunt Minerva. Dear Lord. I imagine she'll be ten times…nah, twenty times worse than old Miss Watson ever was to Huck Finn. Company manners and Bible verses and ladylike this and proper that. I know I've been bad, but have I really been that bad?

I storm into Clara's cabin. "Did you write to my aunt Minerva?" I thrust the telegram at her before she can put down her cup. Coffee splashes the newspaper she's reading.

"Tarnation, Kit," she snaps. "Watch yourself."

"Did you? Did you write her? Did you want to get rid of me so bad you took it upon yourself to write Aunt Minerva?"

Clara takes the telegram. "How could I have written her? I didn't even know this woman existed. Who is she?"

"My aunt. Mother's sister in Philadelphia."

"I thought you didn't have any kin," Clara says, cocking her head and eyeing me.

"Just none worth mentioning." I dip my chin to my chest. "Sorry."

She presses a hand to her temple and shakes her head. "Well, someone knew. Maybe the postmistress or one of those meddling women from the Ladies' Aid or…" She taps her finger against her lips, thinking.

"Miss Sheldon." I groan. "We made a family tree ages ago in history class. Dang her for a busybody."

Clara sets the telegram on the table and squints at me. "Well, let's have it. What's she like?"

I tell her about Aunt Minerva. About her fine house and fancy friends. "She's high society," I say at the end.

"Married?"

I shake my head. "Papa called her a spinster, but Mother just said she was 'independent.'"

Clara's eyebrow goes up at that. She looks around the cabin. I do too, trying to imagine it through Aunt Minerva's eyes. A sheen of dust covers the splintery wood floor, and the tabletop is nearly buried in newspapers, maps, and books about mining. Clara's unmade bed lists against the corner, another pile of books perched on the floor next to it. Our washing hangs on a line between this room and the one in back. I picture my unmade cot. "She's not going to like this," I say.

Clara shrugs. "It's clean." She runs her hand across an empty spot on the table and blows off the dust that coats it. "Mostly. There are no mice or vermin at least. And it's serviceable." She studies my face. "We have nothing to be ashamed of. But, mayhap her coming is for the best. This really is no place for a girl."

I stand up straighter. "How can you say that?" I cry. "She's going to haul me back East and dress me up like some sort of prig—all ruffles and choking collars and fancy walking shoes. She'll send me to private school and make me take elocution lessons and fold my hands in my lap and sit just so…" I shake my head. "Besides, I've got work to do here. I told Sheriff Earp about Tom's claim. I told him I'd find some evidence to prove Mr. Granger murdered Papa."

Clara sighs. "It may well be for the best. All this talk of evidence and revenge. I don't know that it's healthy for a girl your age." She clears her throat, and her gray eyes go serious. "I doubt I'm a proper influence on you, Kit. Granger is a dangerous man. Dealing with him is not child's play."

"Someone has to," I mutter.

"Not necessarily."

"But you said…" I think of all those times Clara came to our tent shouting about "standing up" and urging Papa to do something—anything—to make the mines safer. "You said people had to stand up."

Clara's shoulders sink. She looks down at her hands. Tears streak the sides of her face. "I'm a silly old woman. A silly old woman who should have kept her mouth shut."

I slam my hand against the table. "You helped get him killed, Clara. You, me, Tom—all of us. And now, all of you just want to turn tail and slink away. That's why you want me gone, so you don't have to pretend to fight anymore." I sniff back tears. "You're a coward. All of you. Chicken-livered, yellow-bellied, stinking cowards."

I choke on the last words and run from the table, out the front door, and all the way to Old Joe Smiley's stable. I climb into my stall, desperate to rest my head against the bay horse's mane and cry and cry. But she's gone. A roan stallion takes her place. He rolls his eyes at me and puffs out his chest. When I try to pet him, he pins back his ears and paces and stomps, then he lowers his head and shoves me right out of the stall and into the dirt. I crawl past Arnie's motorcar and into an empty stall. Crouching in the corner, I sniff the air, desperate for the comfort of hay and horse sweat, but it's not the same.

Nothing's the same.

Aunt Minerva's coming whether I like it or not.

*　*　*

I creep back to Clara's sometime after midnight. She's still up, reading on her cot. She puts down her book and watches as I make my way across the cabin and into the back room. I'm nearly asleep, still fully clothed, when she blows out the candle, and I hear her whisper, "Good night."

The smell of bacon and eggs rouses me the next morning. "Thought you'd need a hearty meal today," Clara says. She doesn't ask me where I spent my time last night, and I don't offer any information, though I bet the straw in my hair gives me away.

Clara has already finished her breakfast by the time I've fed and watered the animals. I bolt mine down, change into my skirt, and position myself on the porch to await Aunt Minerva's arrival without uttering a word.

If my silence bothers Clara, she doesn't let on.

By nine, Clara has placed a pack on Sal and is leading her down the road without so much as a "See ya later." I pick at a bent nail in the porch and pretend I don't care. Inside, I'm sobbing.

By eleven, my skirt is covered in dust and burro hair, and I have sketched maps of Goldfield and Baltimore in the dirt with a stick, only to stomp them into oblivion under my feet.

By one, rivulets of sweat claim my back and my arms, and my hair, still too short to hold in a braid, is plastered, damp and itchy, across my forehead. I want to cry, wail, and run after Clara. Instead I curse.

By three, I find Clara's scissors and cut my hair even shorter. I look too much like a boy once again, and I can't wait to see Aunt Minerva's face when she sees it.

By five, I stretch out on the porch. I rest my head against my arms and doze. I've given up thinking about Clara or Aunt Minerva or how any of this looks. Truth be told, I've simply given up.

The buzz of a motorcar wakes me mid-drool. I sit up in time to see Arnie chugging up the road, looking fine in driving goggles and a scarf, while Aunt Minerva perches precariously in the backseat. She clutches her hat with one hand and grasps the top of the door with the other.

A spark of recognition—and maybe even joy—crosses her face when she sees me. I run a hand over my shorn hair, suddenly sorry I took such drastic action.

"My darling," she calls, squinting against the sun.

I freeze in place, hand resting on my head, too surprised at her kindness to believe what I'm hearing. I stare, entranced, and watch as her eagerness shifts to frowning disappointment and, finally, to annoyance.

"What are you doing up there on that porch idling like some linthead?" Aunt Minerva scowls as the motorcar putters to a stop in front of the cabin. "Get down here and fetch my grip before this no-good half-breed drives away with it."

Her tone and the angry glint in her eyes break me from my trance. That's the Aunt Minerva I recognize. I jump off the porch and run over to them.

Aunt Minerva scrambles out of the car before Arnie can turn the engine off. "You and your contraption are a menace to civilized people everywhere," she says, slamming the door.

Arnie shrugs. "She claims she's your aunt."

I bite my lip and nod.

"Some aunt."

I start to nod again, but Aunt Minerva interrupts me by smacking the back of my head and grabbing me up in a sideways hug. I struggle free from her embrace and stare up at her. Confusion, anger, and maybe a little bit of relief fill her face.

"What in the world is the matter with you, Katherine Eve?" Her voice softens just a bit before the hardness catches it again. "I told you to fetch my grip. Or are you so taken with this no-account excuse for a stage driver that you have forgotten your manners completely?"

I roll my eyes.

Arnie smiles, then reaches in the backseat and hands Aunt Minerva's case to me. "Good luck," he whispers. "Pleasure doing business with you," he hollers, tipping his hat to Aunt Minerva. "See you at the stable, Kit." He waves jauntily as he shifts the motorcar into gear. The car bucks, then sputters to a stop. Frowning, Arnie fiddles with the gearshift a moment, then gets out, red-faced and head down, to open the hood. His movements are quick and restless, and Aunt Minerva's smile is smug as she watches him struggle with the car.

"Let's leave the help to their work," she says, turning away from Arnie and walking up the steps to Clara's cabin. "Careful with my grip."

As I struggle up the steps with Aunt Minerva's bag, I hear the car's engine catch. I turn to watch Arnie backing the car around in a slow circle. I mouth my *sorry* to him and wave as he backs down the road toward town.

Aunt Minerva stands on the porch, shaking the dirt from her fine woolen traveling dress. She takes off her green feather hat and holds it in front of her. The feather sways under the weight of all the dust. She gives it a shake, then fastens it back on her head. "That boy is a menace. I couldn't believe my ears when he said he was a friend of yours." She gives her skirt another swoosh and clicks her tongue in disgust. "A working boy—and half-breed at that. I don't know what Sister was thinking, moving you to a place like this."

Aunt Minerva clicks her tongue again the instant she enters Clara's cabin. All the things I noticed yesterday are still there: the dirt on the floor, the unmade cot, the teetering piles of books. To that is added the morning's unwashed breakfast dishes, a new stack of newspapers, and a strange cat, stretched out in the middle of all of it, casually licking a paw.

The surprise of the cat—coupled with my unsettled nerves at seeing Aunt Minerva after all this time—nearly undoes me. I choke back a fit of giggles and shoo the cat off the table. I snatch it up and carry it out the door. I scoop a piece of leftover bacon from one of the breakfast plates and set both the meat and the cat down on the porch. "Come back in a day or so," I whisper to the cat.

"There's no way Aunt Minerva will eat at the same table as you."

Aunt Minerva roams around the room, running a gloved hand first along the table and then across the back of one of the chairs. She locates a wooden stool in the corner, removes a newspaper from the seat, takes her handkerchief from her pocketbook, and wipes the entire stool off, top to bottom. When she has finally scrubbed the handkerchief black, she perches on top of the stool and surveys the cabin like a queen surveying her land. "Sister wrote that conditions were harsh, but I had no idea."

"It's not so bad." I wonder what she would have thought about our tent cabin with its dirt floor and single room. Clara's cabin, with two separate rooms, a cooking area, and real wooden floor and roof, looks like a mansion in comparison, despite its current disheveled state. "Things have been busy since Papa was..." I trail off when I see Aunt Minerva's lip curl.

"Killed in the street like the dog he was?" She shakes her head. "Poor Sister. What in the world did she ever see in that man? A failed shopkeeper. A failed factory worker. And now? An attempted murderer and a thief, if the papers your teacher sent me are to be believed. Lord in heaven."

I bite my lip and busy myself with tidying up the table. It's best not to talk back to Aunt Minerva when she's in a state. She'll only take it as an excuse to light into me, and I have a feeling that lecture's coming soon enough. My guts churn with unspoken words as I conjure up my company manners—which have gone long unused out here—and offer her a glass of water.

"I wondered when you'd ask."

I pour a cup from the bucket next to the cookstove, taking

extra care to replace the oilcloth covering the top when I set it back down.

When I present the water to her, Aunt Minerva wrinkles up her nose and refuses to take it. "I believe I will pass," she says with a sniff. "Show me where I am to sleep. I would like to freshen up before this woman you are staying with returns home."

I lead her to the back room. I fill a bowl with water and lay out a towel for her to wash with. I try to sift out some of the sediment that dulls the water, but it's no use. "The water's not dirty, ma'am," I explain when she frowns. "It's just thick." At least that's what Papa said when Mother and I looked in horror at our first bucketful of Goldfield water.

Puttering around the cabin, I pick up while I fight the urge to take off—to run away and hide so that she can't take me back East. I listen to Aunt Minerva rage about the dust, the wind, and the harsh desert air. I find myself wanting to tell her that it's not so bad. That you get used to it, but I don't. She'll just laugh.

"I should have brought more face cream," she says, after scrubbing her face with the towel. "From the looks of your complexion, I imagine asking if you have any is an exercise in futility."

"I…uh…I don't have any, ma'am."

"No, I don't suppose you do. Perhaps the woman you have been staying with has some extra lying around."

I picture Clara's face—her leathery skin, her wonky eye. I'd sooner wager that Clara has a mattress lined with gold certificates than that she is in possession of a single ounce of beauty cream, but there's no use telling Aunt Minerva that. "Perhaps she might" is all I say.

Chapter Eighteen

Clara comes in while Aunt Minerva is lying down on my cot with a cold washrag spread across her forehead. Clara looks around the cabin, her expression wary as she takes in the cleaned-off table and made-up bed.

"What did you do with Buster?"

I shoot her a questioning look.

"Orange fellow. Long whiskers. I found him snuggled up next to your burro last night. Looked like he could use a home."

"I put him out. Aunt Minerva would have had a fit if I let a cat stay in the house. Especially one sprawled out in the middle of the supper table."

Clara rolls her good eye. The wonky one stays steady, pinned on me. "Last I checked, this was my cabin, not Aunt Minerva's," she mutters. "I thought you'd like a critter that you could have inside. A pet." She shrugs, clearly confounded by my actions. "Besides, he looked like a good mouser, and you seemed worried about cleanliness last we talked."

I hang my head. She's right. I would have liked an indoor pet, but what's the point of it now that I'm leaving? "Sorry, ma'am. I think he's sleeping under the porch. Want me to go fetch him?"

Clara turns an ear to the other room where Aunt Minerva mutters filthy this and disgraceful that under her breath. "Nah. On second thought, you may have done old Buster a favor. There's a decent chance you might find me sleeping under the porch before this night is over." She winks at me.

I smile back. "Sorry." And I am. I'm sorry about the cat, and I'm sorry about Aunt Minerva, but what I'm most sorry about is calling Clara all those awful names yesterday.

"It's okay," Clara says. "I take it she's arrived?"

"Yes'm."

"Welcome to my home, Miss Minerva. I trust you've made yourself comfortable," Clara hollers toward the back room. "We're having sausages and yeast bread for supper, and some tomatoes I picked up at the greenhouse. Or we will, once Kit here gets the fire going."

Aunt Minerva's muttering stops. I busy myself at the cookstove, nervous about her meeting Clara. Clara is just about everything Aunt Minerva hates in a woman: loud, opinionated, wiry, and tough like an old rooster. She can tend the mules, read a map, and prospect for gold as good as any man. Heck, she can even drink whiskey better than most of the men down at the Northern Saloon, if the night she fixed up Papa's arm was any indication.

It's not like Aunt Minerva is without gumption, though. After all, she managed to get from her big house in Philadelphia all the way to Nevada on her own with no masculine help to speak of. Unless you count Arnie, of course, and I am pretty sure Aunt Minerva would not. In any case, she seems to be taking care of herself—and everyone around her—just fine.

Aunt Minerva emerges from the back room while I wrestle the sausages into the hot frying pan. I keep my eyes on the pan, telling myself I'm watching for spatter, but I'm really afraid to see Aunt Minerva's face as she takes in Clara for the first time.

"I want to thank you for caring for my niece," Aunt Minerva says as she crosses the room to shake hands. "It was very generous of you." Her voice is smooth, kind almost, and I take my eyes off my work to look at the two of them.

"It was no trouble," Clara says. "Kit's been a real help to me."

If I wasn't so shocked at my aunt's gracious smile and words, I would have laughed at being called help. But the real kindness Aunt Minerva is showing Clara has put me in mind of Mother, who went out of her way to be sweet and generous to everyone. "Blessed are the merciful," she used to tell me. "Just pretend for the tiniest moment that you are them—and that you see their struggles through their eyes."

I don't think I have ever been very good at seeing things through someone else's eyes.

And now, Aunt Minerva is shaking Clara's hand.

I barely eat for watching Aunt Minerva and Clara converse. They talk as if they are old friends, and Aunt Minerva, though picky about the food and the water and the dust, does not seem to mind or even notice Clara's overalls or braided hair or knee-high men's boots.

I, on the other hand, am nearly overwhelmed with shame for falling into such a slovenly state. My clipped hair is grimy from the wind and dust; my skirt is worn thin and hangs too short on me now, showing all of my ankles; and my still-bare feet are smudged with dirt and God knows what. I am in no way the fine young woman Mother wanted me to be. What must Aunt Minerva think of me? What must Mother think of me—watching all this time as I slip further and further from the promises I made her?

How can anyone be a lady in such a sorry place as this?

Aunt Minerva excuses herself for bed right after dinner. "It's been a dreadfully long day," she explains. She turns to Clara. "I hate to impose further, but you wouldn't happen to have any face cream? It seems I've used the last of mine trying to combat this dry weather."

"Grab that jar from by my bed there," Clara instructs me.

Shocked, I return with a jar of Pond's cold cream.

"It's the best we've got—though don't take my poor face as proof," Clara says, gesturing at Aunt Minerva to take the jar.

"Thank you," Aunt Minerva says.

"You use face cream?" I cry.

Clara smiles at Aunt Minerva before she hisses at me, "Of course I use face cream. I have a face, don't I? What do you take me for? Some sort of barbarian?"

Since I have nothing to say to that, I choose to say my good nights. I fetch a blanket off the cot and make a spot for myself on the floor in the corner nearest the cookstove, where I spend the evening growing a bruise on my hip and wondering what has happened to make Clara and my aunt bosom pals—and how their newfound friendship will affect me. One thing is for sure. I will have to work doubly hard to get Clara to help convince Aunt Minerva I need to stay.

* * *

Aunt Minerva wakes resolved to attend the morning's services at the Presbyterian church. "You realize it's not a real church," I explain over breakfast, determined not to let her see more of the town than is absolutely necessary. Maybe if I can convince her that Goldfield isn't that bad, that I can be trusted to grow up fine and cultured here under Clara's watchful eye, she'll let me stay. I know it's a long shot, but it's all I've got. "I don't know if you'll be comfortable there. It's a tent. A big tent, surely, but still a tent."

"God is not particular," Aunt Minerva says as she picks her way through a plate of fried ham and nearly stale bread. "Get dressed."

Together, we whisk past Saturday night's trash and the still-drunken rabble sprawled outside the various saloons lining the way to the church tent. A few men leer as we pass, and more than one calls out, but neither Aunt Minerva's gaze nor her step wavers. We turn onto Fifth Avenue in record time.

God may not be particular, but Aunt Minerva is. She doesn't even make it to the entryway of the church, where folks stand in their somewhat shabby Sunday best, before taking my hand and turning back toward Clara's. "Perhaps we will do Sunday service at home today, as God surely intended."

"But I thought…"

She shakes loose of my hand. "You should have told me how people dress for church here," she says, looking down at her own gown—white and high necked and, despite having traveled across the country smashed in her grip, fresh and wrinkle-free.

"But some of the women are dressed fine." I purposely don't say *ladies* because the best-dressed women idling in front of the church are Leslie and her mother, wearing gowns I am sure they had made in San Francisco.

Perhaps it was Mrs. Henderson, still wearing her flour-sack apron, that threw Aunt Minerva off. "And Mrs. Henderson wears that ratty old apron everywhere. She's always ready to catch a pig or dispatch an unruly chicken." I gulp, thinking of poor Henry the rooster. "She's eccentric like that."

Or maybe it was the saloon girls. Even with their faces freshly scrubbed and their bodices laced up, they still look like they'd be more comfortable at the bar flirting than in the pew praying.

I was right about keeping Aunt Minerva out of the main part of town. No good will come of it. Still, her change of heart fills me with relief. I am nearly certain that had I entered that tent after such a long absence, God would have struck me down. Or even worse, some busybody would have commented to Aunt Minerva about my ill attendance. I'd never hear the end of that.

Aunt Minerva continues down the sidewalk while I gawk at the saloon girls and consider my near-escape. The click of her heels grabs my attention, and I quicken my pace to catch up with her.

"I do not know what's become of your manners," Aunt Minerva begins as soon as I reach her side. "You've grown coarse and ignorant in your time here. I don't know if it's a result of running with thieves and low-class boys who are nothing but trouble—and trouble in a motorcar no less—or if it's simply the environment. Reprobates and hoodlums and loose women all around. In either case, Philadelphia will be good for you."

She pauses to adjust her gloves, and I use the break to catch my breath. Aunt Minerva doesn't. She just keeps lecturing. "I have located a private academy in Philadelphia that has agreed to admit you, despite it being closed to newcomers and you having no family ties of significance save myself."

Private school. It is just as I imagined. I groan at the thought. I'll never fit it there. I can't even fit in here.

Once her gloves are secure, Aunt Minerva sets off walking again. "Of course, a well-placed donation helped, but that may not be enough if you do not alter your attitude and begin acting like a lady.

"I've also talked with some of my friends. Not the details, of course." Her pace slackens, and she looks me in the eye. "And I do hope you will manage to hold your tongue about your father, Katherine. No one needs to hear such talk. There will be rumor enough to satisfy the busybodies."

I jerk back. "That's not fair. He didn't…" I begin, but before I can get the words out, Aunt Minerva is moving again.

She quickens her gait, and the cadence of her speech quickens with it. "In any case, the ladies have agreed to take you up and prepare you for the cotillions, afternoon teas, and garden parties that fill the summer schedule. I imagine we will have to go back to the basics—sitting, standing, dining properly, speaking with gentlemen, that sort of thing. There will be enough study to engage your days until we are all removed to the seashore to escape the city heat and take in the restorative energies of the beach season. You can start school proper after that."

"It sounds like a danged lot of work to me," I mutter. I raise an eyebrow. "I doubt I'll be very good at it." I jut my chin out, letting the challenge hang in the air between us.

"It surely will be work," Aunt Minerva says, brushing aside my threat. "The elocution lessons alone will be a challenge, and having dined with you, I can see instilling proper table manners will take some time. Still, some of it will be simply heavenly," she says, dodging a drunk man staggering up the sidewalk.

I can't imagine how any part of that could be heavenly. The ocean, perhaps. It would be nice to see an ocean. Of course, most things would look heavenly when compared to here. I reckon, through Aunt Minerva's eyes, Goldfield looks like hell itself. And I need to figure out a way to change that opinion fast.

Chapter Nineteen

Aunt Minerva takes to bed with a headache immediately upon returning to Clara's cabin. I guess she figures God has given up on keeping tally of church attendance here, and I don't argue the point. As we are to leave tomorrow, I'd like the time alone to complete some errands of my own, since I'm no closer to convincing Aunt Minerva that I should stay. I sneak an apple out of the food basket and head straight to the stables to say my good-byes to Arnie.

"The boy's off with his motorcar," Old Joe Smiley says, emerging from the bay's stall with a pitchfork in hand.

"I just wanted to say good-bye. I'm most likely leaving for Philadelphia tomorrow and won't be coming back."

Joe wipes his palm on his dungarees and shakes my hand. "Good luck to you, miss," he says. "I'll keep an eye on your friend and that bay you like so much."

"I thought she was gone." I show Joe the apple. "I brought this for that surly stallion in her stall."

"He left this morning, but the bay'll be back tomorrow." He takes the apple from me. "I'll be sure she gets it." He turns back to the stall and digs through the hay. He holds the worn copy of *The*

Adventures of Huckleberry Finn. "You take this," he says, pressing it into my hands.

"But LM and Arnie…"

"Take it. I'll explain anything that needs explaining." He spits a plug of tobacco into the dust at his feet. "It's my blasted livery, ain't it?" He picks up his pitchfork and walks to the back of the stable. "If you don't want to be covered in muck, I suggest you get along."

So I do, though saying good-bye to the stable and Old Joe Smiley makes me sadder than I ever would have imagined. I meander back to the cabin, clutching *The Adventures of Huckleberry Finn* to my chest and generally feeling sorry for myself.

Clara is not at the cabin when I return, nor is she coming back before morning, Aunt Minerva informs me. "She left you a note." Aunt Minerva hands me an old assayer's report. "On the back."

I flip the paper around. I recognize Clara's writing immediately. The same careful script she used to sign Tom's note.

> Watch after yourself in the big city and know that it
> is as filled with goodness and vice as the place you are
> leaving. Be true to your gut, and remember that a lady
> is more than fancy clothes and big houses. I will hold
> a place for you as long as I walk the earth.
> Your friend, Clara

My friend, Clara. Those words reach inside my chest and pluck at my heart. Strange I never really thought of her that way until now, and sadder still that I never treated her as anything more than a crazy old lady who let me sleep on her cot.

Tears prick my eyes as I think about the way I just accepted her kindness without a thought or a grateful word. I shake my head in shame and wonderment at all the cross words I've had with her since Papa's death and how calm and caring she's been despite my rude mouth and defiant ways. And now I don't even have the chance to say good-bye or I'm sorry or even thank you.

Aunt Minerva interrupts my sorrow by reminding me that we leave bright and early the next morning. "The stage departs at six."

She means the old stage. The one pulled by horses that takes nearly half a day to get to Tonopah. "Arnie can get us there in two hours with his motorcar, and I'm certain he'd offer a discount, us being friends and all." And our poor bottoms will not be bruised clear through from bouncing on a board seat all day, I think, but refrain from saying that out loud because Aunt Minerva would surely protest my mentioning her bottom.

"I do not trust that half-breed friend of yours," Aunt Minerva says. "He'll leave us stranded in the desert while our train is pulling out of the station."

I cringe at the word *half-breed*.

"Arnie is Shoshone," I say, emphasizing the word. "And he's a fine boy." I glare at Aunt Minerva, daring her to argue with me. When she doesn't, I scoop up *The Adventures of Huckleberry Finn* and stomp out of the cabin.

I'm antsy and angry and so full of energy that I walk back into town. I stop at the streetlight on Crook Street. I lean my back against the light pole and slide down until I'm sitting on the ground. I open up *Huckleberry Finn*. I flip through the book, thinking I'll stop at a random page and see if Huck has anything to say that might make all of this a little easier.

I fan the pages of the book. My thumb catches on a piece of notebook paper folded up and tucked inside. I take it out and unfold it. In careful square letters across the top, it says: *This may help you.*

I furrow my eyebrows. *What in the...*

Listed below the words, one after another, are names. Men's names. I scan the page. I don't recognize the first two, but my heart jumps when I come to the third and nearly bounces out of my chest when I read the fourth. Jesse Perkins and Tom Perkins. Tom and Jesse! Why are they on this list?

I keep reading. I don't recognize the next person, but the last name on the list is Westchester.

I turn the paper around in my hands. Who would have stuck a note like this in *Huckleberry Finn*? Arnie? Nah. He'd have just given it to me. Old Joe Smiley? He doesn't seem like that kind of guy who'd sneak things into books. Besides, the writing doesn't look like a man's hand. I stare at the *J* on Jesse and the *K* on Kennedy. They both have a swirl to them, a flourish that looks more like a lady's writing. Fancy and quick, but studied too. Purposeful and pretty. More big-city finishing academy than boomtown tent school.

I look at the list again. There are six names on it, and I know three of them. That can't be a coincidence. I need to talk to Arnie. He's the only other person who knows about the book. Maybe he knows something about the note too. Clearly it's a clue. A clue to catching Mr. Granger. Now I just need to find out what it means.

I tuck the note back into the book for safekeeping and get up. I race back to the stable to see if Old Joe is still there or if Arnie's returned, but the place is empty, save for a couple of horses and a mule.

I wind my way through town, running through the list of names in my head until I find myself in front of Mr. Granger's big stone house on Fifth Avenue. I stand in the street, peering through the glass window at Mr. Granger, sitting in a chair, smoking a pipe, and reading the newspaper. An electric light illuminates his head, and he looks so comfortable and so content surrounded by that light that for a moment I find him very nearly holy.

I pull the paper out of the book and fumble it open. I squint in the dark, trying to read the list of names again. I know this has something to do with Granger. I just know it.

Perhaps it's the sight of Mr. Granger—sitting in his fine house without a care in the world—that sets my mind on its path. Or maybe it's my anger at Aunt Minerva, who is too blind and stupid to see Arnie as the enterprising boy and good friend that he is. Quite probably, it's the gift of Huck Finn himself that's got me thinking daring and defiant thoughts. In any case, a wave of possibility, choler, and rebellion carries me back to Clara's cabin and face-to-face with Aunt Minerva.

"I'm not going back East with you," I tell her once I've roused her from her bed. "I'm not ever going to be made into a fine lady anyway, so I may as well stay here and figure out a way to prove to people that Papa was murdered." I shake my paper at her. "I think I've been given a clue."

Aunt Minerva smirks. "Who do you think you are? Some sort of diminutive Nellie Bly?"

"Nellie who?"

"Bly. She's a newspaper…oh, never mind!"

I start again. "I'm staying. I aim to see Mr. Granger punished, and if I have to lie, cheat, and steal to do it, that's damn well what I'm going to do."

Aunt Minerva starts at the word *damn*, and her smirk shifts into a frown. "Katherine Eve Donovan…" Her voice is slow and steady, but her eyes flash with anger. "You will shut your mouth and…"

"I'll shut my mouth, but I'm not going with you. I don't take any pleasure in talking back to you, ma'am…" Now, that's not exactly true. There is a little pleasure to be had in standing up to Aunt Minerva, but there is no real joy in it. I know she is only trying to do what she supposes Mother would want. She's only trying to get me out of Goldfield and on to somewhere safe where folks say please and thank you, where mothers don't die of pneumonia and fathers aren't gunned down in the street.

"Mother would stay and fight," I explain. "No matter how low-down you think Papa was, Mother knew him to be a good man. She would want other people to know it too."

Aunt Minerva glares at me. "You are just like your father. Stupid and stubborn and more trouble than you are worth." She smooths her nightgown likes it's a dress. "I imagine you will come to a similar end," she says before turning back to the cot. "I bid you good night."

My cheeks flush. "You're stu…" I begin. Then I stop. There's no use getting ugly; I've won. "Good night, ma'am," I stammer, shocked and a little impressed at my own behavior.

I collapse into a chair, suddenly exhausted by the day and by my decision. I put my head down and drift off to sleep with the list of names running through my head. "Tomorrow, I'll start looking for these men," I promise myself before sleep overtakes me.

* * *

I awake with a crick in my neck and Buster the cat suckling my ear. I shove Buster off me and get up. I am fiddling with the cookstove, warming up last night's coffee, as Aunt Minerva emerges, dressed in her fine woolen traveling suit and carrying her grip. "The stage will pick me up at the end of the road," she says.

She sets down her case and reaches into her handbag. She takes out a small bundle of coins, counts out five, and places them on the table. Buster jumps up and bats at them with his paws, knocking them to the floor one at a time.

Aunt Minerva watches him for a moment, then sighs. "Telegraph when you come to your senses. I will wait in Tonopah for a few days. But only for a few days, Katherine Eve. Heed my words. If you do not arrive in Tonopah before my train leaves, that will be the end of it. I will not make this offer again. Lord knows the last thing I need hung around my neck is an ungrateful child."

I cross my arms. I wouldn't telegraph her if she were the last person on earth. I set my jaw. "Bye."

She picks up her grip and heads to the door. "Perhaps a little more time in this horrid town will do you good. Perhaps it will remind you of what you're missing." Her eyes snap, and she takes a deep breath. "Be sure to let your teacher and that Father Dermondy know what happened here. I don't want anyone thinking I'm the sort of person who would abandon a child in a godforsaken place like this—even if they are a bunch of Papists." She flips her skirt, settles her hat firmly on her head, and walks out the door without a backward glance.

I watch her go, partly relieved to see her leave and partly guilty for putting her through the whole ordeal. I'm sorting through my joy and shame when I remember the picture I found at our old cabin. I fish it out of my keepsake box and race to the door, desperate to reach her before she makes the corner. I catch up to her just as I hear the stage rumbling up the road.

"Here." I thrust the photograph into her hand. "I think Mother would have wanted you to have it." It's a picture of Mother leaning against our old wagon, the one Papa drove us here in. She's smiling, a real smile, full of hope and promise and love.

I remember that day. We had just pulled into Tonopah and were listening to people talk about the town of Goldfield and how everyone here was striking it rich. It was a party of sorts, and the photographer was showing off his new camera, taking pictures of arrivals and departures, of children on ponies, and men holding handfuls of gold ore. The good cheer and hopefulness of the place jumped from person to person like a spring cold, and we caught it.

I remember how Mother and Papa laughed as we crossed the desert the next day, talking about the fortune we would find and all the fine things they would buy once they had money.

The three of us had a grand time, singing and laughing and making plans. Maybe if Aunt Minerva could see that her sister had known joyful times, even if she'd never written home about them and even if they'd only lasted a short while, she wouldn't be so sad or so angry about all of it.

Aunt Minerva holds up the picture. She shakes her head—a

mighty sorrowful shake—and crumbles the picture in her hand.

I reach out a hand to stop her, but it's too late. The picture is ruined.

"Sister always was a dreamer. I guess that's something you got from her."

She tosses the picture in the dirt, only to bend down to retrieve it as the stagecoach rumbles up to us. She tucks the ruined picture into her sleeve and climbs into the coach, leaving her grip for the driver to tie on top.

"Have a safe trip," I call. It seems my company manners are still intact, though Aunt Minerva's appear to have deserted her. She neither replies nor looks my way, though I can see her, stooped shouldered and tearful, through the window as the coach drives away.

The sight of her fading into the distance makes me sad. I walk back to the cabin on heavy legs. I have a lot to figure out, and suddenly I feel much older than my thirteen years.

Chapter Twenty

If Clara is surprised to see me when she gets home, she does not let on. "Put some coffee on and give Sal some barley, will you?" she says when she walks in the door. "We are plumb worn out."

I do as she says, though I linger a bit, petting Sal and Jasper and letting them know I am here to stay, despite what I told them yesterday. When I return to the cabin, Clara is hunkered over the cookstove, frying up a pile of flapjacks and bacon.

"How'd she take it?" Clara asks, and I know by her tone that she's not talking about Sal and the barley.

"Better than I'd expected." Which is true. Aunt Minerva didn't faint when I said *damn* or force me kicking and screaming into the stage. She took my news and my defiance like the lady she is, and I guess even I have to respect that. "She said she'd stay in Tonopah for a bit in case I changed my mind."

Clara piles flapjacks and bacon on my plate, then sits down and begins eating her dinner straight out of the frying pan. "I checked out Tom's mine," she says between swallows of food. "I'm no expert, but that's one heck of a rich hole if you ask me. It's no wonder Granger is trying to get his hands on it."

I'm not surprised. Tom isn't one to lie—even if his regular

manners aren't that great.

I fumble through a pile of newspapers and come up with *The Adventures of Huckleberry Finn*. I pull out the folded-up paper and hand it to Clara. "I found this."

Her eyebrows go up as she reads and stay that way until she refolds the paper and hands it to me.

I stuff it back in the book for safekeeping and tell her of my meeting with Old Joe Smiley.

"Joe's not one to talk in riddles," Clara says. "If he has something to say, he comes right out and says it."

"That's what I thought. The only other person who knows about the book is Arnie, and he's not secretive like that either."

"You sure that note was meant for you?"

It's a reasonable question. The note could be for anyone, really. At least it could be for LM or whoever owned the book before I found it in the stable. But that doesn't make sense. The only hands that have touched that book in months are mine and Arnie's and Old Joe Smiley's, but he doesn't count.

"It must have been. Tom, Jesse, and Mr. Westchester's names are on it. I'm sure I was meant to find it. It's the only thing that makes any sense."

"Did you recognize any of the other names?"

"No."

"Me neither." She rubs her chin. "Well, maybe one. J. Martin. That might be Jack Martin, but he won't be any help. He died months ago."

I put my fork down and gawk at her. "Was he murdered?"

"Pneumonia."

"Dang."

"But we could start looking for the others. They might know something that will help. I'll start asking around."

"And I'll go by the newspaper office. Maybe Mr. Westchester will have an idea."

"Mayhap he will." Clara yawns a wide gaping yawn that shows she's missing more than just her front tooth. "And mayhap you'll do the dishes while I get some shut-eye."

"Mayhap I will." But first I have to figure out some things, including how to get a job. I cannot live off Clara's kindness forever.

* * *

I am up early the next day, earlier than I ever managed to get up when I had school and earlier than Clara who still snores softly on her cot in the corner. I prepare the coffee for her, setting up the muslin bag of coffee grounds and readying the water. I round up the coins Aunt Minerva left and stack them next to Clara's coffee cup. Then I scribble out a note.

> I am loath to use Aunt Minerva's money, but I want to
> give it to you in the hope that it will cover some of my
> room and board until I can earn my own keep. Thanks
> for taking me in, Clara. You will surely be rewarded.
> Your friend, Kit

I smile with satisfaction as I sign the note. Sometimes doing the right thing feels good.

I walk into town, determined to find Mr. Westchester—and just as determined to get a job. It is only fair that I pay my own way. Clara did not exactly beg me to stay, and I have a feeling her budget is stretched far tighter than she lets on.

I make a mental list of my skills: spelling, reading. I can write a pretty good essay, and I know quite a bit about American history and politics. I can even relay a few geography facts if I'm pressed and if I stick to North America.

I study the businesses I pass on my way to the newspaper office. Saloons, stores, banks, hotels, assayer offices, and brokerage firms. I am certain none of these places have much call for a thirteen-year-old girl who can spell words like *acquiesce* and knows the name of President Roosevelt's pet badger. (It is Josiah.)

Perhaps I could get work at one of the restaurants in town. I am a lousy cook, but I could wait tables or clean up or something. It doesn't really matter; anything will be fine and a great improvement over spending my days at that useless school. Well, near about anything. I'd rather not have to work in a dance hall or delouse the linens at a tent hotel like Jenny DeMillo does every day after school. The last thing I need is a head full of lice, thank you very much.

But first, I must find Mr. Westchester.

I enter the *Goldfield Times* office and look around the room. At first glance, it looks the same as last time. Newspapers are piled on desks and chairs, and books and stacks of paper are scattered across the floor.

The Shoshone woman dusts some shelves in the corner, and once again, she turns and smiles at me. Once again, I wave. And once again, our friendliness is interrupted.

"What can I do for you?" a voice growls from behind a machine. I turn to see the bearded old man who slept at his desk the last time I was here. He bends over a machine, squints, and curses under his breath.

"I need to talk to Mr. Westchester."

The man looks up from his work. "Westchester?" He scowls. "No-good louse. He's no longer in our employ."

"No longer…?"

"Fired. He was fired. Or quit. I don't remember exactly how it went. In any case, he's not here." The man sweeps his arm out in a wide arc, gesturing at the empty office. "No one's here, which is why I'm fooling with these dad-gummed letters when I should be out doing something useful or taking a nap."

I rub my hand over my eyes as the news settles in. "Where'd he go?"

"Where'd who go?"

"Mr. Westchester. Where'd he go?"

"How in tarnation would I know? Away." He flutters his hand in the air. "He left. They all left."

"Did he leave Goldfield entirely, or did he just leave the *Times*?" I cross over to the table and stand behind him. A hot, thick scent fills the air, and I can't help but breathe it in. A mix of ink, oil, hair grease, and sweat—a combination that smells surprisingly good. The way I imagine hard work and a sense of purpose smells to people who pay attention to that sort of thing. The room practically vibrates with energy as this man works, placing letters on a cylinder.

I peer over his shoulder and watch. After a minute, I notice that the letters are forming words—only the words are written in reverse so that *Railroad Rumors Have Ring of Truth* is written *hturT fo gniR evaH sromuR daorliaR.* The whole thing looks like some sort of spelling game Miss Sheldon would never let her students play. I can't wait to try it.

"Do you have to think backward?" Curiosity pushes my disappointment about Mr. Westchester out of my head.

"Nah. You get used to it. The *p*'s and *b*'s can be tricky though." He motions me to come closer and look.

I move a pile of newspapers from the stool next to him and take a seat. I peer into the wooden trays lined out across the table. They are full of tiny metal letters. He chooses a letter and places it in the cylinder, repeating the process until the word is spelled. Then he puts in a blank piece of metal and chooses the next letter. Before long, an entire news story is written out on the machine as if by magic.

I clap my hands and laugh. "Can I try?"

"The next word is *future*," he says, gesturing to the trays.

I make a picture of the word in my head. I find the tray with the letter *e* in it and proceed to place the metal letters on the cylinder, one by one, until *erutuf* is set in place.

"Not bad. Most folks can't do it without muttering like a surly drunk or writing the word down on paper. It's a shame you're not a boy. I could use a printer's devil around here."

I frown and try to make sense of what he says. "What does being a boy have to do with putting letters on a cylinder?"

The man shrugs. "Printer's devils are always boys. A rough-and-rowdy newspaper office is no place for a girl."

I look around the room. "Seems like this office is no place for people at all," I say. "Where'd everyone go?"

"Away," he says, doing that fluttery thing with his hand once again. "All the union talk had everyone on edge. The killing pushed 'em right over it. Your buddy Westchester didn't help matters—sneaking that article about that injured miner and his poor slip of a girl past me while I was recovering from a long night at the Northern Saloon. Folks were afraid, I suppose, so they left."

I wince at "poor slip," but let it pass. "You're still here, though."

"I have to be." He taps a grimy finger against the masthead of one of the newspapers spread across the table. "Tobias Jeffries, editor in chief. Which means I'm the captain of this newspaper. And any captain worth his salt is duty bound to go down with his ship, you see. So that's what I'm doing. Going down with the ship—one blasted letter at a time." He turns back to his work.

"You sure you can't use any help? I'll work hard and I learn fast." I try to keep my tone even and professional, but I'm sure the quiver of desperation in my voice gives me away.

Mr. Jeffries shakes his head, not even bothering to look up from his task.

I slide off the stool. "Thanks for showing me the machine, at least." I turn to leave but not before taking one more look at the trays and the cylinders. How wonderful it must feel to set all those letters, to have a hand in creating all the words that people will read and talk about. I look over the article again and notice that he's spelled the next word wrong. I start to speak, to point out his error, but he interrupts me.

"If you know of a boy who can spell half as quick as you, send him my way."

I don't answer, and I don't tell him about the error. I guess he'll figure it out when tomorrow's paper is printed and people wonder what in the world a *railroab* is.

Serves him right. A boy, indeed.

* * *

I decide to combine my errands. I will inquire about a job and Mr. Westchester at the same time. I start my search around the corner from the *Times* at the Brown Palace Hotel.

"We have no need for a girl," the desk clerk informs me before I can even ask about a job.

"Not even a maid?" I cringe as I say it, disgusted at the thought of cleaning up after strangers. Still, a job is a job, and I do know how to sweep and mop and make a bed.

"You are far too scrawny to handle a maid's duties," the clerk says with a sniff. "Now, away with you."

"You don't, by chance, have a guest by the name of Mr. Westchester staying with you?" I lean over the desk, trying to sneak a peek at the registry.

The clerk draws the book closer to him and lays a hand across it. "We do not give out information about our guests."

"I don't need information. I just want to know if you've seen him. Small man with round glasses. Carries a little notebook in his breast pocket."

The clerk closes the registry with a bang. "We don't give out information about guests," he repeats before shooing me out the door.

I resume my search, inquiring at restaurants, the bakery, even— horrors—the laundry, but either no one wants to hire a girl with skinny arms and no experience or no one wants to hire a girl. Worst of all, no one's seen Mr. Westchester.

Larson's Department Store is my last real hope.

I pause out front of the store, checking my reflection in the window glass. "Smile," I urge myself as I shake the dust off my skirt. "Be friendly and sweet." I run my hand through my hair, cursing myself for cutting it so short once again. I shake my head at my reflection and stick out my tongue. "You look like a boy, and an ugly one at that," I mutter. "No one's going to hire you."

My mouth hangs open at the thought. Of course no one's going to hire that girl in the window. Not Mr. Larson. Not the clerk at the Brown Palace Hotel. And not the editor of the *Goldfield Times*. But Mr. Jeffries would hire the boy version of that girl. He said so himself.

All I have to do is become a boy. And, really, how hard can that be?

Chapter Twenty-One

I spend the next two days rounding up clothes. I find a shirt in the discount bin at Larson's Department Store—a steal at five cents because it's missing nearly all of its buttons—and use an afternoon to scavenge buttons and sew them on. I've about given up on finding a pair of britches that will fit when I spy some pants hanging on a clothesline across the street from the town wells. Truth be told, I consider snitching them. I could cross the yard and have those pants off the line and in my bucket before anyone notices; I am certain of it. But I don't. Instead, I walk right over and knock on the door.

"I wonder if you'd consider selling that pair of pants?" I ask, polite as you please, pointing to the clothesline.

The woman looks me up and down. "What do you want with those old pants?"

"I…" My mind swims with lies that would put even Huck Finn to shame. A little brother whose last dying wish is a new pair of pants. A school-sponsored charity drive to clothe the poor. A friend who was robbed at gunpoint by a pants-stealing bandit and is hiding around the corner in his skivvies. "I need them for a disguise I'm putting together."

She looks at me hard, like she's considering something. "You aren't aiming to cause any trouble, are you?"

I drill my big toe into the dirt and try to make my eyes wide and innocent-looking. "No, ma'am. I'm just going to play a little joke on a friend."

"You're not planning on sneaking into one of the saloons, are you?"

This time my eyes widen for real. "No, ma'am. I wasn't planning on doing anything like that."

And I wasn't. At least not until she suggested it.

"Tell you what. You fetch me a couple of buckets of water from the well over there, and you can have those pants." She ducks back inside and returns with two empty buckets.

I cross the street, amazed at my good luck. In no time at all, I have the buckets filled and delivered and the pants folded neatly under my arm. "Thanks," I call to the lady as I walk away.

"I better not hear of you causing any trouble," she yells at my back.

"I'm sure you won't." Which isn't a total lie. Though I'm fairly certain I'll cause some trouble, I'm pretty sure she won't hear about it. It's a good-size town after all.

I race to the cabin, grab my broad-brimmed hat and the shirt I got at Larson's, and wrap them up with the pants. I snatch up my copy of *The Adventures of Huckleberry Finn* too, just in case. I head straight to the stable and wait for Arnie. Knowing it could be a while, I pull the book out of my bundle, find a soft spot next to the bay, and flip the pages to Chapter Eleven. In minutes I'm right there with Huck, who is dressed like a girl in a calico gown and a sunbonnet, twitching and sweating in some women's house as he tries to get information out of her.

Sometime after sunset, Arnie pulls up in his motorcar. He kills the engine and gets out. Despite his fine driving clothes, he is covered with a sheen of dust and mud. He swats both his linen coat and his goggles against a post, knocking the dust out before hanging them on a nail just outside the stall. He dips a hand in the bay mare's water trough and splashes it on his face and arms, cleaning off some of the grime. He's about to take his shirt off when I clear my throat and stand, the book still clenched tightly in my hand.

"Hello there," he says, fastening the buttons he'd loosened on his shirt. "I thought you left town."

"Changed my mind."

He nods, like that makes perfectly good sense.

"I'm trying to get a job." I walk out of the stall and stand next to the car. "I was hoping you would help me." I unfold the pants and shirt and hang them over the railing.

He looks at the clothes, then back at me. A slow smile spreads across his face. "What's your plan?"

His green eyes twinkle as I tell him about Mr. Jeffries and the job as a printer's devil. "Let's see what we've got to work with," he says, shoving the clothes at me and motioning toward a stall. "I'll be lookout." Arnie turns his back to me and walks a few paces toward the door.

I duck into the empty stall. I put the pants on first, pulling them on underneath my skirt. I slip the skirt off, careful not to drop it in the muck. Then I slip out of my blouse and tug on the shirt. I am a mess of armholes and mismatched buttons for a minute but quickly get it all straightened out. I look down. I guess it's good I don't have a shape yet. Leslie Granger would never get away with such a ruse, but then again, Leslie wouldn't have to.

I shove the hat on my head and step out of the stall. "Well?"

Arnie looks me up and down. He adjusts the shirt collar and stands back. He frowns. "What are you going to use for shoes?"

I look down at my bare feet and shrug.

"You need shoes if you're going to work in an office."

He's right. Bare feet may be okay for school and for shopping, even for funerals, but if I'm going to work in a newspaper office, I'm going to need proper shoes. Boy shoes.

Arnie disappears into the back corner of the stable. When he returns, he tosses me a pair of boots. "They're my old ones."

I slip them on and wiggle my toes. "I'll have to wear extra socks and shove some newspaper in the toes, but I think I can make them work."

"Let's see you walk."

I stroll down the middle of the stable, casual as you please.

Arnie shakes his head. "You look like a girl. Walk heavier. Like this." He paces back and forth a few times.

I copy him.

"Heavier. Like you have lead in your boots. And don't move your hips so much."

I imagine my spine is one heavy stick—stiff from pelvis to neck. When I walk through the stable again, I make the boots clomp with each step, which isn't hard to do since they are at least three sizes too big. I think I'm getting the hang of it. A little chill of excitement runs up my spine. This might actually work.

After half an hour of pacing back and forth, Arnie finally says, "Okay, let's try it out on some people."

I follow him out of the stable and onto the street. I copy his movements, hands stuffed in pockets, eyes squinted. I nod at everyone we pass, and a few people nod back. I concentrate so hard on walking heavy and stiff that I forget to look where I'm going when we cross the street, and I nearly crash into a lady crossing in the opposite direction. Luckily, Arnie catches me by the arm before I send us both sprawling into the mud.

"Too much beer," he explains to the woman with a smirk and a tip of his hat.

"Sorry," I croak, trying to make my voice low like a boy's.

Arnie snorts back a laugh. The lady frowns at both of us and hurries out of our way. "I guess she believes you're a boy," Arnie says, laughing. "Or she thinks you're a sick frog. In either case, it's not a bad start."

I laugh along with him. Not a bad start indeed.

I spend the next day practicing being a boy with Arnie. I can slouch, spit, and scratch nearly as good as he can. And I've always been pretty good at swearing. After we've practiced all the basics, we run through the things that gave Huck Finn away when he dressed like a girl: throwing, sitting, catching things in my lap. I don't think the opportunity to thread a needle will come up, but I practice that too—holding the thread and poking at it with the needle instead of the other way around.

The one thing I can't do is talk—at least not in a way that sounds remotely like a boy.

But I think I can work around that. If Mr. Jeffries asks, I'm just going to tell him that my throat was injured because I smoked too much when I was younger. That's why I sound like a girl.

Besides I'm not looking for a job as a singer. I just want to be a printer's devil.

* * *

First thing in the morning, I slide into my pants and shirt, stuff Arnie's boots with newspaper, and pull my hat down tight on my head. I march right into the newspaper office, letting the door slam behind me. I clomp across the floor like I haven't got a care in the world. "I hear you're looking for a printer's devil," I say when I reach Mr. Jeffries desk. "And I'm just the man for the job."

Mr. Jeffries peers up from the paper he's reading and yawns. He looks me up and down. "Can you read?" he asks, narrowing his eyes.

"Of course," I sputter.

"Spell?"

"Sure."

"Clairvoyant."

I take a step back. "I can't see the future, sir. I didn't think that would be a requirement for the job."

Mr. Jeffries rolls his eyes. "Not are you. Can you spell it?"

"*C-l-a-i-r-v-o-y-a-n-t*."

"Backward."

I clear my throat. "*B-a-c...*"

"No." He settles back in his chair and sighs. "Spell *clairvoyant* backward."

It takes a great effort for me not to smack myself in the head. Of course. "*T-n-a-y-o-v-r-i-a-l-c*," I spell.

Mr. Jeffries purses his lips and nods. "Not bad. You're nearly as quick as a girl who was in here a day or so ago. Not quite, but close. What's your name, son?"

"George Peters." Why not? If it's a good enough pseudonym for Huck Finn, it's good enough for me.

"All right, George," Mr. Jeffries says with a twinkle in his eye. "How's ten dollars a week sound?"

Like a fortune! I can barely contain my excitement. "Wonderful, sir," I squeak. "I mean, that'll be just fine," I say, forcing my voice down a register.

A smile flickers across Mr. Jeffries face. "Can you start today?"

"Sure."

"You remember…I mean, you know how to use one of these things, George?" he asks, pointing at the printing press.

"I sure do."

"Good. Here's some copy." He hands me the piece of paper he was reading. "Why don't you get started?"

I read over the page. He could use a handwriting lesson or two from Miss Sheldon, but I can mostly make everything out. "Is that an *i* or a *j*?" I ask, pointing at the wobbly script.

Mr. Jeffries squints at the page. "Whichever one makes sense in the sentence," he grumbles.

I take another look. "Oh, it's a *z*."

He frowns and shoos me off with a wave of his hand. I hear him mutter, "My writing's not that sloppy," as I take a seat at the printing press.

The day flies by in a blur of words and ink and paper. My fingertips are stained black from the ink, and my mind is filled with backward words like *ecremmoc* and *ytinutroppo*. I can't wait until tomorrow when I can see all those words I set in print.

Plus ten dollars a week! I think of all the things I can buy as I race over to the stable to tell Arnie my good news. Food, boots, even a new dress, though I will have little cause to wear it as I am now George Peters, boy printer's devil—or at least I am five days a week and a half day on Saturday.

"You got it!" Arnie races over to hug me as soon as I walk into the stable.

My toes tingle and my face flushes when his arms go around me. I squirm loose. "How'd you know?" I stammer. "I haven't even gotten a chance to say anything."

"It's written all over your face." He rubs his thumb across my cheek and holds it up, smudged with black ink.

He hands me a towel, and I head over to the water trough to scrub my face. I tell him all about Mr. Jeffries and the job while I wash. "The pay is good. Plus I get to see all the news before anyone else. Today there was an article about the railroad coming. And another about Mr. Granger opening up a new mine, which reminds me…"

I dig *The Adventures of Huckleberry Finn* out of my pocket and pull out the paper stuck inside. I hand the list of names to Arnie. "Do you know anything about this?"

Arnie scans the list and shakes his head. "I gave a Mr. Kennedy a ride to Tonopah a few weeks ago. Could be the same guy." He flicks the paper with his finger. "Where'd you get this?"

I tell him the whole story, starting with finding the list in the book and ending with searching all over town for Mr. Westchester.

"You think these people have something to do with Granger killing your father?"

I nod. "I know Tom and Jesse. They were in a fight with Granger over a claim. Now they're gone. Maybe it has something to do with that."

Arnie hands the note back. "Well, there's no time like the present," he says, slapping the dust off his britches and grabbing his hat.

"For what?"

"To find the first fellow on the list. Wendell Harrison."

I slide the note back into the book and straighten my hat. I follow Arnie into the street. "Where are we going?"

"The best place in town to hear news. The Northern Saloon."

I laugh. "You think they'll let me in?"

Arnie shrugs. "Your outfit worked on the newspaper man. No reason it shouldn't work on a bunch of drunks."

I follow him onto Crook Street, concentrating on my walk and trying to catch glimpses of my reflection in the store windows. "Maybe if I don't talk much."

"That would probably be best," Arnie agrees as he fishes some beef jerky out of his pocket. He tosses me a piece. "Better eat up. You don't want the beer going straight your head."

Chapter Twenty-Two

If people really do roll over in their graves when the living do something they'd object to, I can pretty much guarantee that Mother is spinning like a top in hers right now. The thought of Mother flipping around in her grave is nearly enough to make me hightail it back to Clara's quicker than you can say "drink and debauchery." Arnie must sense my hesitation because he grabs me by the shoulder and steers me through the swinging doors.

The Northern Saloon is so crammed with people that no one even looks my way as Arnie and I weasel through the crowd. The saloon is huge. Bars line the walls, and there must be a dozen men pouring drinks and taking money. Opposite the bars, men and women swarm around big wheels with black and red squares that spin and spin.

"Roulette," Arnie explains as we walk by one of the wheels. "A sure loser of a game."

The chorus of groans and swear words that erupt when the man spinning the wheel announces, "Red fifteen," makes me think Arnie's right. Still, I like the energy of the place. People's eyes shine with expectation and excitement. It feels like anything could happen. My chest thumps with thrill of it all.

Never in my life have I seen such a whir of activity—not even in Baltimore. The saloon is filled near to overflowing with a mishmash of people shouting over pool tables, hunkering over card tables, and swearing over dice games. Miners bend over games or lean on the bar in their tattered shirtsleeves, chatting casually with finely dressed mine owners and crisply pressed government officials. Workers of every type and size—from bankers to brewery men, and even the boy who brought me the telegraph—drink from glasses and mugs.

Ladies in white dresses and hats with huge bobbing plumes laugh and nod and order champagne, their bubbly voices rising just above the din. Women wearing their feathers on their dresses instead of their hats hang over the backs of chairs, watching card games. A group of men in suits huddles around a table, shouting numbers and writing things down.

"Stockbrokers," Arnie says, nodding in their direction. "They come to trade nearly every night." He grabs a seat near the men. "They know everything going on in town," he says, shoving a chair toward me. "They might be worth listening to."

I sit, fanning the air with my hand. The stench of cigar smoke mingled with sweat and face powder has my head reeling and my eyes watering. I alternate holding my breath and taking in tiny sips of air. It seems to be working until a gust of flowery perfume overtakes our table. A girl with heavily rouged cheeks and a blouse that shows more than it covers launches herself in Arnie's lap. She places a bottle and two small glasses on the table, then reaches up, pulling off Arnie's hat and setting it crookedly on her head.

"How's tricks?" she asks Arnie with a wink. "That car still running?"

"Yep. Should have your last payment end of the month."

The girl grins wide, revealing a crooked front tooth smudged with lipstick. "I'll drink to that." She picks up the bottle and begins to pour.

My eyes go round. A twinge of irritation cuts into my side. *Who is this girl?*

Arnie slips a hand over the top of the second glass. "Just the usual tonight. I have to get up early and meet the train."

She rolls her eyes. "Always such a spoilsport." She finishes her drink, then fiddles with the hat, taking it off and placing it back on Arnie's head. She adjusts it, moving it over and forward a little, so it sits cocked to the side, nearly covering Arnie's left eye. She smiles that wide grin again. "Who's your friend?" she asks, pointing her chin at me.

I stare blankly at her, too afraid to speak.

"That's George. He just started working at the *Goldfield Times*."

"A newsman. It's been a while since we've had someone from the *Times* in here. Aside from Mr. Jeffries, of course." She holds out her hand. I give it a halfhearted shake. "You sure you don't want something stronger than Arnie's usual?" she asks, smacking him on the arm as she gets out of his lap.

I pull my hat down lower and shake my head, wishing with all my might that I could disappear.

"He don't talk much," Arnie adds.

"You don't say." The girl winks at me and sashays off to the bar.

"Not bad," Arnie says once she's gone. "Casey's got a good eye.

I thought she might see through your cover."

"It probably helps that the lights are low in here," I offer. "And that she didn't get too close."

Arnie blushes.

He blushes again when Casey returns with our drinks. She slides a mug in front of each of us. "Two usuals."

Arnie picks his up and takes a long drink. I eye mine warily.

"May as well get it over with," he advises. "Folks get suspicious if it looks like a man doesn't enjoy his beer."

I grasp the mug and try not to think about my last experience with alcohol and the coughing fit that followed. "Does it burn?"

"Nah." He takes another gulp. "Smooth as candy."

I close my eyes, wrinkle my nose, and say a quick apology to Mother. Finally I take a drink. But the bitter taste doesn't come. Instead it's sweet and spicy. "Sarsaparilla," I say, laughing. "You tricked me."

Arnie grins. "Told you it was like candy."

We sit quietly, watching people and sipping our drinks. "Any idea what he might look like?" Arnie asks.

"None. All I've got is the name."

"Maybe Casey can help." Arnie waves the girl back over.

She returns carrying two more mugs. "You better pace yourselves. You don't want all this sugar keeping you up late."

"We're looking for someone named Wendell Harrison. You know him?" Arnie asks.

Casey purses her lips. "Harrison," she mutters. "I don't know a Wendell Harrison, but I do know a Pete Harrison." She cranes her neck around like she's looking for someone.

"Casey, table three!" a bartender calls out.

"Give me a second," she barks back. "Can't you see I'm busy here?" She scans the room. "There he is," she says, pointing to a man leaning against the piano. "Hiya, Petey! Get over here."

The man looks up, surprise clear on his face. He makes his way over to our table. He's halfway across the room before I recognize him. It's Peter—the assayer we drove in from Tonopah. I nudge Arnie with my foot and smile. "We're in luck."

Peter recognizes us right away. "Arnie," he says, shaking his hand, "and Kit?" He looks at me quizzically.

I glance over at Casey who's grinning away. "I'm kinda going by George right now," I say, taking his hand.

"Of course," he says, nodding like I've just said something sensible.

Arnie gets right to business. "Do you know a Wendell Harrison?"

"I should, considering he's my brother. What do you want with Wendell?"

"You boys set here?" Casey interrupts, nudging me on the shoulder when she says *boy*.

My face flushes. I have no idea what to say to this girl. Thankfully, I don't need to say anything. Arnie presses a gold coin in her hand. "Much obliged."

"Stay out of trouble now, Arnie. You hear?" She holds his gaze, her eyes serious for an instant before she hikes up her skirt, tucking the coin into a blue lace garter.

Arnie blushes clean up to his ears. "I'll do my best, ma'am."

I shake my head. That twinge of irritation is back—pressing hard into my side. I turn away from Arnie and the girl and direct all of my attention on Peter, who pulls up a chair.

"What do you want with my brother?" he asks again.

I take a deep breath. If I'm going to move forward, I'm going to have to trust the note—and the men whose names are on it. "I think we want his help." I go on to explain about Papa's murder and Tom and Jesse's mine and the note I found in the book.

Peter takes a long drink of his beer. "Wendell's done some engineering work for just about every mine out here. There's a good chance he knows something." He squints at his pocket watch. "He's probably still in the office. Want to go see?"

We squeeze our way through the crowd once more. When we reach the street, I take a deep breath, trying to clear my nose of all the barroom scents. But I don't have long to appreciate the clean air. Peter wastes no time leading us to his brother's office.

* * *

"I know this place," I say when we reach the building. "I see he's gotten his window repainted." I nod to the words painted on the glass. *Harrison Engineering and Assay.* "The last time I was here, it was shot to pieces."

Sure enough, the short man whose office space I barged into the day of the gunfight emerges from the back room, shotgun in hand, seconds after Peter unlocks the door.

The sight of the gun and the man brings the whole day back to me. The thwack of the bullets, the tang of sweat and fear that filled the air. I close my eyes against the memories and will my hands to stop shaking.

"I brought some friends," Peter says.

The short man rests the shotgun against the desk and eyes us warily. "Don't I know you?" he asks, his gaze resting on me.

"Kit Donovan," I say, reaching out to shake his hand. "You saved me from a crazed gunman and a glass of whiskey a while back."

The short man smiles, showing his dimples. "Of course, Miss Donovan. Have you learned any new curse words since I saw you last?"

I blush at the memory. "One or two," I confess. "Though I haven't had cause to try them out."

"Give it time."

Peter and Arnie pass a confused look between them. "We're old friends," Mr. Harrison says by way of explanation. "What can I do for you tonight?" He pulls a few chairs up to one of the tables and motions for us to sit down.

I fish *The Adventures of Huckleberry Finn* out of my pocket and take out the list. I slide it across the table to Mr. Harrison. "Someone thinks you can help me." I tell the story I told Peter at the saloon, only this time I go into detail. I explain about Mr. Westchester interviewing Papa after the mine collapse, about Tom and Jesse's claim being worth a lot of money, about me talking to Mr. Westchester and how Papa said it was going to make trouble, and what Tom said about Papa helping them prove Granger was trying to steal Tom's gold. I tell all of it, and when I'm done, the room is silent and my mouth is dry.

"You think your father found out something and Granger killed him for it?" Mr. Harrison asks.

I nod. "I think there's some connection between the mine collapses and the stealing. Something Papa knew that no one else does."

"And the newspaperman?"

"I'm not sure. I think Mr. Westchester knows more than he let on in his articles. He knew that the union boss was tied up in it somehow," I say, remembering Mr. Westchester's disgust with Mr. Hines.

Mr. Harrison tips back in his chair and runs a hand across his bald head. "How many people on the list do you know?"

"Four, including you. I think J. Martin is dead, and Arnie here drove Charles Kennedy out of town a few weeks ago."

Arnie nods. "Said he was heading east and good riddance."

Mr. Harrison frowns. "Kennedy sold his claim to Granger before he left. Sold it for a song, I hear."

"And you? What do you have to do with Granger?" I can't contain the hope in my voice.

He taps the paper with this finger. "I was the engineer on the Goliath mine early on. The Molly Ann too." He gazes over my head and out the window. "How many people know about this list?"

I look around the room. "Just us. And Clara." I press my index finger against my lips, trying to remember. "Oh, and my aunt Minerva, though I didn't really show it to her. That's it. Well, besides the person who wrote it."

His eyes widen. "You don't know where it came from?"

His alarmed tone makes me sit up straighter. I shake my head. "Found it tucked in the book." I look around the room. A knot forms in my belly. *Could this whole thing be a trap?*

"And you don't know where this Mr. Westchester is?"

"No. He's not at the newspaper anymore. I don't even know if he's still in town."

Mr. Harrison rubs his head again. "This is a bad idea." He stares at me, holding my gaze across the table for a long moment. Finally he gets up and goes to a filing cabinet in the corner. He shuffles through some papers, then returns, spreading a map out on the table in front of me.

"Are you sure you want to know all of this?" he asks, placing his large hand over the map and covering the image. "There's a lot at stake here."

I picture Papa lying bloody and broken in the street. His casket being lowered into nothingness. "I think I know what's at stake, sir," I whisper.

He cracks his knuckles slowly, one at a time, and looks at Peter. "Granger is a dangerous man. This is not child's play."

"I think it has to be, sir." I pause, waiting until he looks at me, hoping he can see that I am serious. "No one else wants to take it on."

He rubs his head again. "Okay, damn it," he says, smoothing the map. "This here is the Goliath mine." His fingers sweep over the map. "This shows where the tunnels are. The direction they plan to expand in. Basically, it's how the Goliath should look underground."

I point to a spot just south of the Goliath. "That's where Tom and Jesse's claim is."

Mr. Harrison squints at the map. "Granger's tunnels all run east to west." He trails his finger along a line that starts at the bottom of the shaft and moves up diagonally. "This is the gold vein," he says, running his hand up and down the sloping line. "See how it starts here on the surface, then runs at a slant all the way down to the bottom of the shaft. See how all the tunnels end when they meet that line. That's where the gold is. There's no plan to dig to the south. The gold is all here." He runs his finger along that slanted line again.

I frown. "But he told Tom their gold really started on his claim. That he could follow the vein from his mine into theirs."

"I'm sure that's what he said, Kit, but look here." He pushes the map closer to me. "The gold Granger's digging lies at a diagonal running east and west. In order to go south, he'd have to dig over or under his own ore and real close to those existing tunnels. You can't do that."

Arnie's eyes go wide. "Would digging like that cause accidents?" he asks. "Would blasting new tunnels that close cause cave-ins in the main tunnels?"

Mr. Harrison's mouth forms a straight line. His eyes are serious. "Exactly, son. It would make the whole place unstable."

I look around. Everyone is quiet. They look dazed. I wonder if I do too.

I lay my palm across the map. "I'd bet anything this is what Papa knew." My skin tingles and my voice shakes. "Now I just have to figure out how to prove it—before more men get hurt."

Chapter Twenty-Three

Clara is still up when I finally make it back to the cabin. Her face is red, and her eyes spark with anger. "Where in the world have you been? I've been pacing back and forth for hours worried sick," she spits out. "I don't care if you have a job; you can't prance around all hours of the night. Not if you plan on living here."

I wait until she pauses to catch her breath, then shove the copy of the map Mr. Harrison gave me in her face.

She pushes it aside. "Whatever that is, it's not a good enough excuse for staying out half the night." She paces again, and her bare feet thump against the floor. "I should have made you go," she mutters under her breath. "I never should have listened to Minerva. I'm in no shape to parent a young..."

"I found Wendell Harrison!" I cry, shaking the map in her face, desperate to drown out whatever else she might say. "We've figured out what Papa knew. We've figured out why Granger killed him."

I spread the map out on the floor and show it to her. "Granger's been stealing Tom and Jesse's ore. He's digging secret tunnels under his existing ones and sneaking into their claim from underneath. Then he's digging out their gold. That's why the mine is unsafe.

That's why they've had all those cave-ins. The secret tunnels are causing the others to collapse."

Clara draws in a sharp breath and sits down on the floor next to me. "No wonder he wanted to keep Tom and Jesse from sinking a shaft. Chances are they'd have run right into his secret tunnels." She rocks back on her heels and shakes her head. "He's stealing gold, and he's putting all those people's lives at risk to do it."

"Papa must have found out about it. He must have said something that night…"

"And Granger shot him," Clara finishes the sentence for me.

I try to nod, but I can't. I cover my head with my arms and sob.

Clara lets me be. When I finally stop, I'm a mess of tears and snot, but she hugs me anyway. "Wouldn't your mom and dad be proud of you now," she whispers in my ear. "Wouldn't they just be so proud."

The tears roll down my cheeks. "I'm sorry I'm so troublesome, Clara. I really am," I whimper, nestling against her. Gratitude washes over me. A sense of duty follows it. I owe Clara so much for the care and comfort and general kindness she has shown me. She's sacrificed her privacy and perhaps her well-being to take care of me. I aim to show her that she was right all along when she said someone needs to stand up. I aim to make her proud.

* * *

The next morning, I wake swollen-eyed from crying, but lighter somehow. Hopeful. I stash the map and the list of names in my keepsake box and show Clara my hiding place. (As if she wouldn't know where to look if she needed to—under my cot isn't much of a hiding place, but it's better than nothing.)

"We'll figure something out," she assures me before I head out the door for work.

I spend the day reading articles and setting type. I'm slow and distracted and have made so many mistakes that Mr. Jeffries says, "Go on. I'll finish up," before the clock has struck five.

"I'll do better tomorrow, sir," I promise.

"You'd better," Mr. Jeffries grunts.

His words hit me like a punch. I trudge down the street, feeling sorry for myself. I've barely gone a block before self-pity turns into shame. I turn back to the newspaper office, disgusted with myself. It is not fair to stick Mr. Jeffries with my work. I will offer to finish it myself—even if it takes all night. Or I can tidy up the newsroom until it really is quitting time. In either case, I won't shirk my duties.

I'm nearly to the office when I hear the crack of pistol shots. I crouch low and dart out of the street. I duck behind the Bank and Trust building and peek around the corner. More gunshots echo through the streets, but I also hear something else—the faint ting of a bell.

Fire!

I run in the direction of the shots. Men and women, boys and girls pour out of their houses, tents, and businesses and run in the same direction. Some carry buckets; others haul washtubs and teakettles. I even see one small girl carrying a tin cup full of milk. I want to scream at the girl to go back, that it's not safe, but I don't. I just run.

Groups of people crowd around every well and faucet in town, filling buckets and pots and basins. I think I catch a glimpse of

Leslie in one of the lines, but before I can be sure, a man from the Texas Saloon thrusts a bucket of water in my hand. Casey from the Northern Saloon shoves in right behind me, and together we run to Columbia Street and take our places in a bucket brigade that is splashing water on the Nevada Hotel.

Waves of heat roll off the nearly finished building site. Flames flicker up the frame and leap across to the buildings on the right and left. People stream out of the office building next door, eyes wild with fear. Some join our line, but most just back away from the building and stand silently in the street.

"Where's the water truck?" the man in front of me growls. His soot-covered face is black. His bloodshot eyes glow with heat and fear and what looks like anger. Just as I'm about to shrug my reply, a cheer erupts around me.

The water truck has arrived! Men swarm the truck, pulling out hoses and pumping water. Streams of water douse the building in front of us. We cheer.

But too quickly, the water flowing from the hoses slows, first to a trickle, then to a drip. "Pull that tight," one of the men shouts, shaking the hose. But it's already straight; there are no kinks in the line.

"We're out of water," the man yells.

The crowd groans.

Buildings up and down Columbia Street are ablaze. Flames lick the rooftops along Fifth Avenue. A woman shrieks as the fire spreads to the general store, igniting a barrel of flour and threatening a display of kimonos draped over a table on the sidewalk.

"It's no use," the man in front of me cries as what's left of the

Nevada Hotel collapses in a whoosh of smoke and smoldering ash. "The whole town's going up."

I squint through the smoke, trying to see how far the fire has spread, desperate to know if the stable is all right. My stomach tightens. If the mare or Arnie or poor Old Joe Smiley are hurt, I don't know what I'll do.

I cast around for something to throw on the flames, but it's no use. All we can do is watch helplessly as building after building smolders and ignites.

Then, out of the corner of my eye, I spot movement. Mr. Ulmer of the Little Hub Saloon is soaking blankets in a keg of beer and hanging them on the side of his building to protect the wood from the approaching flames. Before long, more kegs are rolled out, and we are back in business—only this time, instead of using water to douse the flames, we throw buckets of beer.

After what seems like an eternity, the fire is contained. I run a hand over my face, surprised to feel tears. I look at the scene in front of me. Hot ashes smolder where buildings and houses once stood. The places that escaped the flames droop under wet blankets and scorched roofs.

Stunned, I join a group of people milling around and assessing the damage. A good portion of the business district is gone. Nearly twenty buildings and countless tents are destroyed—including four lodging houses, two hotels, and—worst of all—the sweet-smelling San Francisco Bakery. The Bon Ton Millinery is gone too, which means no fancy new hat for me. I can't help but think that Mother would have found that fact sorely disappointing.

Casey finds me in front of the smoke-filled hole where the

millinery once stood. "They're saying it started here," she says, hooking her arm through mine. "Gas leak."

"They'll never rebuild," I say, more to myself than to Casey. But I'm not really thinking about the folks who own the millinery or the bakery or even the Nevada Hotel. I'm thinking about us—about Papa and Mother and all we lost in Baltimore. "It's too hard," I murmur. "Too much to come back from."

Casey frowns. "You'd be surprised. Folks around here tend to rise up, no matter what knocks 'em down."

She glances up and down the charred street. "It may take them a few days though. Guess you'll have to keep wearing this sad old lid," she says, snatching the hat off my head and slapping it against her thigh.

Dust and smoke puff around us. Casey's bloodshot eyes sparkle. She settles the hat back on my head. "Cheer up, Georgie boy," she says with a wink. "No one was killed, and buildings can be rebuilt. The real question is, how am I ever going to get the stench of beer out of my hair?"

I laugh. She has a point. The whole town smells like beer and burned toast.

I excuse myself when I spot Old Joe Smiley standing by a water truck. "How's the stable?" I ask, breathless for news.

He smiles. "Safe and sound." He adjusts his hat, then stares out across the town. "It's amazing what can be done when folks pull together, ain't it?"

I ponder his words as I walk back to the *Times* building. I am pleased to see that it escaped the fire. Mr. Jeffries paces along the sidewalk in front of the office, a wet handkerchief pressed against his nose and mouth. He hustles me inside.

"You were there? You saw it all?" he asks through the cloth. He pulls out a chair and shoves me into it.

"You weren't?" I croak, taking in his clean clothes and soot-free face.

He flutters the handkerchief in front of his face. "Asthma. Smoke like that'll kill me. But you! Did you talk to people? Do you know how it started? What buildings burned? Is anyone hurt? Killed?"

I nod. "I was in the bucket brigade, so I guess you can say I had a front-row seat to the whole thing." My chest swells with pride.

"Excellent." He shoves a pad and pencil at me. "Write it all down."

I look at my dirty hands. "Maybe I should clean up first..."

He presses the pencil into my hand. "No time for that. Get it on the page while it's still fresh in your mind."

I grin. "Really?" I feel nearly giddy as I sit down to write. An hour later, I hand him the paper.

"Conflagration," he reads with a smile. "Good word, but it might be a little much for our readers. How about we call it an inferno instead?" He reads through the rest of the article in a rush. "This is great," he says. "A real firsthand account. Tomorrow you can go out and get the details. Loss estimates. Amount of water used. Maybe even an interview with good old Bert Ulmer himself. Human interest. People will like that. But this," he says, waving the paper in front of me, "this will be perfect for tomorrow morning's edition."

I'm so excited I want to cheer, but I don't think he would like that much. Instead, I smile so big it feels like my cheeks will burst.

Mr. Jeffries heads over to the printing press and starts organizing the letters. He seems to have forgotten me entirely until a coughing spell overtakes me. "Why don't you go home and clean up," he advises, once my hacking subsides. "I'll take it from here. Besides, you smell like a brewery, and it's making me thirsty."

* * *

A copy of the morning's paper lies next to the printing press when I get into work the next morning. My story is on the front page. I pick up the paper with shaking hands, so excited to see my words in print that I can barely read them.

"Town Bravely Battles Towering Inferno" the headline reads, and below that, "George Peters, the *Times* Newest Reporter, Gives His Firsthand Account of the Fire."

I gasp. "Newest reporter?"

Mr. Jeffries's lips twitch beneath his mustache. "Don't let it go to your head," he warns. "There won't be a raise, and you'll still have to do the printer's devil work."

"But I'm really a reporter?" I cock my head and eye him carefully. He better not be joking.

"Yes. Yes. So stop reading and get out there and interview folks." He tosses me a little notebook—like the one Mr. Westchester carried—and a stubby pencil. "Get the details. Damage estimates. Insurance numbers. Find out what started it and what happened with the water truck—and see if the story about the parrot is true."

"A parrot?"

He waves his hand, pointing to the door. "Yes, a parrot. Now go."

I spend the day wandering downtown, talking to the weary men and women who lost their homes and businesses to the fire and tracking down the story of the parrot who was brought to safety, only to fly back into the burning house to die in his cage. I think even Henry the rooster has better sense than that, despite him being an ordinary chicken and not some fancy exotic bird from who knows where.

I stop at the Hub Saloon and interview Mr. Ulmer about his brilliant idea to use the beer. "Even the temperance movement ladies will herald you a hero after that stunt," I tell him as he blushes.

I also interview the head of the volunteer fire department as he treats his crew to a drink. He explains why the water ran out. "The whole town was filling buckets. All the faucets were being used. The pipe's only three inches wide," he says, showing me the width with his fingers. "It can't take that much use and still get water to the fireplugs."

"I think there are at least two stories here," I tell Mr. Jeffries after I've organized my notes. "A general piece on the fire and a separate feature about Mr. Ulmer's quick thinking."

"Write 'em up." Mr. Jeffries rises from his desk, hitches up his pants, and heads for the door. "Just leave them on my desk. I'll look them over tonight," he says. "If you need me, I'll be at the Northern."

I settle down to work. The smell of ink and paper, and the scratch of my pencil soothes me. I feel at home for the first time since we left Baltimore. The realization sends my head reeling. Home. I didn't even know how badly I missed it.

It's dark by the time I've finished writing the stories. I set them carefully in the center of Mr. Jeffries's desk and head out into the night. I know that I should go straight to the cabin—no use worrying Clara—but I'm still buzzing from the excitement of being a real-life reporter. I decide to take the long way home and see if I can find Arnie on the way. I'm sure he would love to hear my good news.

I wander up Main Street toward the stables. I take my time, nodding to people and peering into store windows, thinking about what I'll buy just as soon as I get my first paycheck. When I see Arnie's car parked in front of the Nixon Block building, I stop and look up and down the street, but I don't see him.

I'm trying to decide whether or not to drop into the Northern Saloon and look for him when the flicker of a candle catches my eye. I peer into the window of the Louvre Restaurant, and there, seated just on the other side of the glass, is Arnie. He looks sharp. Crisp shirt. Combed hair. A real dandy. I make a fist, preparing to tap on the window and wave, but I stop before my knuckle touches the glass.

Leslie Granger sits across from him. I watch as her lips part and her mouth opens. She's laughing. And so is he. Arnie is wearing a fancy shirt and grease in his hair, and he is laughing with Leslie Granger.

My eyes sting as I back away from the window and stagger across the street. Stupid, ugly Leslie Granger. And stupid, greasy-haired Arnie. I run until my heart threatens to explode, then I run faster.

I feel like I'm dying.

I feel like Huck Finn after the steamboat crashes into the raft and he and Jim get separated.

I feel like I've lost my best friend.

Chapter Twenty-Four

I toss and turn all night, trying to make sense of what I saw. How does Arnie even know Leslie? And what in the world would possess Leslie to go around with a boy like Arnie? He's not rich or elegant or from some important family of mucky-mucks who brag about keeping horses in Virginia and a house in San Francisco. He's Arnie. A dressed-up version of Arnie, to be sure, but still, just Arnie.

After turning it around in my head every which way, I give up. I'll just have to ask him. No use getting all worked up and upset over what might easily be nothing—at least that's what Mother would advise. "Better to ask and know the truth than go through life wondering and wishing," she would say whenever Papa hesitated to approach a customer about an unpaid bill or a man about a job. And she was nearly always right. But, somehow, I don't think this is nothing.

I go to the livery stable first thing, hoping to catch Arnie. I'm in luck. He's sitting on a rail in front of the bay horse's stall whistling a tune when I walk up. "Beautiful morning, isn't it, Kit?"

I scowl. "Don't you have to go to Tonopah?"

"Eventually." He rubs the bay mare's head and whispers something in her ear.

"Why are you so happy this morning?"

Arnie smiles, a stupid, wide-mouthed, glazed-eyed grin. Then he blushes.

I roll my eyes. "I saw you last night." I tap my foot—a foot that's wearing his cruddy old boot—and wait.

He just stands there, grinning.

I sigh. "At the Louvre…I saw you." I can't believe he's going to make me say her name. My mouth purses as I form the sounds. I'm certain my nose wrinkles in disgust. "I saw you with Leslie Granger."

"Isn't she something?" Arnie sighs.

"Something!" I seethe. "Leslie Granger? She's several kinds of somethings."

"I think she's the tops. Smart. Funny. And a looker to boot." He eyes me curiously. "What's not to like?"

Spots clutter my vision. *A looker!* I kick the rail. "Where do I start! She's Leslie Granger. Daughter of Hiram Granger." I give him my meanest, most sarcastic look. "Remember him?"

Arnie jumps off the rail and gathers up his goggles and scarf. "Come on, Kit. She's not her father."

"She might as well be. She's spoiled and rude and…" Flashes of Leslie cloud my head. Leslie sneering. Leslie ordering the kids to drag me off the step. Leslie convincing everyone to make fun of me, to ignore me, to hate me. "She once threw a rock at me," I sputter, ducking my head and willing myself not to cry.

Arnie's mouth curves into what I think might be a smile. It goes back to a frown when I glare at him.

"But she's not her dad," he says, sighing. "Besides, she's mad at him herself. She told me…"

"I don't care what she told you." I shake my head for a long moment. "I can't believe you're doing this. I can't believe you'd squire around Leslie Granger. Not now. Not after you've helped me. Not after everything we've…"

"I like her," Arnie says flatly. "And I think she likes me too." He fiddles with the knobs on the motorcar. "Besides, it's really not any of your business. One doesn't have anything to do with the other."

I stand, gape-mouthed, as he turns the crank and starts the car. I'm still standing gape-mouthed when he backs it out of the stable and drives away.

I splat down in the mud and tug his boots off my feet. I fling them across the stable. "Damn you!" I scream at the top of my lungs—not entirely sure if I'm cursing Arnie or Leslie or maybe myself.

It turns out Arnie is just like Huck Finn—and not in any of the good ways. He's impulsive and selfish and has horrid taste in girls. He's got himself stuck in a blood feud between me and the Grangers, and I'm afraid it's not too hard to figure out who he's likely to side with when things get tight.

A sour taste fills my mouth. Mr. Harrison was right. This really isn't child's play. I swallow around the lump in my throat, then square my shoulders and stand. I walk across the stable and gather up the boots. I pull them on my feet, then push up my sleeves and march toward the door. I'll just have to go it alone. I inhale deeply and let the smell of hay and oats and horse sweat bolster my spirits. Then I stride into the street, resolved to handle all of this on my own. Who needs friends anyway? Especially if they're silly and lovestruck and totally lacking in good sense and good taste. Not me. That's for sure.

* * *

"Stupid boys!" I mutter when I get to the newspaper office and realize Mr. Jeffries isn't there.

The Shoshone woman peeks her head out of the back room and smiles at me. "You're working here now," she says. Her voice is so low and quiet that I have to lean forward to hear her.

I nod. "They call me George."

She smiles and holds a finger to her lips. "I can keep a secret," she says with a wink. "Stupid boys don't have to know."

I smile weakly.

By the time Mr. Jeffries comes in, I've helped Marta clean the entire office and have told her the whole story of Arnie and Leslie and the total betrayal that he's inflicted on me. "He's a traitor and a liar and a stupid grinning dandy—and I don't even like him anyhow," I decide when we take a break for coffee.

Marta smiles. "Don't be too hard on him. Love is strange." She smiles across the room at Mr. Jeffries. "Take me and him," she whispers. "I always thought I'd marry a great man. A leader. Someone with passion. Who knew I'd fall in love with a fat man who sits at a desk and reads?" She gives a little shrug. "But we've been married twenty-three years now, so something must be right."

I glance over at Mr. Jeffries and shrug. "Love is stupid, and so is Arnie."

Marta pats my arm and takes my coffee cup. "Back to work now…George," she says loudly. "The news waits for no man. Isn't that right, dear?"

Mr. Jeffries holds out a paper. "Right you are," he says, smiling an actual smile at her. "Especially the news in Goldfield."

The news in Goldfield does keep moving, and some of it is even interesting. Most of my work involves setting print for advertisements and the "Comings and Goings" section, though, and even seeing my work in black and white doesn't make "30% off beans" and "Mr. and Mrs. L. Baker departed Goldfield for Tonopah by auto yesterday" exciting.

One of the things I like best about the job is reading newspapers from all over the country. Mr. Jeffries has them sent in so he can keep up with national events and see what his brothers at papers like the *Bisbee Daily Review*, the *Sacramento Record-Union*, and the *Denver Republican* are up to. A lot of it is similar to what happens here: socials, music evenings, new buildings, gold strikes, deaths, and fires.

I've already gotten two ideas for stories from reading the articles. One about the Ladies' Aid Society's fund-raising efforts, and another about the trouble a Colorado mining town has been having with a new group of activists.

Today, though, I couldn't care less about what's happening in any city other than here. I'm tired of waiting around and trying to figure out my next move against Granger. I'm ready to act.

I'm reading through an old copy of the *Los Angeles Herald* when an article about a mine collapse in Pennsylvania catches my attention. It's short. Three sentences in all. One to tell the story of the seventeen men killed and the one who was injured. One sentence to say that the injured man will probably die, and another to report that the bodies have been recovered.

I've barely set the *Herald* down when another article—this one from a Montana newspaper—outlines the gruesome death of seven men in a mine explosion. This article is much longer—nine sentences in all and full of blood and guts and people stuffing body parts into sacks. I lean back in my chair, imagining this man, Nels Wampa, according to the paper, just doing his job carrying dynamite to the men tasked with opening up the shaft, when *bam*, he's blown to kingdom come. I start to mutter a silent prayer for the lost men, though I have sincere doubts that God is listening, when the beginning of a plan seizes me.

People should know who these men are, and they should know them by name. Not just Nels Wampa, but the other six too. And the eighteen men in Pennsylvania. And not just the dead ones. The ones who survived. The ones who went back to work the very next day despite being banged up and scared and too tired to even walk, let alone wield a sledgehammer. People should know them. Should know their stories, and the stories of all the men working the mines here in Goldfield. It's only a matter of time before the people of Goldfield are reading about seven or seventeen of their own men dead in a mine collapse.

"Maybe we could do an in-depth report of a miner's life," I suggest to Mr. Jeffries. "Go into the mine with him. Follow him around. See what his life is like on a regular day. Show how dangerous the work is. How people risk their lives every single day for a little bit of gold." I fumble through a stack of papers. "One of the temperance movement papers did something similar a while back. Only they had a reporter shadow a bartender, and then he wrote about all the bad things that happen in the saloon. Fights and gambling and abused women—everything the temperance people complain about but don't get to see because they refuse to go into such places."

"Sounds more like a stage play than a news article."

"People love stage plays. You could spread the story out over a month—one piece a week or something. Think of all the newspapers you'd sell. I'd bet it would even get picked up by one of the papers back East. You could call it *Life Underground* or something like that."

Mr. Jeffries strokes his beard. I see his gaze flicker toward the ledger where he tracks subscriptions. "Investigative reporting in Goldfield," he says. "I'll have to think about that."

* * *

While Mr. Jeffries thinks, so do I. I even run the story by Clara one night at dinner. "Investigative reporting, he calls it," I explain. "I'd follow the miners around, day and night, and even dress like them—kind of poor and grimy, so I'd fit in. Then later, I'd write up the story with all the details of what it's like to be in the mine."

Clara looks at my clothes and raises an eyebrow. "You've certainly got the poor and grimy part down. I thought you were going to buy new clothes with your earnings."

"This week," I promise. I've already used most of my money to buy Clara new boots and some overalls and even a new dress, which made her tear up and tell a story about a dress her husband bought her as an anniversary present years ago.

"My Malcolm would have loved this," she said, patting me on the arm. "He had a thing about little blue flowers."

Most importantly, I'm saving up to buy Papa a real headstone. One with swirling vines and big block letters.

I'm still thinking about the newspaper article when I go to bed. Telling the men's stories feels important all on its own, but maybe

I can kill two birds. Maybe I can get some information about Granger's operations. Maybe I can even stop something horrible from happening at the Goliath. The thought of sneaking around behind Granger's back makes my stomach turn. Still, one must "sacrifice for the story," as Mr. Jeffries says. "Truth will out" and all of that.

I imagine it's the idea of truth willing out that gets me poking through my keepsake box. I pull out Mr. Harrison's map of the Goliath mine and think about those tunnels running east and west and all the men down there working to get the gold out. How many know about the secret tunnels? How many know that the entire mine could collapse on their heads any time? Do they know that they're stealing gold from the neighboring mine? Or are they all just victims of this—like Papa and Tom and Jesse and everyone else on my list?

If only I could find out what's really going on in the Goliath mine! All I need is someone to track out the secret tunnels and draw a map showing where Granger is really digging his gold.

The thought keeps me up. I wonder if I can pull it off. It's one thing to fool Casey and even Mr. Jeffries, but an entire mine full of men? I think of all the ways it could go wrong and whisper most of them to Buster when he comes looking for a place to snuggle. Of course, it's not like I have a choice—not really. After all, there is no someone. There is only me.

By the time the sun hits the horizon, my mind is made up. All that's left is to convince Mr. Jeffries that an in-depth report of life in the mines is exactly what the *Times* needs—and that I'm just the boy for the job.

"I thought you just wanted to follow some fellow around," Mr. Jeffries says when I tell him my new idea.

"I think this idea has more market appeal," I say. "Think about all the people back East who would love to learn what the inside of a real gold mine is like."

"How are you planning on getting into the mine?"

I hold up a copy of the *Tonopah Daily News*. "Granger just put in an advertisement calling for men at the Goliath Mine."

Mr. Jeffries sighs. "You're not exactly a man."

"Close enough," I snap. "Besides, they might need some boys to act as nippers. I can fetch tools and hold lanterns or even swing a pickax if it comes to that."

"You really think there's a story there?" His dark eyes grow serious. "Maybe something more than a day-in-the-life piece. Something with substance?"

I match his thoughtful look with one of my own. "Mr. Westchester seemed to think so." I catch my mistake and stumble on. "I mean, didn't a reporter here write some articles about Mr. Granger's mine being dangerous?" I try to keep my eyes wide and innocent.

Mr. Jeffries averts his gaze and tugs at his beard. "Something like that," he mumbles. "But that didn't work out so well."

"I don't think Mr. Westchester knew what he was looking for."

His brow furrows. "Don't tell me you do?"

I shrug. "I might."

"Nah." He fumbles with some papers on his desk. "It's a bad idea. Too…controversial." He looks at me. His eyes are somber. "You're just a kid."

I return his look. "There's more to me than meets the eye."

He shakes his head slowly. "You really have to do this?"

"I think so."

He sighs, then reaches in his desk and tosses me a handful of coins. "Get yourself outfitted. Gloves, some bandannas for the dust, a helmet if you can find one."

I tuck the coins in my pocket, triumphant and more than a little nervous.

"You know I'd go in if I could." He flutters a hand in front of his face. "That dirt would be the end of me, though."

"Your asthma. I know. Still, you'll print it up? Whatever I find?"

Mr. Jeffries runs a hand across his cheek. He looks tired—and old. "I'll print it. Just be sure you have some facts to back you up."

"I will."

"Get on with you then," he says, pointing toward the door. "Ah, hell, wait a minute. I'll walk you out. I could use a drink."

Mr. Jeffries grabs his hat. He sticks a sign that reads *At the Northern* in the window and locks the door behind him. I follow him to Exploration Mercantile. "Remember the helmet," he says, pressing a few more coins in my hand. "And don't forget to take notes. The story starts now."

I pat the notebook in the pocket of my shirt and smile.

"And for the love of Mike, stop smiling," Mr. Jeffries says as he continues down the sidewalk. "Keep your mouth shut and your ears open."

Chapter Twenty-Five

"You're very quiet tonight," Clara observes after supper. "Long day at the paper?" She rubs Buster's face while she talks. The cat collapses under her pets, stretching his long body across the table.

I consider telling her the truth, but then I remember all the stories about how her husband was killed in a mine collapse and all the times she fought with Papa about speaking up about how dangerous the Goliath is and I say nothing. Even though she didn't bat an eye when I decided to dress like a boy to get the newspaper job and she never once blamed me for getting kicked out of school or scolded me for defying Aunt Minerva, I don't think she'd be too keen on me going into the mine. Especially not this mine.

"I'm just tired." I force a yawn. "Mr. Jeffries wants me to come in early tomorrow."

"Then off to bed with you." Clara lights a candle and extinguishes the lantern. "I'm going to stay up and read some." She pats a thick book titled *A Manual of Mining*. "Who knows, maybe old Ihlseng here will help me figure out a way to keep Granger from stealing that claim."

I find her asleep at the table the next morning, Buster wrapped around her head like a turban. I ease the book out from under her arm and place it next to the burned-out candle. Buster refuses to budge, so I simply drape a blanket over Clara's shoulders, pack my lunch quietly, and leave without stepping on the creaky board. I stop to feed Sal and Jasper and the chickens and to grab the gloves and bandannas I stashed behind the cabin. "Wish me luck," I whisper to the critters before leaving.

I hustle out to the Goliath Mine site east of town, grateful that Clara is still asleep and won't wonder why I'm going the wrong way to work. The place is already jam-packed with men and boys itching to be hired. So much for being early.

I squeeze my way to the front of the group. A gang of boys gathers to the right, so I ease my way over there, careful to position myself not so close that they'll notice me, but close enough that anyone else can tell I belong. I shift my weight from foot to foot, hoping to burn off some anxiety.

We stand around for about forty minutes. Some of the men shout greetings to one another. Others stand quietly. Many of the men have the drawn cheeks of a person who hasn't eaten in a week. All of the boys have the same hollow-eyed look.

Finally, Mr. Hines emerges from a building and stands on a scaffold next to the shaft. "We'll take ten men today," he shouts, looking over the crowd.

The men groan. "Only ten," a man near me mutters. "I walked all the way from Tonopah, and they only want ten men." He shuffles away from the group without another word.

Mr. Hines starts pointing at people and gesturing for them to come up. It's clear he's picking the strongest of the lot. The youngest. The ones without the hollowed eyes or drawn cheeks. Around me, men cuss and holler—but none of them get called.

"How many boys?" a small voice pipes up.

Mr. Hines glares at him. "Three." He points at two large boys near me. They look like twins—same ruddy face, same red hair. "You two gingers will do," he says. "And we need a small one. Someone quick." He surveys the group. "You."

My heart leaps, then catches. He's pointing to the dark-haired boy beside me. The boy bolts forward. "Sorry," I whisper as I stick my foot out and hook him by the ankle. He trips, sprawling into a group of men who don't even try to catch him.

"Oof." "Watch out." "Get off." The men protest and shove him to the ground.

"He can't even walk!" I yell, pushing forward through the crowd. I stop in front of Mr. Hines's scaffold. "I'm fast, and I'm strong. I'm worth two of him."

Mr. Hines ignores me and scans the crowd.

"C'mon, sir," I holler. "Give me a shot. You won't be sorry."

"Ah, give him a try," one of the men on the scaffold prods. "What's the difference?"

Mr. Hines grunts and points his finger at me. "You better be as quick as you say."

I nod my head, shift my hat a bit lower to hide my face more, and hustle forward.

The boy I tripped spits in my face as I rush by. I shudder and wipe it off as I move through the crowd. I can't blame him for being mad.

One of the smaller boys gazes at me, jealousy clear in his hungry eyes. "Lucky dog," he mumbles as I pass him.

I agree, though I am scared as all get-out. Knees shaking, I line up with the rest of the men in front of the shaft.

"There will be no pilfering," Mr. Hines says from his perch. "Anyone caught stealing ore will be dealt with…severely. Lunch pails will be brought up immediately after your break." He looks around and points at me. "That's your job, nipper. Bring up the pails, pick up broken tools, fetch anything anyone needs."

He whispers to a man at his side, who then gestures toward another group of men. Five men hustle out and line up next to the shaft. "These men will help you Johnny Newcomes get settled," Mr. Hines shouts. "Two new men for each helper. Let's move!"

Everyone scrambles to their proper place, and before long, men and boys pile into the cage that carries the workers down into the mine.

When it's my turn, I hold my lunch pail against my chest with shaking hands and step into the cage. The metal elevator groans mightily as men fill in the space around me. I close my eyes as the wires creak and the cage descends into the darkness below.

Something sharp pokes my side. I open my eyes. There in front of me, with a shy grin plastered on his face, is Arnie.

"Looks like we had the same idea."

"I…uh." I can't believe he's here. I start to smile, maybe even clap with joy, but then I remember that I'm mad at him—and that I am a man down here. Men don't clap. "Does your girlfriend know you're here?" I say with a sniff.

Arnie rolls his eyes and looks away. "Of course. Been working here for over a week now." He looks around and lowers his voice. "Figured it would be a good way to look around—maybe see the tunnels and all." He shrugs. "I guess you thought so too."

"I guess I did." *And I bet I thought it before you did,* I think, but I feel my anger slacken a little. Maybe I've been a little hard on him.

"Hang on," a man yells. The cage jolts to a stop. We file out. Before my eyes have adjusted to the dark, Arnie is gone.

My first job is to light the candles used for warming the lunch pails. I move through the tunnels, finding the planks that hold the candles. Each plank has a circle of nails with a candle in the center. I light the candle, and the men place their lunch pail on the table made by the nails. The candle keeps their lunch warm or heats up water for tea or coffee.

Apparently there is no way for me to escape women's work. Even when I look like a boy, I'm stuck fixing people lunch. Fixing lunch and chasing off the long-tailed rats that scuttle through the tunnels and try to steal food from the pails. Papa never said anything about rats, and truth be told, if I had known there would be rats down here, I might have pitched the whole plan. Fearing for my life is one thing. Fearing that I will be torn apart by rats is another matter entirely.

Once the candles are lit, I run around the tunnels fetching tools and picking up broken chisels and picks to take back to the blacksmith for repair. Thanks to Mr. Harrison's map, I already had a pretty good idea of how the tunnel system works.

The Goliath is divided into four levels, with tunnels running east to west. Parts of the tunnels are wide—spacious even—and grown men can walk without bending over at all. Other sections are tiny. So dark and tight that crawling in them takes my breath away. I can see why Mr. Hines wanted a small person for this job. I have to slump my shoulders and lean way over to get to the farthest section of one of the smaller tunnels.

I don't see how the men can work in some of these places, but they do. Tall men bend nearly in half in some places, while others lie on their stomachs, scraping at the rock wall with a pickax. At the far end of Tunnel Three, Arnie and another man drill holes in the rock. Arnie clutches the drill bit with both hands, while the other man swings a gigantic sledgehammer down on top of it, pounding it into the rock.

The hammer rings against the steel drill bit. *Ching. Ching.* I flinch every time the sledgehammer comes crashing down, closing my eyes, then opening them to see if Arnie is still in one piece. He always is, but I don't know how. I would love to ask him how he can stay so still and be so trusting. One wrong move, and that hammer will smash his hand to pulp. But, since I am mad at him, I keep my questions to myself. I simply set up his candle and lunch pail like he's just any other worker and move on down the line.

A whistle blows at noon, and the men put down their tools in what looks like one motion. They sit in small groups, eating their lunch and talking about the work, the gold, and the mine owner's problems. "They're pulling lunch pails," the miner who was working with Arnie says, nodding at his metal bucket. "Cracking down on thieves. Before you know it, they'll be searching us."

Arnie cuts his eyes in my direction. "What do you mean, searching?"

"Changing rooms. Some places make you change clothes whenever you enter the mine and again when you leave it. Keeps you from sneaking ore out in your pockets."

He unbuttons his shirt—revealing a separate shirt underneath. The front of the shirt—right over his stomach—is one large pocket

212

where he's been stashing gold all morning. He buttons it back up and pats his stomach. "Looks like fat—and I guess it is. Fat of the land." He laughs at his own joke. A couple other men join in.

My hand grasps the top of my shirt. Searches? Changing rooms? I better find what I need—and fast.

After lunch is over, I scurry around, picking up everyone's lunch pails and sending them up in the cart. I save mine to take up with the last bunch, but when I try to pick it up off the shelf, it won't budge. I brace my feet against the wall and tug. Still nothing.

I look closer. Someone has nailed my lunch pail to the shelf. My face flushes with a mix of embarrassment and anger as the men in the section burst out laughing. "Johnny Newcome!" they shout.

When the din dies down, Arnie hands me a crowbar. "They did mine when I started too," he confides with a shrug. "Welcome to the Goliath."

I'm so exhausted by the time work is over that I barely make it back to Clara's cabin. I wash up in the animals' water trough, careful to get the dust and grime cleaned off my forehead and out of my ears before Clara gets a good look at me. I eat supper in silence, not even noticing what I put in my mouth.

After supper, I scribble some notes in my book, trying to capture the claustrophobic feel of the tunnels, the dust, and the smell of earth, blasting powder, and sweat. I tear out the pages and fold them in half. I fall asleep at the table and only wake when Clara prods me with her foot.

"To bed," she says. "And tell that Mr. Jeffries to ease up on your hours. You're too young to be this tired."

I'm pretty sure I owe Papa an apology for all the nights I

complained about him falling asleep right after supper. I'm pretty sure an apology isn't nowhere near enough. Still, it's the best I can do. *Sorry, Papa.*

* * *

Thank the heavens for Henry. He crows me awake just in time to get dressed, throw some lunch together, and run to the *Times* office. I slide the article I wrote last night under the door, then race out to the mine.

I arrive just in time to climb on the last cage ride down. This time, I keep my eyes open, noticing where each tunnel begins. I count by thousands under my breath, trying to gauge how much distance there is between each tunnel and how much time it takes for the cage to go all the way down the shaft.

Mr. Hines rides down to the third level with me. I'm a little afraid he might recognize me, but he doesn't even look my way. Once we climb out of the cage, he says, "Give me a candle." He bows his head, showing me the candleholder fitted on his helmet. I light one and place it in the holder. He slides down the wall into a sitting position and unfolds a map.

I bend over, pretending to organize my candles. I kneel next to Mr. Hines, fussing with the candles and trying to sneak a peek at the map. It's hard to see in the dim light. I make out the word Goliath and some arrows pointing down. That's it. I strain to see more, but Mr. Hines folds up the map and stands, shoving it in his pocket.

"What're you still doing here?" he barks. His candle shines into my face. He grabs me by the collar and hauls me to my feet. "Get moving, or I'll get another boy to do this job."

I resist the urge to kick him in the shin with my heavy boot. Instead, I scowl and hurry away, but not before I make a mental note of which pocket holds the map.

I hope to sneak out of Tunnel Three and explore the rest of the mine, but Mr. Hines never leaves our level. He keeps moving back and forth, running his hands along the tunnel walls and inspecting the ore the men are pulling out. Near the end of the day, he pulls a blaster over to the drill site. "Let's blow it now."

"What about next shift? Things will be pretty shaky for a bit."

Mr. Hines shrugs. "Mr. Granger wants three more feet."

The blaster sighs and wipes sweat from his forehead. "All right." He blows out a long breath before turning from Mr. Hines to me. "Fetch me an explosive."

I run to the cage and ride it to the top. I grab a tube of black powder and carry it back to Tunnel Three carefully, the Montana article about the explosion rustling in my head. I don't exhale until I hand the tube to the blaster. I stand back as he inserts a fuse in the tube and stuffs the tube into one of the holes Arnie and his partner drilled yesterday.

The blaster clenches his jaw and glares at Mr. Hines. "You sure you want to do this now?"

Mr. Hines smirks. "There's a line of men who'd be more than happy to do your job if you're feeling skittish."

A hush falls around us. I notice I'm holding my breath and exhale sharply. Just how dangerous is this? I look at the men gathered around me. They all have the same look on their faces—anger flashes in their eyes, but there's something shimmering just behind it, something like defeat. I shiver. Images from the news article rise up and take over my mind. Bloody arms and heads and bodies blown to bits too small to identify. I push them away and stare at the man, wide-eyed, terrified of what will happen next.

The man shakes his head. His neck muscles pulse. Finally, he holds up a hand and clears his throat. "Fire in the hole!"

Men drop their tools where they're standing and run through the tunnel toward the cage. I follow, hands covering my ears. The walls shake, and the air fills with the acrid scent of burned powder and the tang of sulfur. I bury my head in my arms and huddle against the wall, certain the whole place is going to collapse around us. My breath rasps. I squeeze my eyes shut and try not to whimper. I don't look up until a hand clutches my shoulder.

"It's okay," Arnie says. "We're okay."

I wipe my nose and nod. "Okay," I echo as I follow him into the cage.

The elevator carries us back to the surface. The men are quiet. Their eyes spark with anger. "Stupid, dangerous decision," one of the men mutters. Some nod. Others look away. All refusing to meet one another's eyes.

There's more going on here than just secret tunnels and stolen gold. Much more. And I have a feeling I don't have a lot of time to figure it out.

Chapter Twenty-Six

Today starts the same as yesterday—with a cock-a-doodle-doo-inspired jump out of bed, a weary run to the *Times* to drop off my story, and an even wearier run to the mine. Again, I'm the last one in the cage, only this time neither Arnie nor Mr. Hines accompanies me on my ride down.

The timbers creak and groan as I work my way through the tunnel, picking up tools and fetching tins of water. The dusty air puffs around me with each step, and even with a bandanna wrapped around my face, my nose and mouth are filled with grit.

After lunch, when I'm taking the empty pails up to the top, I begin exploring the other tunnels. I wind my way through the first two tunnels quickly—noticing how they connect at the ends in a large cavernous area the men call a stope. The walls shimmer in the lamplight. The white quartz sparkles, and I can just make out little gold flakes clustered on the rock. It looks magical, yet the men hardly seem to notice it as they shovel ore into the carts.

I eavesdrop on the miners as they work, picking up bits and pieces of conversation at each level. The men work steadily. The night shift blew a wider hole in Tunnel Two, and now the men are mucking out the hole. "We need to go farther east," one of the men observes. "Color's pretty thin here."

"Color's thin everywhere." A tall miner swipes a filthy rag across his sweaty brow. "Davie in Tunnel Three says they haven't pulled out anything worth shouting about in weeks. I'd wager the whole place is played out."

"Can't be. Granger just hired on ten new men. Why'd he do that if the vein is played?"

The tall man stuffs the rag into his back pocket. He places both his hands on his lower back and stretches. "Beats me." He yawns and picks up his shovel. "But then, Granger ain't paying me to solve his problems."

The whistle blows before he can get back to work. "Quitting time." He grins. "Looks like he's not paying me to shovel dirt anymore either." He tosses his shovel into the railroad cart and climbs in after it. The other men do the same, and they all let the burro pull them and the cart through the tunnel and to the cage. I can't help but think of Jasper and his ruined eyes. Poor burro.

I crouch in the corner, waiting for them to leave. I watch as the cage full of men makes its way to the top and back—emptying out the mine of ore and people with each trip. Finally the shaft is quiet. I have less than an hour until the next shift starts coming down.

I gather up some tools and make my way to the cage. If anyone sees me, I figure I can claim to be checking the tunnels for a lost pickax. Candles and lanterns flicker along the tunnel entrances, lighting the way for the next shift. Once I'm certain that everyone is gone, I climb into the cage. This time, I ride it all the way down—past the fourth tunnel and into the darkness below. From what I remember from Mr. Harrison's map, I should be able to ride the cage all the way to the bottom of the shaft without seeing another tunnel.

Before I get to the bottom, I spot what I think is an opening. I stop the cage at a small, poorly lit tunnel and climb out. This entrance is darker than the others. Quieter too.

My heart pounds in my chest as I stare into the darkness. The only sound I hear is the click of rats' claws. I imagine the place is swarming with them, and the thought of long-tailed rats swishing along the ground sends chills through me. I fumble for a candlestick. My hands shake, and it takes three matches and one burned fingertip to get it lit. I breathe a sigh of relief when the flame flickers against the darkness, then panic as my breath makes the flame sputter. It stays lit, though. I hold the candle out in front of me like a weapon, hoping that the light will scare off any rat that thinks my ankle might make a tasty snack.

I press my shoulder against the rock wall and make my way through the tunnel, trying to ignore the creepy shadows the candlelight casts against the rock. I only go a couple of feet before I trip over a pickax. I get up from the ground and look around. The tunnel seems to end here. I shine my candle on the wall, expecting to see the same wide, cavernous spot that marks the end of all the other tunnels. The spot where it butts up against the vein of gold. I examine the wall, but I don't see any quartz.

I do see the entrance of another tunnel, though. A very small tunnel. And if my sense of direction isn't completely fouled up, I'd swear on Papa's grave that it's running south.

I scrunch down and peer into the tunnel. It's small, cramped, and dark. Way dark.

My mind flashes to memories of the Goldfield cemetery, of Mother's and Papa's caskets being lowered into the ground. I inhale sharply, more screech than breath.

I shake my head—trying to chase the thought away. "It's just a tunnel," I tell myself. "No different from the one you were just in." My hands tremble as I put the candle in my mouth, and then keep trembling as I crawl into the opening. It's a tight fit, even for me, and made tighter by the chunks of rock and old wood that litter the ground.

I crawl for what feels like forever. Every now and then, dust skitters down from above. I conjure up images of spiders and rats and nearly turn around. In an attempt not to think about what critters might be falling onto my head, I try to recite every poem Miss Sheldon had us memorize. I mumble the words as I crawl along. Wordsworth, Burns, Shakespeare. I even throw in some Poe, but that just scares me more and gets me wondering if anyone ever died in here.

It looks like the kind of place people have died in. Dark. Lonely. In fact, it feels like the kind of place a ghost would love. Everything is close in, like the edges are pressing into each other, and it's dank. The ground smells wet and feels cool beneath the palms of my hands, but the air is hot—like someone left the door to the cook-stove open.

I swipe at the sweat that's dripping in my eyes and shiver. I sincerely hope no one has ever died here—and if someone has, I hope they passed peacefully and are not at all wrathful and angry and looking for someone to take it out on. "Sorry about the Poe. Maybe some Dickinson," I mumble, by way of an offering.

But all I can think of is "Because I Could Not Stop for Death," and nobody wants to hear that—not me and certainly not some poor ghost.

So I shut up and keep crawling, pausing only to examine the timbers that are placed every few feet to hold the place up. I wish I would have thought to count them. Then I'd have some way to tell how far I had to go on my way back, and some sense of how long this was taking. It feels like way too long. I decide to use the timbers as a guide. If this place doesn't open up in the space of ten timbers, I'll turn back, I tell myself. When it doesn't, I decide to push on. Ten more, I promise myself. Ten more timbers and I'm going back. I'm about to make that promise to myself one more time when a flicker of light catches my eye.

I flinch and crouch lower. I lick my lips, wishing I had some water. I didn't expect anyone to be down here. I fight the urge to turn back. I gulp in some air. *Just a little farther*, I promise myself.

Heart thumping, I crawl faster, squinting against the darkness. As I get closer, I make out shapes. First, a lantern. Then a pickax and a couple of canvas bags. Finally, I see the shadows of two men.

I watch as one man scrapes dirt from a rock wall. The wall sparkles with quartz. Patches of gold cover the rock face. The sight of it is beautiful enough to make me gasp. I press a hand over my mouth, too late to still the sound.

A man whirs around. "Who's there?"

The second man picks up the lantern. "Where?"

"In the tunnel. I thought I heard something."

"Probably just rats." He waves the lantern in my direction. "Wait. When did rats start carrying their own light?"

My skin goes clammy, and I feel the sweat pooled under my arms turn cold. *He saw me!* I scream silently. The fear of being caught seizes my brain, and I can barely think, let alone move. Stiff with terror, I fumble with the candle and press my fingertips against the flame, extinguishing it.

The man with the lantern comes closer.

I drop to my stomach, trying to make myself smaller. Before I can shimmy backward, though, the timber nearest me groans and a cloud of dust whooshes around me. I throw my hands up over my head, wishing that I bought that danged helmet Mr. Jeffries had gone on and on about. *Dang Mr. Jeffries and his good ideas.*

Rocks thud all around me. Something heavy crashes against my forearm, and I cry out in pain.

The light swings around again. A man emerges from the shadows. "Who's there?" he growls. He holds a pickax in one hand, and even in the dim light, I can tell he's more than ready to use it.

I crawl to the place where the tunnel widens out and scramble to my feet. "I'm...uh...the nipper," I stammer. "Mr. Hines sent me." I force myself to meet the man's eyes. "Said someone had a broken drill bit down here."

The man shakes his head. "Worthless Hines. Luke's pickax snapped last night." He walks back to the wall and grabs the tool.

"I don't suppose you brought a replacement?"

I shake my head. "He said drill bit."

"Idiot. Well, be sure to let him know it's going to cost us time. Two men and one pickax ain't exactly a recipe for fast work."

"I will."

The man holds the lantern up to my face. "Looks like you took a bit of a beating." He moves the light lower so he can see my arm. "You okay?"

I look down at my arm. My shirtsleeve is shredded, and my forearm is gashed wide open. Blood and flesh and I don't want to think about what else seep from the wound.

My stomach turns. I close my eyes and press my forehead against the wall.

"Bashed it up pretty good," the man says. He takes me by the shoulder and steers me to where the other man is still working. He reaches in his lunch pail and pulls out a canteen. He splashes some water on my arm and uses his bandanna to wipe away some of the blood. "There's not enough light here to pick out the splinters, but that should clean it up some." He wraps another bandanna around my arm and ties it so the gash is mostly covered. "Have Doc give it a look when you get topside."

"Much obliged."

"You catch your breath, then head on out. I don't know what Granger and Hines are thinking—sending a boy way out here. I hope he's paying you triple."

"Nah, just regular nipper wage."

The man shakes his head. "The deadliest tunnel in the place, and you're getting rook wages. You need to learn how to negotiate." He stands and grabs the broken pickax. "I'll haul it out myself. Might have one or two more bangs in it after all."

He joins the other man at the wall while I cradle my arm and try to work up the nerve to go back into the tunnel. I look around the cavern. It looks like every other stope—minus the railroad cars and burros. The men's lunch pails rest along one wall—a plank already set up to heat them. Extra candles lie next to the plank, along with a booklet of matches. A man's long-sleeved shirt is folded neatly nearby. The edge of a piece of paper peeks out from under the tail of the shirt.

I look at the men. They're engrossed in their work. The rock wall nearly glows with gold, and the chunks of ore they stuff into their canvas bags are bigger than baseballs. I stretch out my legs and pin the piece of paper beneath the heel of a boot. Then I skid my boot along the ground, sliding the paper toward me. I scoop it up and shove it down the front of my shirt without unfolding it.

I light my candle from theirs and hustle to the mouth of the tunnel. "Thanks again," I call as I drop to my knees and crawl away as fast as my hurt arm can manage, desperate to get back before the next shift starts. I have no idea how long has passed since I entered the tunnel. *Surely not a whole hour*, I pray.

I finally emerge and race to the cage. It's still there—just as I left it. I breathe a sigh of relief and turn my attention to the paper.

I hold the candle in my mouth again, and fish it out of my shirt with my good arm. I open it. A less detailed version of Mr. Harrison's map stares back at me. The shaft is marked, and so are the tunnels—including the short one I'm standing in. Two more tunnels are inked in on the map. One leads off this fifth tunnel to the south. It must be the one I just crawled through. Another branches off from the middle of the third tunnel. It's sketched in—the lines are faint—but they also point south.

I squat down and take a closer look at the map. I whistle, long and low, as the entirety of Granger's plan becomes clear to me. I'd bet just about anything that Granger is planning a second secret tunnel. A tunnel running off the third level. Maybe that's why Hines was hanging around there yesterday. Maybe they're planning to close off the third tunnel and use it to dig into another spot in Tom and Jesse's claim.

I fold the map up carefully and slip it into my back pocket. I climb into the cage and ride it to the surface, trying to decide what to do next.

Arnie waits at the top of the shaft. He opens the gate on the cage as soon as it stops. "Where've you been? I've been looking all over for you..." His eyes rest on my arm. Blood seeps through the bandanna. He reaches out to touch it, but stops himself when I flinch away. "What happened?"

"One of the timbers gave way. It's not a big deal." I walk to a corner, gesturing for him to follow. I slip the map out of my pocket. "I found a secret tunnel. And I found this."

Arnie looks at the map. His green eyes widen. Then, in one movement, he yanks the map out of my hand and shoves it deep into his lunch pail.

"Hey," I protest. "Give it back."

Arnie catches me by the shoulder and turns me around. "They're searching everyone," he hisses. "Checking for thieves." He gestures toward a group of men standing in line in their underwear. "They're making everyone strip down. Then security is going through their clothes piece by piece. We've been out here over an hour now."

Over an hour. No wonder there were no workers in the mine when I came up. I had no idea I was in the tunnel for so long.

I look over at the men in line again. My hand clutches the top of my shirt. "But, I can't..."

"I know." Arnie's face is grim.

"You!" one of the security men calls. He points a fat finger in my direction. "Get down here."

I look at Arnie. His eyes look wild—desperate. I wonder what mine must look like. I walk slowly over to the guard, my hand still clutching the collar of my shirt.

"What're you two conspiring about?" the guard asks. He adjusts his grip on his rifle and juts his chin at Arnie.

"Nothing. Just...you know. Talking."

"Get over there," the guard says, motioning the tip of his rifle in the direction of the group of men. "Strip down to your skivvies. Smitty'll go through your clothes."

"You've already searched us," Arnie protests. "We were just hanging around waiting for our friend to get done." Arnie turns to the guard called Smitty. "Remember? I was clean?"

Smitty nods. "Yeah. I already got that one." He looks over at me. "I didn't see the boy with the hurt arm, though." He shrugs. "Maybe I just didn't notice him."

Mr. Hines stands next to the guard with the rifle. He looks at Arnie and me, his eyes wary. "Search them both." He takes the guard's rifle from him. "You do it, Carson."

I back away, my eyes wide with fear.

The guard jerks Arnie's lunch pail from his hand and paws through it. He takes out the map. He stares at it for a minute, then hands it to Mr. Hines. Mr. Hines's face goes pale.

"Grab him!" Mr. Hines yells at the guard. The guard snatches Arnie by the shoulder, pulling him into his chest. He wraps his other arm around Arnie's neck.

A scream lodges in my throat. I stand frozen in place, too shocked to do anything but stare.

As Arnie struggles beneath the guard's grip, Mr. Hines picks up Arnie's lunch pail. I watch as he reaches in his pocket and pulls out two rocks. He drops them both in the bucket, then holds it in the air for everyone to see. "Looks like we caught ourselves a thief," he says.

Something about the word *thief* wakes me up. The scream that was lodged in my throat comes out as a roar. I snag the handle of the lunch pail with my good arm and wrench it from Mr. Hine's grasp. I swing the pail, whacking first Mr. Hines and then Carson in the head with the metal bucket. "Run, Arnie!"

I sprint through the crowd. Half-dressed men jump away from me as I wind my way around them. I'm nearly through the group when I hear the *thwap* of bullets hitting the dust in front of my feet. I stop just short of getting shot in the foot. Anger courses through me as I curl my hand tighter around the handle of the lunch pail. I pivot in a wide circle, looking for someone else to hit.

"The next one goes in your head," a calm voice warns.

I look up and see Mr. Granger standing on the running board of his motorcar, his rifle aimed right at my face.

With shaking hands, I drop the lunch pail into the dirt. A group of men seize me by the arms and drag me back to Carson and Mr. Hines.

Arnie slumps against a wall, his arms wrapped around his middle. His face is a mess of blood and tears.

"What'd you do to him?" I scream, kicking at the men nearest me. "What did you do to Arnie?"

"Search him." Mr. Hines nods at Carson.

I slide to the ground next to Arnie. Carson looms over me. His hands grasp the collar of my shirt. Fear grips my chest. I slink back, scooting across the dirt on my butt. I windmill my legs, kicking blindly. "I'm a girl!" I scream. "Get off me, you no good coot. I'm a girl!"

Carson jerks his hands off my shirt. "What the hell?"

I fling my hat off my head and sit up. "I'm a girl, you idiot." I kick him one more time in the shin and jump to my feet.

A murmur rises through the crowd. Carson and Mr. Hines take a step away from me. "What in tarnation…" Mr. Hines says, scratching his head. "Get her out of here." He looks over at Arnie, still slumped against the wall. "And take this thief to the sheriff."

Carson and another man grab Arnie and haul him into a wagon. They look at me. "Miss?"

"I can get in myself."

I climb in the wagon and hunker down next to Arnie. "You okay?" I whisper. I pat his arm. "Please be okay."

Arnie shakes his head, but he's not looking at me. He's looking at Mr. Granger, who is still standing on the running board of his car. Granger's jaw is tight, and his eyes are clear and hard, full of recognition and hatred—and they are staring right at me.

I muster up all of my courage and meet his gaze. "I know what you're doing," I shout. I point an accusing finger at him. "This is just the beginning."

Chapter Twenty-Seven

By the time we've pulled up in front of the jail, bruises blossom all over the side of Arnie's face. His breath comes in shallow gasps. "He's dying!" I yell when Carson comes to the back of the wagon.

He climbs in and lifts Arnie's shirt, poking at his chest and sides. "Broken ribs. Hurt like hell, but they don't usually kill a fellow." He helps Arnie to his feet and carries him out of the wagon and into the jail.

I run in after them.

"…caught stealing," Carson is explaining to the deputy. I recognize him. It's the surly fellow from before. The one who ran me off when I came looking for help.

"Where's Sheriff Earp?" I cut in.

The men ignore me. "Granger's pressing charges. Wants to make an example of this one."

The deputy nods. "Looks like he already has." He grabs Arnie by the arm and shoves him into the cell.

"Stop!" I run into the cell and catch Arnie before he stumbles to the floor. I ease him onto the cot before I turn around. I walk right up to the deputy and look him in the eye. "Where is Sheriff Earp?"

The deputy smirks. "Home. Sick. He left me in charge." He

pulls me out of the cell and slams it closed. The clang of metal striking metal echoes through the room. The deputy locks the cell with a flourish, then twirls the key on his finger before returning it to his desk drawer.

"He's hurt. He needs a doctor."

"Doc stops by every morning around ten." He peers into the cell. "Guess we'll see if he lasts till then."

I edge closer to the cell, my glance darting between the desk drawer and the lock on Arnie's cell. "You can't just…" My voice quavers.

He presses his knee against the desk drawer and smiles at Carson. Carson fumbles in his pocket. He pulls out a twenty-dollar gold certificate and hands it to the deputy. Then he turns to leave.

"Pleasure doing business with you," the deputy calls after him.

Mr. Carson jams his hat down on his head and slams the door.

"I reckon it's time for you to leave too," the deputy says. "That is unless you want to make a payment—maybe ease your partner's stay a little."

I don't even bother to search my pockets. I know they're empty. And I doubt my payment would do little more than line the deputy's pocket. I'm fairly certain it won't buy Arnie much comfort tonight. "You're as corrupt as the rest of them."

The deputy erupts from the desk and seizes my sore arm. He hauls me to the door.

My stomach lurches. I pull back, trying to wriggle away, but he holds me tight. "I'll be back for you, Arnie." I catch the doorjamb with my good arm and hold tight, twisting my head to look back at him. "I won't leave you here."

The deputy shoves me out the door. I stumble down the steps and fall into the street, smacking my arm on the ground. My eyes fill with tears. "To hell with you!" I grab the nearest rock and throw it at the deputy. He closes the door just in time, and the rock smacks the wood, right where his head should have been.

I throw three more rocks before the throbbing in my arm forces me to stop. I haul myself to my feet, cursing the deputy, Mr. Carson, and the rain that has just started to fall.

Using my good arm, I snatch an empty milk crate off a nearby porch. I lug it across the street and set it against the wall behind the jail where I can stand on it without being seen. I peer through the barred window. I can just make out Arnie lying on the corner bunk where I left him.

The cell is filthy, a fact that didn't register when I was keeping Arnie from falling. Rags lie scattered across bunks, and the floor is littered with mouse droppings. The air is heavy with the smell of rotten hay and manure from the livery stable next door. If Arnie's injuries don't make him sick, this place surely will.

"Arnie, can you hear me?" I whisper through the window. I press my ear against the bar and listen, but all I hear is a faint groan. "Arnie?"

Despondent, I plop down—right in the mud. Tears cascade down my cheeks. "I'm sorry," I whisper. "I didn't mean for this to happen. I didn't mean for any of this to happen."

I think about the last few months. Mother's death. Papa's murder. And now Arnie, beaten and left in a jail cell. All of it is my fault—in one way or another—and no matter how hard I try, I will never make any of it right.

I brush away my tears and climb back on the box. I peer in the window, but I can't see anything in the dim light. "Arnie?"

I don't want to leave, but eventually I do. I stagger home through the pouring rain, too tired and too heart-worn to care that my clothes are drenched and the bandanna has slipped off my swollen arm and fallen somewhere along the way. I reach the cabin, surprised that no light shines through the window. I hope Clara didn't come out to search for me—not in this weather.

I run up the steps. The cabin door is open—flapping in the wind. I grab the handle and pull it closed behind me. I crash into what must be the table and barely make out the shape of the lantern sitting on Clara's chair. I fumble with it, lighting the wick in the dark. Buster mews as the lantern light fills the room. Next to him, Clara sprawls on floor. A pool of blood surrounds her head like a halo.

No, no, no! I knock the stool over in my hurry to get to her. Clara groans when I touch her side. Her eyes flicker open, and she struggles to sit up. She tries to speak, but the words are too faint. I lean in.

"Water," she whispers. "Water."

I stumble to the water bucket and look for the dipper, but it's not there. I pour a cup of water directly from the bucket, spilling most of it. I hold Clara's head still, careful not to touch her battered cheek. She winces when I put the cup to her lips, but manages to suck in a drop or two.

"You…have…to…go," she sputters, pausing to take a rasping breath between each word. "He'll…kill…you."

"Can you stand?" I gingerly place a hand under her arm.

She struggles to her feet. She stands, resting her weight on me.

"Oh," she cries, and collapses back to the floor.

"Clara!" I shove my hand on her chest, searching for a heartbeat. It's there. Faint but steady.

I race outside. Jasper's ears perk backward at the sound of my footsteps. I look around for Sal but don't see her in the driving rain. "I guess it's just us." I slip a rope around Jasper's neck and lead him to the front of the cabin and up the steps. I bring him to a stop right next to Clara.

"I need you to bend down a little," I tell Jasper, tugging gently on the rope. The old burro bends his knees and lies on his side. "Good boy!"

I wrap Clara in a blanket and half carry, half drag her across his back. I cover her with an old raincoat and say a quick prayer that it will keep her from getting a chill on our way to the hospital. I also curse the rain. I urge Jasper to his feet and lead him carefully through the cabin and out the door.

"All right, Jasper. Let's move." Jasper follows as I lead him through the dark streets. I want to run, but I'm afraid the bouncing might jostle Clara too much, and I'm near certain that the sudden exertion might kill poor Jasper. So we go slowly for the longest time, slogging through the muddy streets. I pause every so often to check on Clara's breathing and readjust the raincoat. I nearly cry with relief when the rain changes from a downpour to a drizzle.

Jasper and I trudge through town and out across the open desert. We reach the county hospital just as the sun rises over the hills. I march Jasper right through the doors and into the main hallway.

"Get that mule out of here," a gray-haired man yells from his place beside a patient's bed.

233

I ignore him and tug Jasper forward. "Help, please," I shout. "Help!"

A nurse runs up the aisle. She lays a hand on Clara's neck. "She's alive. Help me get her on that bed." I hold Jasper while the nurse rolls Clara off his back and pulls her onto a bed. "You'd better take that burro outside," she says as she examines Clara's head. "But come back quick. You don't look in too good of shape yourself."

I lead Jasper out of the hospital. I find a bucket and fetch him some water from the well. My hands shake as I tie him to the hitching post next to a couple of horses. "You'll be okay here," I whisper in his ear. "Just act like a horse."

I race back into the hospital tent. The gray-haired man who yelled at me is bent over Clara. The nurse steps away from the bed and leads me to a chair. "She's been pretty badly beaten. Looks like someone struck her with a blunt object. Piece of wood, maybe, or the butt of a gun?"

When I don't say anything, she continues. "She's in and out of consciousness now. We'll clean her up, tend the bruises, stitch up that eye, and immobilize the broken shoulder. We'll keep an eye on her." She lays a firm hand on my arm. "She looks like a tough old thing. We'll just have to wait and see. In the meantime, let's take a look at that arm."

I sit silently while the nurse pokes at the gash on my arm. She disappears for a while, then comes back with a bottle of brandy and tweezers. "This is going to hurt," she advises. She pours the alcohol on my arm and begins plucking splinters and pieces of rock out of the wound.

"It really doesn't hurt much," I reassure her through my tears.

And it doesn't. She's careful and quick. But I cry anyway, remembering the last time there was a gashed-up arm and tweezers heated white-hot.

When she's checked and rechecked that she got the wound clean, the nurse wraps a bandage around it. "That was quite a cut," she says. Her gaze travels to Clara's bed. "And quite a crack on the head. Care to tell me what happened?"

I close my eyes for a long minute, then shake my head to clear it. "Mine trouble," I mumble.

She bites her lip. "Hers looks a bit more like people trouble..."

"You could say that." I consider telling the nurse the whole story. She has kind eyes and gentle hands. But one glance at Clara's still form on the bed stops me. "Will she be all right?"

"Time will tell. Now, what about you? I bet you're starving. Let's get you some food."

"No thanks," I say, ignoring my growling stomach. "I just want to see Clara."

The nurse helps me slide the chair over to her bedside.

"Now we wait and see," the doctor says when I ask him if she's going to be all right. I ask again when he comes to check on her around noon and once more at five. The answer's always the same. "Wait and see."

So that's what I do. I slump in a chair and watch Clara sleep, waiting to see if she's going to make it.

Chapter Twenty-Eight

Clara wakes early the next morning, cussing and calling for whiskey and coffee. "Boy, do I have a headache," she says when she notices me in the chair. She looks around the room. "Hospital, eh? You're going to have to fill me in. I'm a bit fuzzy on the details."

I tell her all I know, and a few pieces come back to her as I talk. "Toughs," she says, as the nurse checks her bandage. "Two hulking fellows waving around a rifle, I think." She touches the side of her face and winces. "Granger's men, I imagine."

The nurse flinches at the name, then ducks her head and busies herself with straightening Clara's sling. I watch her out of the corner of my eye as she fusses over Clara. "That'll do it." She forces a smile that doesn't reach her eyes. Her face is pale, and her upper lip is sweaty. She's scared. I think back to Granger's hard eyes staring at me over his rifle barrel. She's smart to be scared.

Clara doesn't notice. "Now tell me about yours," she says once the nurse leaves.

"Cave-in." I confess my lies—explaining how I convinced Mr. Jeffries to let me go undercover at the mine. I tell her in detail about the secret tunnels, Mr. Hines's map, and how he caught me and Arnie with the evidence. "They beat Arnie something awful too," I say, swiping away a tear.

Clara tries to sit up. "Is he here?"

"Jail."

Clara slumps back in her bed and closes her eyes. "I'm going to take a little nap now," she says. She reaches out a thin hand, and I take it in mine. "You'll stay?"

"Of course," I whisper. "I'll be right here."

I stay, holding her hand until she wakes up again. "I'm going to run back to the cabin and check on the animals," I tell Clara. "You have dinner, and I'll be back before you know it."

She nods. "Maybe peek in on Arnie too?"

"I don't know if he'll talk to me, but I'll try."

I go to the cabin first. I take the lead rope off Jasper and turn him loose behind the cabin. I find Sal way down next to our old tent. She perks her ears at me, then continues browsing the cheatgrass between the tent and Clara's cabin.

"Your loss." I shake a bagful of oats at her. She whinnies and races past me. She's standing next to Jasper at the feedbags when I get back to the cabin. "Smart girl." I rub her ears and let them eat. Buster winds around my legs as I toss some feed to the chickens. I open a tin of fish for him and put some water out. I also grab a tin of crackers and a handful of jerked meat and wrap it in a towel for Arnie.

I start to leave, then hesitate. I go to Clara's bunk and search underneath. There, wrapped in a pillowcase, is Papa's pistol and a box of cartridges. I grab the pillowcase like a sack and stuff the food in next to the gun. Then I secure the cabin door.

I'm heading back to town, trying to figure out what to say to

Arnie, when I see the squatter woman sitting on an overturned bucket watching me as I pass the tent.

"Your friend okay?"

The concern in her rough voice makes me stop. "How'd you know?"

"I saw you hauling her off on that burro." She chews on her lip for a minute, then spits. "Was it those men that did it?"

"What men?" I walk over to her.

"Two big suckers. Came up in a fancy black motorcar. Some dandy in a suit was driving it. He stayed in the car while the other two went inside."

My head roars. Granger was standing on the running board of a fancy black motorcar when he pointed his rifle at me. "Did you get a good look at the man in the motorcar?"

She spits again. "I ain't blind."

"Why didn't you go check on her when they left?" I glare. Fury wraps around my words, making them quick and hard. "Why didn't you help?"

"I didn't think she was home." She glares back at me.

"That's a bunch of horse manure."

She chews her lips some more and shakes her head. "All right. Truth be told, I was chicken." She slumps a little then straightens. "I ain't usually chicken."

Her admission stills something inside me. "You had good reason to be this time."

A toughness crosses her face, and she sets her mouth in a hard line. "I'll keep an eye on the cabin." She pats her shotgun. "Me and Bess here'll deal with any intruders."

I nod. "I'd be much obliged. Maybe you'd take care of the animals too? Just for a couple of days? Nothing much. A little food and water. Maybe a tin of something for the cat."

The woman smiles. "Sure, kid."

I shake her hand. It's small, practically dainty, but hard too. More bone than flesh. "Could you do me one more favor, Sophie?" I pull Papa's pistol out of the sack. "Could you teach me how to shoot this?"

* * *

I don't even bother to knock when I get to the sheriff's office. I just push the door open and walk inside.

The deputy sits at his desk fiddling with a deck of cards. His hand twitches to the rifle resting against the wall. He pulls it closer.

"Did the doctor come?"

The deputy looks toward the cell. "See for yourself."

I run over to the cell door and peer through the bars. Arnie sits on his cot. His face is a mess—bruised and puffy. His left eye is swollen shut. A large bandage covers most of his cheek. I wince and scuff my foot against the floor. "How are you?"

"Okay. Sore."

"Did they check your ribs?"

"Wrapped 'em up tight."

"I brought you food." I hold up the tin of crackers and the dried meat.

Arnie gets up from the cot and walks over to the bars.

"Whoa," the deputy comes up behind me and jerks the food out of my hand. "I've got to approve this first."

He looks at the tin of crackers and hands it to Arnie, who

fumbles with the lid. Once it's open, he stuffs three crackers in his mouth at once. I think he smiles.

Meanwhile, the deputy samples the meat. He hands two pieces back to me. "He can have these," he says as he shoves the rest in his pocket. "I'll be keeping the rest—as payment."

My hands close into fists, and I glare at him. I imagine hitting him, one sharp blow to his stupid smirking face, but contain myself. I turn my back to him and hand the meat to Arnie. "I'll bring more later."

So relieved that he's okay, I nearly bounce with the urge to tell him everything that's happened since I left. I want to tell him about Clara and Granger's men and how we're all probably in bigger danger than any of us could have imagined. But I don't want the deputy to hear. Instead, I just say, "I'll figure out a way to get you out—I promise. But in the meantime, is there anything I can do?"

Arnie starts to shake his head, then hesitates. "Maybe check on Leslie? Make sure she's okay."

I have to stop my jaw from dropping to the floor. "Check on Leslie," I repeat slowly. "Umm, sure. All right."

"And, Kit? Be nice."

I start to protest, but then I see the pleading look in his eyes—or at least the eye that's not swollen shut—and relent. I owe him this much. "I will. I promise."

*　*　*

I hurry back to the hospital to look in on Clara. She's sleeping, so I pull a chair up to her bedside and sit. I'm tired. And I have no idea how I'm going to keep my promise to Arnie. How can I check up on Leslie? If her father sees me, there's a decent chance he'll kill me. I can still hear his voice, all calm and hard-edged. "The next one goes in your head."

And besides, what does Leslie need protecting from? Too many ruffles? An avalanche of money?

More stupid promises. When will I learn?

I doze in the chair, waking when Clara stirs and drifting off when she goes back to sleep. My dreams are filled with images of Leslie's blue eyes begging for help and Arnie's voice pleading, "But you promised, Kit."

The nurse approaches me the next morning. "Go home, honey," she urges. "She's out of the woods and needs her rest. You do too."

I look at Clara. She does seem better. Her breathing is steady, and she's not as pale and clammy as she was yesterday. Still, I don't want to leave her. Granger's men could come back. "No. I think I'll just stay a little longer."

The nurse frowns. "At least eat something."

I take the bowl of oatmeal she offers. Even though it's cold and lumpy, the smell makes my stomach growl. I take a big bite. It tastes awful, but my stomach doesn't seem to mind. "Thanks."

"You're welcome. I also brought you this." She lays a dress on the foot of Clara's bed. "It was my daughter's. I thought it might be a close fit. If you want it, that is."

I look down at my torn shirt and dirty pants. "I guess I'm a pretty sorry sight."

The nurse smiles. "A bath might help. And a nap. There's a washbasin in the room back there." She points to the end of the building, where a curtain separates the hospital floor into another room. "There's also a cot the doctor uses when he has to stay over-night. You're welcome to both."

I don't know what to say. Tears trickle down my face and drip off my chin, splashing in my oatmeal.

The nurse takes the bowl and helps me to my feet. She hands me the dress and gives me a little shove. "I'll stay with Clara while you get situated."

I make my way to the back room. It's tiny—more of a closet than a room. A small cot is pushed up against one wall. A water basin and jug rest on a wooden stand. A towel hangs off the side. A coal oil lamp sits on another small table, heating a pan of wa-ter. The whole thing looks luxurious, and I feel more than a little spoiled—a thought that gets the tears rolling again.

I strip out of my grimy clothes and pour the warm water in the basin. Quickly, I wash. It takes three pans of water to get all the dirt and grime off me and two more to clean my hair. I dry off quickly, shivering despite the summer heat, and slip into the dress. It's pink. Frilly, but serviceable. I imagine the nurse's daugh-ter wearing it to church when it was new, then after it got a little worn, to school. I wonder where she is now.

I throw my bathwater into the alley and warm another pan to clean out the basin. I don't know where to put the towel, so I fold it up and set it next to the washbasin. I ball up my old clothes and shove them in the trash. I'm pretty sure I'm finished being George Peters for a long while.

I imagine Mother breathing a sigh of relief at the thought.

I fully intend to go out and thank the nurse for her kindness, but I end up sitting on the cot thinking of Mother and Papa and

Clara and Arnie. Before long, I'm lying on the cot. I'll just close my eyes for a second, I promise myself, then I'll get up and check on Clara.

I wake to a great commotion. I hurry out of the room and stare out at the hospital floor.

Men on stretchers cry out in pain or lie still and much too quiet, considering the chaos taking place around them. Nurses in starched skirts scurry back and forth, directing the stretcher-bearers to "wait" or "stay" or "bring that one over here."

I press against the wall, frozen with shock.

The kind nurse spots me peeking out from behind the curtain. "Fetch some water, Kit. These men need a drink."

Somehow I make my legs work. I race to the well and fill a bucket. I grab the dipper from its nail and bring it inside with the water.

The gray-haired doctor moves rapidly from one man to the next. "Get those pneumonia cases moved to the back," he directs one of the nurses. "Strip the linens and ready the beds. There's no telling how many more injured men we'll get."

I move among the men offering each a dipperful of water. "What happened?" I ask the first man I come to. His arm is bent in an awkward position, and I steady the dipper for him as he drinks.

"Cave-in," he pants between slurps of water. "At the Goliath."

My fingers clasp the dipper handle. The metal clicks against the man's teeth, and water spills down his shirtfront. "Sorry," I whisper, steadying the dipper once again.

I want to ask more questions to find out exactly what happened, but I need to go on to the other men. I shuffle forward, offering the dipper to the next bloody man and then to the next. The line seems endless, and each new man, each new injury, sends a bolt of anguish through me. Still I move on, forcing a smile and a calming word as I offer the water with shaking hands.

Nurses hustle up and down the line of men, assessing wounds and separating out those most in need of the doctor's care. I try not to get in their way as I pass the water through the group. I move slower than the men would like, but I'm afraid if I rush I will blunder into them, bumping a broken arm or stepping on a hurt foot. So many are gray-faced and woozy already that I couldn't bear it if I caused anyone more pain.

I make a second pass through, having refilled the water bucket. The steady stream of men being unloaded from wagons and motorcars and the backs of mules has slackened. My brain clears a bit, and I use the lull to remind myself to breathe.

"Did you get everyone out?" someone asks the stretcher-bearers as they carry in the last two men.

"We think so. Hines is out there now checking his list."

"Hines." The man nearest me spits, splattering my boot. "Sorry about that," he says. He leans down and wipes it off with the cuff of his shirt. "If you knew him, you'd understand."

I grit my teeth and remember Hines threatening the blaster. "I'm sure I would."

I make my way to the new arrivals. I offer the dipper to a man sitting up on a cot. A dirty bandage covers half his face. I help him lift the corner off his mouth so he can take a drink.

"Well, what do you know? It's the nipper," he slurs through broken teeth. He jerks his head back and takes a look at my dress.

"Whatcha doing in that getup?"

I look closer at his face as he drinks. It's the man with the lantern. The one who was digging in the secret tunnel.

I shrug.

"Told you it was dangerous work." He tries to wink, but the movement makes him wince. "Looks like you got out just in time."

"Are you okay?"

"Better'n poor Luke." He frowns at the other cot where a man lies silent and still. "He took the brunt of it. Probably saved my life, the crazy fool."

"What happened?" My voice shakes, afraid of his answer.

"Hines had us blasting a new hole in Tunnel Three. Supposed to be all hush-hush about it, but then the boss man comes in stomping around about 'Four more feet. Four more feet.' Wants it blasted now. In the middle of the shift." He shakes his head and grimaces. "Stupid thing to do, blasting in the middle of a shift—but maybe he figured since it was only Luke and me in Tunnel Three, it wasn't no big deal."

"So you blew it and…"

"*Ka-bang*. Whole thing comes down on our heads."

"My God." My stomach turns and my hand flies to my face. I gag back the hot vomit that fills my throat.

"Turns out it wasn't just the new tunnel that fell. Most of Tunnel Two came down with it." He sweeps his gaze around the room. "That's where all of this came from."

I look around. "Why do you think it caved in?"

"Too many tunnels, too close together. We had no business putting another one in there."

I try to remember the layout of the mine. "I'm not sure I follow you. You were blasting between Two and Three? Were you trying to connect them?"

"Nah. Look here." He reaches in his pocket, pulls out a piece of paper, and unfolds it.

My breath catches. The dipper falls from my hands and tumbles across the floor. It's the map. Mr. Hines's map.

I fumble for the dipper as he talks. "We were digging here in the middle of Three—going south like we did in Tunnel Five. I don't know. We must've hit a soft spot of ground between the tunnels. Damned lucky the whole place didn't go."

"Damned lucky," I manage, transfixed by the map in his hands.

Just then the nurse comes by. "I'm going to take this fellow with me, Kit."

He gets up to follow. "See ya later, nipper." He crumbles the map and tosses it onto the floor.

I scramble after the paper, then unfurl it and carefully press out the wrinkles. It's all there. The layout of the mine. The two new tunnels.

In the bottom right corner is a small sketch. It looks like it's a picture of the ground above the mine. The Goliath is marked with one square. Then just below it is another square; this one is marked Baby Sister. A key shows how to measure distance using inches.

I gulp in a huge breath of air and release it in one big whoosh. Granger's plan, and it's all here in black and white. The voices fade away, and all I can hear is my heart beating, fast and strong. "I've got him," I whisper as I fold the map up. "I've finally got him."

I move to shove the map in my back pocket. Stupid dress.

Someone really should make a dress pattern with pockets. I hurry over to Clara's bed.

"Quite a commotion." She struggles to sit up, so I help her and adjust her pillow behind her back.

"The Goliath caved in."

"I heard. I was hoping I'd spot those thugs who worked me over." She scans the room. "But one bloody face looks too much like another. Poor bastards."

"I found this." I unfold the map and place it on her stomach.

Clara's gray eyes narrow. She wipes a hand across them. "Things are still a bit blurry. Is this what I think it is?"

I squeeze her hand. "Keep it hidden?"

She folds it up into a tight square and hands it to me. "Stick it in the toe of my shoe. "No one's going to be poking around there." She raises an eyebrow at me. "What's your plan?"

I look around the room. There's so much noise and confusion that I can't think clearly. "I need to talk to Arnie," I decide, "and maybe Sheriff Earp."

Chapter Twenty-Nine

The hospital is too jammed with people for me to stay the night. Once the miners are sorted and treated, their families start showing up, and pretty soon the place is a teeming mess of wounded men, scared, angry women, and dazed kids.

The whole scene makes me want to scream. First at Mr. Granger for causing all this suffering, and then at myself for not stopping him before this happened.

A little while later, Mr. Granger's car pulls up out front. My vision clouds, and the entire room turns red. Part of me wants to stay, to shove the map in his face and call him out the minute he walks in the room, but the other part—the part that is worried for Clara and Arnie and even for me, though it embarrasses me to admit it—knows better. For once, I side with caution.

"Don't let him see you," I whisper to Clara. I help her turn on her side and fluff up the blanket so that most of her head is covered. Then I sneak out the side entrance.

I make my way down the street leading back toward town. I head straight to the jail, hoping that I can talk to Arnie and tell him about the map. My feet stop when I remember my promise about Leslie. He's going to want to know that I saw her, that I spoke to her. He won't be happy to learn that I haven't even tried to find her.

I take a deep breath and shove the swear words trying to work their way out of my mouth back down. I change direction, cutting through side yards and building sites until I get to Fifth Avenue. I walk up Fifth, past the burned buildings and scorched houses, until I get to the Grangers' big brick house on the corner.

The house appears empty. No light shimmers through the windows. I open the iron gate and step into the yard, then ease through the shadows and up the porch steps. I cup my hands against the front window and press my face to the glass.

"You looking for someone, miss?"

I startle and bump my head against the window frame. Terror fills me as I tumble off the steps and crash into the flowerbed.

I hear the swish of a match. Lantern light fills the porch. I rise to a sitting position and see a man sitting on the porch swing. A shotgun rests beside him. "I…uh…I was looking for Leslie. I mean, Miss Granger."

The old man smiles gently. "Miss Leslie left. The whole family left, 'cept for Mr. Granger hisself, and he's over at the hospital checking on the men." The man shifts in the swing. "That's why I'm here guarding the place."

"What are you guarding it against?"

The old man shrugs. "Men, I suppose. Miners mad about the collapse. Drunks looking to stir up trouble." He pats the shotgun. "Mr. Granger wants me to shoot anyone who comes up the path."

"Why didn't you shoot me?" I stand on weak legs and hide my trembling hands beneath the folds of the dress.

He smiles again. The lantern light glints off his white teeth. "I didn't think a bit of a girl like you could cause too much trouble. Besides, between you and me and this here swing, I don't always do exactly what Mr. Granger asks."

I finally take a deep breath. "I think you're the first person I've met in this whole town who can say that," I say with a smile.

"That might be so. If you see Miss Leslie, you tell her good luck from me. I always did think there was more to that girl than meets the eye."

I roll my eyes. Another Leslie lover. And just when I was starting to like him. "Umm. I will." I walk out of the yard and close the gate behind me. Just as the latch clicks shut, the lantern goes out and the porch is dark once again.

At least now I can tell Arnie that Leslie is safely out of town with her mother and brother. She's probably settling into some marvelous hotel in San Francisco or Reno—ordering room service, planning a shopping trip, and not the least bit worried about Arnie or the men lying bleeding and broken at the county hospital.

The thought brings a foul taste in my mouth. I spit to clear it, then spit again to show my anger and resentment toward the whole Granger family.

I begin walking all the way back through town to the jail to tell Arnie the news. By the time I reach the livery stable, a great exhaustion washes over me. Hunger claws at my insides, and I try not to think of how long it's been since I've had something to eat. I bet it's been at least that long for Arnie.

I cast around, trying to figure out how I can get my hands on some food. The hospital, maybe, but that seems so far away. I glance over at the livery. Maybe Arnie's got some grub stashed in his car.

I drag myself into the stable. Arnie's motorcar sits against the far wall. A jacket is folded up on the front seat. I reach in and dig through the pockets. *Jackpot!* I stuff a stick of jerky in my mouth and rest the other pieces on the car. I walk over to the bay mare's stall and whistle low, calling her to me. "Sorry I don't have an apple or something," I say as I rub her muzzle. "But it's been a very long day. A very long couple of days, actually."

A rustle in the next stall catches my attention. A form leans on the rail. I squint in the dark, not trusting my eyes. "Leslie?"

"Kit? Oh, Kit, is it really you?" She rushes out of the stall and envelops me in a hug. "I knew you'd come."

I stumble back, trying to extricate myself from the ruffled embrace. "You did?"

Leslie goes back in the stall and returns with a lantern and a match. "I was afraid to light this in here." She hands both to me.

Very carefully, I strike the match and light the wick. I hang the lantern on the hook, then step outside to bury the match in the street. When I return, Leslie perches on a rail. Her eyes are red and swollen, and her hair is wild. Half is matted to her head, while the rest is frizzy and snarled. She really could use a ribbon. And a comb.

I peek into the stall. A suitcase rests against the wall, and a blanket is laid out in the straw. "What are you doing here?" I ask. I don't bother to keep my annoyance out of my voice.

"I ran away. I just couldn't stay with him…not after this…" She buries her face in her hands and sobs. "How could he do that to Arnie?"

"He didn't just do it to Arnie."

She looks up and wipes the tears from her eyes. Her chin quivers, but she meets my gaze with steady eyes. "I know. That's why I thought the list would help."

"The list?"

"You got it, didn't you?" She goes over to the stall with the bay and starts digging through the straw. "Get out of the way, Athena," she says as she gently shoves the horse to the side. "I left it here in the Twain book."

"You left the list?" I can feel my jaw drop in surprise, and I don't bother to close it. I feel like Leslie just hit me upside the head with a fence rail—stunned and more than a little dumb.

She nods. "Arnie said you were reading the book, so I thought you'd for sure find it there."

"You're LM." I shake my head.

"Leslie Matilda." She frowns. "Hideous, I know. I used to come here and visit Athena every day. Sometimes I'd read."

"Athena." So that's the mare's name. I have to admit, it's not half bad. Certainly not as bad as Matilda. "But, why?"

"Daddy shouldn't have shot your father like that. Not over some stupid gold. Then I met Arnie, and he told me about you, and…I just thought if I could help, I should."

"Even though you knew it could hurt your father—your family?"

Leslie swallows hard. "It just didn't seem right, what he did." She shrugs and looks down. Big tears hang from her lashes. "I don't hate him, Kit, if that's what you think. But I don't agree with him either…I don't know…"

"You love Arnie."

The tears spill down her cheeks, and she nods. "I love Arnie."

I close my eyes for a long minute and let the truth of that settle in me. Leslie loves Arnie, and Arnie loves Leslie. The realization pricks my heart, and I feel something inside me—hope maybe, or just longing—shrivel up. *So, that's that.*

I heave out a long breath and sit down on the rail next to her. "Looks like we need to figure a couple of things out."

Chapter Thirty

Leslie and I talk all night. Mostly about Arnie and her father, and that would have been fine, but—and this is humiliating to admit—I just couldn't let her get away with acting like we were bosom friends all of sudden. Not after every mean thing she's done to me since I came to this dusty old town.

"Why were you so awful to me?" I whisper, interrupting her story about how she and Arnie met. "Why'd you get everyone else to be so mean to me? You seem almost…nice." I nearly choke on the word, but it's true. She does seem nice. And caring. And not at all as stupid and lazy and horrible as I've made her out to be.

Leslie digs her heel into the hay and shrugs. "I don't really know. I just was." Her eyes tear up again, and I can tell by the way she's looking at me that she really wants to hear me say I forgive her.

I try. I even say it in my head, but for some reason the words won't get past my lips. So I pat her leg instead. "That Athena sure likes carrots," I say, nodding at the mare. "We should probably find her some."

Leslie nods, then goes right back to telling me about how fine and cute Arnie is and how funny he looked covered in dust the first time she saw him.

By the time Old Joe Smiley comes in the next morning to tend to the horses, I know way too much about Leslie and Arnie's romance, and we have a solid plan—and maybe the tiniest glimmer of a friendship.

"How's our boy?" Joe asks when he stops to fill up Athena's water trough.

"He'll be better soon, I hope," I say. "I'm going to see someone about him today."

Old Joe looks at Leslie. His lips curl into a smile. "If you ladies want to tidy up a bit, there's a water basin in my office. Comb too."

Leslie's hands fly to her hair. She ducks her head and runs toward Old Joe's office.

Joe turns back to me. "You need anything? Money, maybe? Or a fast horse?"

I shake my head. "Just the use of the stable to bed down is plenty."

Joe spits a stream of tobacco juice on the floor. He scuffs it with his boot. "You come fetch me if you need anything," he says. "I may be old, but I've still got a few tricks up my sleeve."

I smile wide, remembering his shotgun. "I'm sure you do, sir."

I leave Leslie at the stable. "No use risking running into your father," I insist when she starts to protest. "Then you'll be no help to anyone."

I go to the hospital to check on Clara, who's looking much perkier. I tell her all about Leslie and Arnie.

"So, she's the one who left the list of names," Clara murmurs. "Ain't she the dark horse?"

She is indeed. And maybe a useful one, though I hate to admit it.

"Has Mr. Granger been around? Or Mr. Hines?"

Clara looks around, then motions for me to sit on the edge of her bed. "Not since yesterday. And after all the ruckus, I don't expect him to be back."

She leans in closer. "The men near about threw him out on his head—at least some of them anyway." She looks around warily. "A few stood up for him. Said business is business, and all of that. But, I tell you, Kit, if some of these fellows were a little stronger and a little more mobile, I think Mr. Granger would be occupying one of these beds himself."

"I think it's time I talk to Mr. Jeffries," I say with a deep sigh. Truth be told, I've been a little afraid to see him. I don't think he'll be too happy to discover he's had a girl printer's devil all along.

"He was in here last night," Clara says. "Talking to the men. Checking faces. I got the impression he was searching for someone." She rubs her forehead and frowns. "Poor man. I should have realized he was probably looking for you."

The news takes me by surprise. "You sure?" The thought of Mr. Jeffries checking on me eases some of my worry about facing him.

Clara shrugs. Her entire face looks sad. Weary. Dark circles surround her eyes, and her hair looks even grayer than before. "Old brain's still a little muddled, I guess."

I pat her on the hand. "It'll come back."

"Yeah. A few more days, and I'll be good as new." She fiddles with her pillow. "Go see that man," she urges before lying back down. "Ease his mind."

"I will," I promise. "But first I have to get Arnie out of jail."

* * *

"Man's dying," Mr. Larson tells me when I stop in his store and ask for directions to Sheriff Earp's house. "At least that's what folks are saying 'round here."

I think of Sheriff Earp's serious blue eyes and the way his whole frame bent toward me when we talked. "I sincerely hope not," I say, "but I still need to see him."

I find his modest clapboard house at the end of Euclid Avenue. I tap on the front door. Mrs. Earp opens it a crack and peeks out.

"I need to see the sheriff. It's important."

"Sheriff Earp's ill," she says. She starts to close the door, but I shove my foot in the jamb, forcing it open. "Please, ma'am. It's concerning Mr. Granger. And Virgil promised to help me if I asked."

I don't know if it's grim determination or me calling him Virgil that sways her, but she lets me inside. "He's not up for visitors, but if you'll tell me what you need, I will talk to him."

I lay out the story—emphasizing who I am and explaining how Arnie is only in jail because he helped me. "I saw Mr. Hines drop the gold in his lunch pail. He set him up."

She disappears into the bedroom. In a few minutes, she returns. "He'll see you," she says. "But just for a minute."

I step into the dimly lit bedroom. Sheriff Earp is propped in a wheelchair, a heavy woolen blanket spread across his waist. His face is pale, and his shrunken frame is even thinner than I remember.

"Granger's a crook," he mutters through cracked lips. "Write it out, Allie."

His wife sits at a desk and writes something on a piece of paper. She hands the pen and note to him. With a shaking fist, he signs his name and hands the paper to me.

> Release the boy named Arnie on $3.00 bail. Charges
> to be dropped if proof of guilt is not brought to me
> in 12 hours time. Proceedings will resume upon
> my return.

Tears fill my eyes. "Thank you, sir," I whisper.

"You find your proof?" His gaze is still unwavering, despite his watery eyes.

"I think so, sir."

"Good. I'll take great pleasure in seeing him exposed." He sputters into a handkerchief, then slumps back in his chair and closes his eyes.

"Thank you," I say, louder this time, as Allie guides me out of the room. I look at the note. "Do you think he'll honor it?"

She smiles, but her face is full of sadness. "Even Deputy Douglas won't deny Virgil his last bit of official duty. He is a legend, you know."

I race through town and into the stables. Leslie sits on her blanket, staring into space. She jumps up when she sees me.

"Do you have three dollars?" I cry, flapping Sheriff Earp's note at her.

She stares at me, blank-faced, then runs over to her bag. She pulls out three silver coins and holds them up. "Here, but why do you need...?"

I press the note in her hand. "Take this and the money over to the jail. The deputy will have to release Arnie to you." Leslie grabs the note and starts to run out of the stable. "Don't take no for an answer," I call after her. "If you get into trouble, find Old Joe. He said he'd help."

Leslie waves her hand over her head and keeps running.

I can't help but smile. Leslie Granger galloping through town like a…well, like me. Won't Arnie be surprised?

But probably not half as surprised as Mr. Jeffries is about to be.

* * *

I spend my entire walk to the newspaper office trying to gather my courage. I think of Mother saying "Honesty is the best policy" and try to comfort myself with that. When it doesn't work, I remind myself that even Huck Finn admitted that sometimes telling the truth is better than telling a lie.

I can only hope this is one of those times.

I take a deep breath, trying to ignore the thickness in my throat and the pinching pain in my chest. I swing open the door and step into the office. The smell of ink and dust fills my nose and gives me hope. I breathe deeply and look around. Before I can say a word, Mr. Jeffries rushes across the room and swings me up into a hug.

I stiffen at the shock of his arms around my shoulders but soften as his relief and happiness become contagious. "You knew?" I cry when he finally puts me down.

"Of course I knew. I'm a reporter, aren't I? Trained to see through lies and deception and ferret out the truth." He takes a step back and tugs at his beard. "You wrote it all down, didn't you?"

I duck my head and look at my boots. "No, sir."

Mr. Jeffries sighs. "Haven't I taught you anything at all? You get it down while it's fresh—before the details get muddled." He grabs a notebook and a pencil from his desk and hands them to me.

"I could just tell you. You see, I found…"

"No talking. Write." He points to the paper. "Do it now. I'll wait."

I write all afternoon. I don't stop for lunch or coffee or even when my hand cramps up so badly I want to cry. I tell all of it: crawling in the tunnel, the collapse, the man with the lantern, and all the gold glimmering on the wall. I write about the map and Arnie being set up by Mr. Hines and about Mr. Granger pointing a rifle at me and threatening to blow my head off. I write about the filthiness of the jail, about finding Clara beaten and bloody, and about the cave-in and the screams of the men at the hospital that night. I write like my soul is on fire—like Mother and Papa both have a hand on the pencil and are urging me forward.

"That's it." I push the pages toward Mr. Jeffries and close my eyes. *That's the best I can do, Papa.*

I shiver and open my eyes. I reach for the sandwich he brought me hours ago. He reads it while I eat. Every now and then, he pauses to shake his head. When he finishes, he sets the paper down and hugs me across the table.

This time I smile. Who knew Mr. Jeffries was such a softy?

"What about this Mr. Harrison?" he asks. He fumbles through the papers. "The engineer. He still in town?"

"Far as I know."

"Think he'll talk—on the record?"

"He's an honest fellow."

"Even honest fellows balk." He gets up and goes to his desk. He hands me a newspaper. "Speaking of honest fellows, take a look at page six—the Coming and Goings."

I flip to the section and read. *Some of the arrivals in Tonopah yesterday included Arthur Flynn, Frank Williams, H. P. Anders, Mason Lynch, and Markus Westchester.*

I read it again. "Mr. Westchester." My eyebrows flick up. "He hightailed it out of here pretty quick once the mine collapsed."

"Think you're up for a trip to Tonopah tomorrow?"

Heat rushes to my face. Mr. Westchester. He's had a hand in all of this. It's only fair that he tells what he knows. "I guess I'd better be."

"I'll tinker with this and maybe see if I can track down Mr. Harrison. Why don't you go in the back and ask Marta to set up a cot for you." He smiles. "You look like you could use a good night's sleep."

Every muscle in my body longs for that good night's sleep, but I still have work to do. "Nah. I need to go make sure Leslie got Arnie out of jail, and I need to check on Clara." I rub my eyes. "If I find Mr. Westchester, do you think we can get a story together in a day or so?"

He's already back to looking at my pages. He raises his head absentmindedly and nods. "You just bring that louse Westchester back here. I'll handle the rest."

I return to the hospital and find Arnie and Leslie crowded around Clara's bed. I rush over in a panic, only to discover they are playing a particularly intense game of poker.

"What does two of a kind beat?" Leslie asks as she sets her cards down on the bed.

"Not much," I say, winking at Clara.

Leslie jumps up and hugs me. "It worked, Kit! The deputy read the note—oh, you should have seen the face he made—but then he stomped right over and opened the cell. My poor Arnie looked so banged up that I brought him straight here to be checked out."

I look over at Arnie. He does look pretty beat up. Still, it's a relief to see him. "All good?" I ask—hoping he understands that I don't just mean his injuries. I mostly mean our friendship.

"All good." He smiles. "Leslie says you have a plan."

"I do, but I'm going to need your help."

Chapter Thirty-One

"Are you sure you can't come along?" I ask Arnie. Butterflies dance in my stomach.

"Doc says I need to stay put another day or so. Besides, I don't think these ribs would fare well on the road between here and Tonopah. You can drive the car, Kit. You know how. Just go real slow until you get out of town."

"I've ridden in cars dozens of times," Leslie adds, taking my hand. "We'll be fine." She blows a kiss at Arnie and drags me out of the hospital and to the stables.

It takes us a full hour to get the motorcar started. "Maybe it's gas first and then the ignition," Leslie offers after we've adjusted and readjusted everything a dozen times.

I get in and look at the levers and buttons again. I try to remember just how Arnie had them set. I make a few changes, check the brake, then flip the ignition switch. "You crank it this time," I tell Leslie. "My poor arm is about to fall off."

Leslie scurries to the front of the car. She turns the crank and looks at me.

"You have to turn it harder," I yell. "And keep it steady."

She rubs her hands together and tries again. The motor roars.

Her eyes go round. "Woo-hoo! I…"

"Get in!"

She scrambles into the passenger seat.

I release the brake slowly and feed it a little gas. The car lurches forward. The engine sputters but doesn't die. I add more gas, and we coast right out of the stables and onto the street. *Steady. Just keep it steady.*

"Help me watch for horses—and people," I shout as we turn onto Main Street. We crawl down the road.

"Old women are passing us," Leslie observes. "Babies too." She points at a toddler staggering up the sidewalk outside the Palm Studio.

"Arnie said go slow until we get out of town," I say through pursed lips. "So that's what I intend to do, old women and babies be damned."

"Hey, Kit. There's the newspaper man." Leslie pokes my shoulder.

I flick my gaze off the road for a second. Mr. Jeffries is standing on the sidewalk outside of the *Times* office. "Good luck," he calls.

I want to wave in return, but I don't dare. Instead I keep both of my sweaty hands tight on the steering wheel and face forward. I don't relax until we're out of town and on the road to Tonopah. Even then, my back and shoulders are still rigid and tense.

"Keep an eye out for rocks," I advise Leslie. "Don't let me drive over any big ones."

Leslie is a pretty good navigator. She points out problems early and isn't at all girlie when it comes to fixing flat tires.

"I always thought you were kind of prissy," I admit after

we've spent the better part of an hour patching a particularly bad puncture.

Leslie wipes a drop of sweat from her forehead, leaving a streak of grime across her cheek. "I usually am. Spoiled too."

"But now?"

She shrugs her thin shoulder. "I said some pretty terrible things to Daddy. Unforgivable things, really. Not that it matters, but I'm pretty sure he won't be buying me a new dress anytime soon." She stares out across the desert for a moment.

"Arnie's smart," she says, wrinkling her forehead. "And he's going to be rich someday. I'm sure of it. But he's not rich now, so I am going to have to figure out how to do things myself. Cooking, cleaning—and fixing punctured tires." She shrugs again, like she's not entirely sure what's in store for her.

I make a face, but I have to give her some credit. She seems determined. "I think it will hold," I say, giving the tire another look. "Let's get this on. Then you can crank up the car. Get those hands broken in for all the cooking and cleaning that's coming your way."

Leslie wrinkles her nose and sticks her tongue out at me.

I stick mine out too, and we both burst out laughing.

Between tire punctures and my slow driving, we don't pull into Tonopah until around noon. The narrow streets are crammed with motorcars and wagons, and people weaving in and out of traffic. I consider parking the car on the outskirts of town and simply walking, but Leslie is afraid some desperate traveler might steal the car, so I drive all the way to the middle of downtown while Leslie hangs over the side, waving her arms and shouting, "New driver, stand back!" over and over. By the time we get halfway through town, people are so intent on getting out of our way that the streets are nearly clear—which kind of annoys me as I'm just starting to feel comfortable maneuvering this thing.

I park the car in front of the courthouse and get out. Leslie and I look up and down the street. The sidewalks swarm with people. Building after building lines the main street, and more are being built as we watch. "Where should we start?" Leslie asks.

"Saloons, I guess." I begin to walk up the street, nodding curtly at people and trying to choose a likely place.

Leslie grimaces but follows me to the door of a building that looks like it was built yesterday using whatever scrap material the owner could round up. "Not here," she begs, tugging at my arm.

"We have to start somewhere." I try to shrug her off, but her grip is too strong.

"How about over there?" She points to a building across the street. The fancy lettering on the window reads Mizpah.

I crane my neck and look up at the five-story building. "It's a hotel—and a fine one at that. I don't think we'll find Mr. Westchester there."

"There's a bar too." She drags me across the street. "You look in the bar, and I'll check out the hotel lobby. Maybe someone's seen him."

I roll my eyes and sigh. "Then we're going to the real saloons. And the dancing halls. It's the only way we're going to track him down."

Leslie nods, but by the way she holds her mouth, I can tell she's not pleased with my plan.

We walk into the lobby of the Mizpah Hotel. Leslie turns to the left, toward the front desk, while I veer right to the bar. I pause, mesmerized for a minute, and watch a group of finely dressed ladies clamber into a grand elevator. I stare at them as the door closes. Soon an arrow above the elevator doors begins to move, showing the floor the elevator stops on. All the way to five. I inch toward the elevator doors, tempted to ride it up myself just to see what it's like, but a sharp cough from the direction of the bar catches my attention and reminds me of my real purpose here.

I enter the bar and pause, waiting for my eyes to adjust to the dim light. It's early afternoon, but the place is crowded. A few men sit at the tables, reading the newspaper and eating lunch. Others stand at the long mahogany bar. More than a couple look up, but I ignore them. I push my shoulders back and stride right up to the bar.

The bartender frowns but comes over to where I am standing. "You can't be here," he says, loud enough for the men standing nearby to hear.

I straighten my back and widen my stance. I'm not going anywhere.

He looks around sheepishly, then leans in closer. "What do you need?" he asks softly.

"I'm looking for a man. Bookish. Wire-rimmed glasses. Looks like he should be back East somewhere teaching school."

The bartender narrows his eyes. "Reporter?"

I nod.

He points to a table in the far corner of the wide room. "Been there the last two days."

I squint, trying to make out the figure sitting in the dark. I move back slightly and blink. I can't believe it. "That's him," I murmur. "Thanks."

Light-headed, I make my way to his table. He doesn't look up until I slide a chair over and sit across from him. Then his tired eyes shine with recognition—and guilt.

"Hey."

"You shouldn't be here." He ducks his head. "I can't help you."

"I think you can." My voice is louder than usual. Harder.

He fumbles for his drink. "I tried. I really did." He finishes his whiskey and gestures to the bartender to get him another.

I lean back in my chair. I press my lips together and search for the right words. "But we have proof now. Maps that show Granger is stealing gold. Maps that show where he's dug tunnels that have made the whole mine unstable."

Mr. Westchester peers at me over the wire rims of his glasses. His eyes glimmer in the candlelight. "How'd you get the map? Nobody would do more than hint about a map…"

I sit up a little straighter and let pride slip into my smile. "I just happened to come across one someone was finished with."

"And the union?"

"Was in on it. Mr. Hines really is a…What did you call him? Apos…traitor?"

"Apostate." Mr. Westchester smirks. "I really wanted to work that into an article somehow."

"Now's your chance. Mr. Jeffries sent me to fetch you back."

He takes off his glasses. He pulls a handkerchief out of his pocket and wipes the lenses. "You can tell him I said no way in hell."

My cheeks flush. "You have to." My voice shakes. I bite my cheek and try again. "The mine collapsed. Men died. My father…"

Mr. Westchester holds up a hand. "Whoa, there. All I…"

"Whoa nothing." I lean forward and grab him by the wrist. My fingernails sink into the back of his hand. "You started this. You came to us."

"I did my job!" He wrenches his hand free and points a finger at me. "You were the one who came to me. You're the one who wanted your name in the paper."

I slide my hand off the table and cross both arms in front of me. My face burns, and I feel sick. Sweaty and shaky and too hot all over. He's right. I did come to him. I shift my gaze, unable to meet his eyes. "You should have warned me." The words come out in a croak, and I want to pull them back, to pull all of this back, but I can't. "We need you," I whisper.

Mr. Westchester presses a trembling hand to his forehead. His eyes are wet. He nods quickly, then fumbles with his glasses. "Jeffries, huh?"

I cover his hand with mine, softly this time, stilling the rattle of his fingers against the table. "Yeah. He figures between us we can come up with a pretty good article outlining exactly what's been going on at Goliath Mine all these months."

He puts the glasses back on his nose and looks at me. "A tell-all. He's really willing to do this?"

"He's raring to go. Said I was to bring you back today, and we'll try to get it out tomorrow—day after at the latest."

"How'd you even know I was here?"

"Newspaper. 'Comings and Goings.'" I grin.

"Damned busybodies." He gulps down the whiskey the bartender slides in front of him. "Give me a moment to settle up and grab my hat."

"I'll wait for you at the front desk." I hesitate. Uncertainty prods me. I lay a hand on his arm and wait for him to look me in the eye. "You're really coming, aren't you?"

Mr. Westchester looks away. He rubs his chin, then meets my eyes again. "I really am."

"There might be trouble." My stomach clenches. I don't want to make him change his mind, but I don't want to force him into something that might get him hurt—or killed.

He glances at the whiskey glass. "I know."

"Okay." I take a deep breath and let it out in a *whoosh*. "I'll be at the front desk."

Leslie is talking with an older man in a fine gray suit when I walk up. "Kit," she says, squeezing my arm. "This is Mr. Ericson. He's offered to help us."

"No need." I shoot a suspicious glance at Mr. Ericson.

He returns my gaze without a flinch or a shrug. "It is no problem. Young ladies like yourselves should not go near the places men frequent. It's dangerous."

I relax a little. He really does seem sincere. "It's okay. Turns out you were right," I tell Leslie, nearly choking on the words. "Mr. Westchester was here after all. He should join us any minute. He's paying his bill."

Leslie squeals in delight. "I told you…"

A richly dressed lady swoops in, taking both of our attention. She glides over to Mr. Ericson and tucks her hand in the crook of his arm. "I hope I didn't keep you waiting, Richard. The elevator was simply too crowded. I decided to take the stairs."

I jerk my head back and gasp. "Aunt Minerva!" I stammer. "What in the..."

Recognition and relief flicker across her face. She smiles and reaches toward me. "Katherine. Is it really you?"

I stagger back a step. "What are you still doing in Tonopah?"

She smooths her skirt. "Lovely to see you too." She frowns. "Don't stand there gaping at me like an idiot. Where are your manners?" She taps me on the head with her fan.

I slam my mouth shut, feeling my teeth click together. Fortunately I manage to miss my tongue. "I thought you went back East..."

"Well, I planned to. But there's so much happening here. So many opportunities." A small smile crosses her lips as she gazes out the window. "Besides, I've made some good friends." Her brow furrows and the far-away look disappears. She turns her attention back to me. "And, there's you, of course. Did you really think I'd leave my only niece in the wilds of Nevada?"

She doesn't give me a chance to answer. Instead, she smiles at Mr. Ericson. "Richard, this is my niece, Katherine. Katherine Eve, Mr. Richard Ericson, my architect."

"Uh...pleased to meet you," I manage. "This is my...this is Leslie," I offer.

Leslie dips in a perfect curtsy.

"A pleasure, Leslie," my aunt coos. "Aren't you lovely—and what a fine example you set." She turns to me, eyebrow raised. "Perhaps some of your grace will rub off..."

I spot Mr. Westchester waiting at the door. "I'm sorry, Aunt Minerva, but we really must be going back to Goldfield. We have some business to see to."

"Yes, well, as do I. We were just going to check on the construction of my new house." She turns toward the door, then pauses. "Perhaps a private word, Katherine. Excuse us for a moment," she says, smiling at Leslie.

I glance longingly at the door before following Aunt Minerva to a small lounge area off the lobby. I fidget nervously as she sits in a chair, arranging her skirts around her. She nods, indicating that I am to take the chair opposite.

"I really do have to go," I protest.

"Sit, Katherine." She sighs. "This will only require a moment." I sit.

Aunt Minerva leans forward. Her eyes are serious, her gaze piercing. "How are you?"

"I'm fine." I fight the urge to roll my eyes. She wants to do polite company talk, now?

"And Clara? I haven't heard from her in a while. She had planned to visit last week…"

"Clara knew you were here?" I can't believe it. I can't believe Clara would spy on me for Aunt Minerva, but one glance at Aunt Minerva's steadfast face and I know it's true. I shake my head. Talk about betrayal. I wonder if Clara told her I got kicked out of school or that I was pretending to be a boy.

"Don't be dramatic, Katherine. Of course I kept in touch with her. I am your aunt. And I like her." A small smile flickers across her lips. "But clearly something is the matter. What is it?"

I push my bruised feelings aside. "She was hurt pretty bad. Granger and his men..." I stand. "That's why I really have to get back. There's been trouble and..."

Aunt Minerva's face goes pale. She clutches my arm. "Is she all right? Does she need..."

Aunt Minerva's reaction startles me so much that I don't jerk my arm away. "She's doing better. Talking and joking and complaining about the food."

Aunt Minerva closes her eyes and mutters, "Praise God." She opens her eyes and grasps my arm tighter. "Do you need anything? Money? Help? Richard has access to a motorcar. Perhaps he would..."

My brow wrinkles. *What is she up to?* But my suspicion fades with one look in her eyes. She's sincerely worried. Some of the tension I've been carrying around falls away. "No." I place my hand over hers. "It's kind of you to offer, but I'm okay. We're just really close to uncovering it all. Granger. The union. Maybe even Papa's murder." I glance toward the door. "I really do need to go."

Aunt Minerva stands. She smooths her skirts, then pats me on the shoulder. "You'll contact me soon? Let me know everything is all right?"

I nod.

"And tell Clara I will come to Goldfield for our visit. Next week. I'll wire you."

"Have them deliver it to the *Times* office." I break away and head to the door. "And read the newspaper. Things are about to get interesting."

Chapter Thirty-Two

We make it back to Goldfield in record time—thanks to my increased confidence with the motorcar and Mr. Westchester's help with tire punctures. I drop Leslie off at the hospital. "Tell Arnie thanks and that I'll leave the motorcar at the stables," I say. "And tell Clara she owes me an explanation about Aunt Minerva."

I smile. It will be fun to tease Clara about it, but truth be told, I don't mind. It's kind of nice to have people looking out for you, even if they are doing it in secret.

I park Arnie's car at the stable, and Mr. Westchester and I walk to the newspaper office.

"Ahh...just in time," Mr. Jeffries says. "Wendell and Peter were just here. I got some great details about mine engineering and setting up tunnels." He chews on the end of his pencil, then scribbles something on the notes in front of him. "It looks like you were right, Kit. Tunnels too long and too close. Tunnels practically bisecting other tunnels. It was a recipe for collapse."

I half shrug. "Would have been better if we caught it before the place caved in."

He looks up from his papers. "Still, it's good work." He tugs on his beard, then turns to Mr. Westchester. "So, I see you made it back to us." He eyes him for a minute. "Sober?"

Mr. Westchester nods. He crosses the room, hangs his coat on the chair of his old desk, and takes a seat.

Mr. Jeffries runs a hand over his head. "All right then. Let's get started. Westchester, I want you to look at Kit's notes here. See how they jibe with yours."

"Kit, you man the printing press. Start with this." He hands me a sheet of paper. I scan it. It looks like the facts about the collapse. How many men injured. How long it took to dig them out. "One man died," I say, shaking my head. "Did you get a name?"

"Luke something." He fumbles through some papers on his desk. "Fields. Luke Fields."

"Oh." My eyes well up with tears. I can't help but wonder if he had a family, if he had a son or a daughter somewhere angry and afraid, just like me.

"Some fellow name of Jackson said he died a hero. Pushed him out of the worst of it. Makes for a hell of an obituary."

We spend the rest of the evening writing, arguing over words and phrases, going over facts, and setting type. My hands are black with ink, and we're all exhausted and more than a little cranky when the last page rolls off the printing press. Still, it feels good to finally be doing something.

"Do you think this will work?" I pull a newspaper out of the pile. "Do you think anyone will even care?"

Mr. Jeffries looks from me to Mr. Westchester and back again. "'Hain't we got all the fools in town on our side?'" he says with a wink.

I laugh harder than I should. "So you have read *The Adventures of Huckleberry Finn*."

"Of course, my dear George Peters. Now help me get these in stacks. The newsboys will be here any minute."

Sure enough, two wiry boys tumble through the door, wiping sleep from their eyes. "We want them all gone before eleven o'clock," Mr. Jeffries says. "And no selling them off to some high roller at the Northern who's trying to impress a girl. Regular sales—do that, and there's a bonus in it for you."

The boys shove folded papers in their sacks—their tiredness forgotten at the word *bonus*. They sling the full bags over their arms and step out the door, already crying, "Special Edition. Mine collapses. Corruption, theft to blame. Read all about it…"

My chest swells at the words. I take a deep and satisfied breath and let it out slowly. I stand next to Mr. Jeffries, watching them go. He rests a hand on my shoulder. "Now we wait."

* * *

And sleep. At least, I think I've been sleeping when I finally raise my head off my desk, groggy and dry-mouthed, and look out the window.

Arnie is running across the street—hands clutched to his side. He tears into the office, slamming the door behind him. "They're coming," he pants. "Men. Lots of them." He turns to the window and looks out. "And they look mad."

I jump up from my chair, my heart beating wildly.

"Get in the back," Mr. Jeffries shouts as he reaches for his rifle. Marta scurries into the back room. The door clicks closed behind her. Mr. Westchester adjusts his glasses and takes a pistol out of his desk drawer. He walks across the room to stand next to the printing press.

"I said go," Mr. Jeffries yells.

I know he's talking to me, but I ignore him. I pull Papa's pistol out of the pillowcase I stashed beneath my desk. I move to the far wall. I kneel down behind the table, pop six cartridges into the chambers, and close the cylinder. I prop the heavy pistol on the table, just like Sophie taught me, and point the barrel at the doorway.

"Here they come," Arnie says. He steps away from the window and takes a place near Mr. Westchester.

The back door slams. We all turn, weapons at the ready. Marta's black eyes shine as she walks into the room, a shovel and a shotgun cradled in her arms. She tosses Arnie the shotgun and moves next to her husband. He wraps an arm around her waist in a quick hug, then lifts the rifle to his shoulder.

We wait, watching the men through the window. They seem to be arguing at first, then someone pulls open the door and the mass of them crash inside.

"Who's in charge here?" the large man barks.

Mr. Jeffries steps out from behind his desk. Marta's arm reaches out, touching his shoulder, then drops back to the shovel handle. She hoists it to her shoulder like a baseball bat.

"Is what you printed true?" The man holds up the paper.

"I stand behind every word."

"And Hines really knew about it all?"

"Looks that way."

"No-good bastard." Another man rushes forward, pushing his way to the front of the group.

Heart pounding, I adjust my pistol so the barrel points at him. I notice that the others have done the same.

The man's mouth opens in surprise. He raises his hands above his head. "Sorry," he says, taking a step back. "No need for bullets. Just expressing an opinion is all."

The large man steps forward again. "I have some men here you might like to talk with." His glance moves to Mr. Westchester. "Interview and what-not. Some work at the Goliath. Some work at Granger's other mines. They might have some stories about secret tunnels and late-night digging that would interest you." He looks around the room. "That is, if you all will put your guns down and give a listen."

My pulse slows down a little. We look at one another. Mr. Jeffries nods, and I slacken my grip on the pistol. Together, we all lower our weapons. Marta turns and walks to the back room. She returns without the shovel and begins making a pot of coffee.

Mr. Jeffries offers the large man the chair in front of his desk. "If you men will be patient, Mr. Westchester, Kit, and I will talk to you one at time. Arnie, could you get some money out of my desk drawer and run to the bakery for some pastries? I'm sure these men could use a bite. Then you head back to the hospital. You've done a good job today."

Mr. Jeffries, Mr. Westchester, and I listen to the men's stories all day long. When more men stream in, we listen some more, taking notes and matching up dates and times with one another. By midafternoon, the women begin to arrive. Some carry babies; others trail toddlers behind them. They tell the stories their husbands were afraid to tell—unpredictable explosives, fires caught just in time, faulty timbers, and faked inspections.

"I'm so glad you're doing this," a young woman tells me when she gets up to leave. "I've been scared every day my Barry's gone off to work there. I just knew he was going to get covered up down there and I'd never see him again." She takes the handkerchief I offer and dabs her eyes. "Bless you." She pats my cheek. "Bless you."

I take her hand and squeeze it as tears streak down my face. "I'm just glad I could help," I murmur.

We write more articles. Articles about the families. Articles about the mine inspector who took a stage out of town hours after the collapse and has not been heard from since. And articles about the union and reorganization.

We also hear from the small miners who have claims near Granger's other mines. Their stories are much like Tom and Jesse's. Now, many insist that Granger's other mines be checked for tunnels leading onto their claims. "He's probably been robbing us all blind while we've been sitting on our thumbs waiting for the court to sort things out," one of the miners tells me.

"Tonopah's sending over a mine inspector tomorrow. Maybe you can talk to him." I scribble the name on a scrap of paper. "Not sure where he's staying, but I'd bet cash money you'll be able to find him at the Northern come nightfall."

We work late into the night, setting the print and getting the paper ready for tomorrow. At midnight, Mr. Jeffries calls it a day. "That's it. Sleep, eat, drink if you have to," he says, fluttering his hand toward the door. "The rest will wait until tomorrow. I'm going home to Marta. Kit, you take the cot in back. I don't want you wandering the streets this late."

"You never minded before."

"You weren't a girl before," he says, tugging at his beard again. His soft eyes make mine a little teary.

As I settle into the cot, I give thanks, for perhaps the first time ever, for being a girl. I'm so tired that I don't think I would have made it even as far as the stable—let alone all the way to the hospital. And I give thanks for Mr. Jeffries and Marta and even Mr. Westchester. They did good work today, and as Mother would say, they will surely be rewarded.

Chapter Thirty-Three

I wake long after the sun has come up. Men run up and down the street, shouting. I grab Papa's pistol and race to the front room. I crouch down and scooch over to the window.

Groups of men line the street. Some are holding signs with slogans like *Bosses Beware!* and *Safe Mines Now!* Others hand out leaflets. All are chanting, "An injury to one is an injury to all."

I stash the pistol, then unlock the door and join the crowd on the sidewalk. Mr. Jeffries holds up his coffee cup in greeting. "Fine morning for a strike, isn't it?" He smiles. "I hear they have Hines on the corner of Ramsey with all the other criminals. Want to take a walk and see?"

I rub the sleep from my eyes as we worm our way through the crowd. "It's like the Fourth of July," I say as I jump out of the way of a boy riding a unicycle.

"It kind of feels like the Fourth, doesn't it? Jot a note. I think that might make a good headline."

I hold out my empty hands. "No pockets."

"Dresses." Mr. Jeffries sighs. "Let's get Marta to sew some pockets on there for you."

We round the corner to Ramsey Avenue. The crowd is even

thicker here. Mr. Jeffries cuts through the throng of people, barking, "Press. Coming through. Excuse me. Official business." In seconds we're directly across from Mr. Hines.

He stands in the same place I stood just a few months ago, a piece of wood tied around his neck. *Traitor, Liar, Thief* is written on the board in bright-red paint. It looks heavy. The rope has already cut into his neck, and his shoulders are slumped. His eyes are vacant, and his gaze never leaves the ground.

He's not tied to the post, but he has been roughed up. Bruises mark the side of his face, and his lower lip looks split. I imagine the threat of more pain is enough to keep him in place. I can't help thinking that he's lucky to be alive. I wonder if he's smart enough to realize that himself.

I look around the crowd for Stewie. I catch a glimpse of him peeking around the corner of the Exploration Mercantile building. Our eyes lock. For once, he doesn't sneer or yell or throw things. Instead, he ducks his head and disappears behind the building.

I stare at the space he left. My mouth feels dry. "I think I'm going to go check on Clara," I tell Mr. Jeffries. "Meet you back in the office in an hour."

"What? Oh, sure." His eyes never leave Mr. Hines. "Poor sucker got off easy," he mutters. "I'd hate to see what they do if they get their hands on Granger."

I make my way back to the hospital slowly, tapping my fist against my lips as I try to figure out exactly what I'm feeling. How can I be happy to have exposed the truth about Mr. Hines and Mr. Granger and still sad for Stewie Hines, who never spent a minute feeling bad for me?

I'm still trying to sort through my rambling thoughts when I turn the corner to the hospital and crash right into a man coming out of the door. I jerk back, an apology already on my lips, only to see Mr. Granger's ashen face staring down at me.

"You…" I sputter. My hands go to my side—automatically trying to search my pockets for something I can use as a weapon. Stupid dress! I look around, but the street in front of the hospital is empty.

Granger staggers back a step. He pulls his hat low, so that it shields the side of his face, and glances toward the hospital door. Then he reaches a hand toward my arm.

"Don't touch me," I growl. My voice is low and steady. My body is calm. I don't flinch and I don't run. I simply stand there on the sidewalk. Hands balled into fists, breath slow and even—I meet his eyes and startle to see that they are filled with tears.

Voices shouting, "Bosses beware! Safe mines now!" cut through the silent street.

Granger's eyes go wide. "Don't let them get me!" His entire body shakes. "Please!"

I think about Mr. Jeffries's words. Would the men really kill Mr. Granger if they found him? I glance up the street. A group of men holding signs gathers at the intersection. All I have to do is yell, and they will be on Granger in a hot minute.

I turn back to him. "There's no place to run. You have to know that. We've sent the story to papers in San Francisco and Reno and even Denver."

Granger drops to his knees. His hands seize the hem of my dress. "Please. I don't want Leslie to see. I don't want her to see what they'll do to me."

My mouth goes dry. I cast a long look at the hospital door. There's no way she won't hear the commotion. No way she won't come running to see what it's about. I think about Stewie. How destroyed he looked hiding behind that building. I picture Leslie's bright eyes. Her quick laugh. I glance at the men at the end of the street again. If they don't kill him outright, they will hurt him and hurt him bad.

"Okay," I say, exhaling slowly. I position myself between Mr. Granger and the picketing men. "The police will catch you soon enough."

Mr. Granger jumps to his feet. "Bless you," he whispers. He darts down the street. I close my eyes so I don't have to see him go. I stand in the street for a long time, thinking about what I've just done.

No one will believe that I let the man who killed Papa go.

I don't think I believe it.

Still, for the first time in months, I feel free. A smile tugs at the corner of my mouth. I can almost hear Mother say, "Well done."

* * *

Things are quiet inside the hospital. Most of the beds are empty. The men who remain are the worst of the cases—and most are drugged and sleeping. Even the group around Clara's bed is somber.

"You just missed him," Leslie says. Her eyes are red and puffy.

"Who?" I ask, pitching my voice high and making my eyes wide and innocent.

"Her dad. He's leaving town. He wanted her to come along." Arnie reaches for Leslie's hand and pulls her to him.

"And you refused?"

Leslie nods.

I turn in a circle to hide my smile. "He got away?"

Clara grabs my hand, stopping me mid-turn. "He won't get far. Charges have been filed. I wager he'll be arrested soon enough." Leslie begins to cry again, but Clara smiles and feigns a chipper tone. "And Leslie's going to stay with us."

Of course she is. I guess, like Huck Finn, I am in it and in it for good. "'Might as well go the whole hog,'" I say, quoting Huck Finn though no one seems to notice. "I hope you don't mind being a little crowded."

"It's only temporary," Clara continues. "Until we can get ahold of her mama or…" She looks at Arnie and winks.

Arnie blushes, but a smile plays on his lips when he looks at Leslie.

Ugh. I made peace with them being all lovey-dovey. Can't they keep the gushy stuff to themselves?

"I also sent a telegraph to Tom and Jesse in Oregon, letting them know what's going on. Mayhap we'll hear from them in the next day or so."

"Do you really think they'll come back?"

"It's a good claim. I trust they'll want to see what it can produce."

I smile, thinking how happy Papa would have been at the thought of his friends' fortune. "When do you get to come home?"

"Well, I reckon I've been lollygagging long enough. I think I can convince Doc to turn me loose this afternoon."

Tears well up behind my eyes. I swipe them away. "Good." I turn to Arnie. "Will you give Clara and Leslie a ride to the cabin? I'll meet you all there for supper."

"We can have a bit of a party," Clara says.

A whisper of a frown crosses Leslie's eyes. I reach out and grab her hand. "A welcome home. Who knows, maybe I'll even teach you how to fry up some bacon."

Leslie sticks her tongue out at me, and something like a laugh escapes her tear-stained face.

Arnie smiles over the top of Leslie's head. "Thanks," he mouths.

"No problem," I mouth back. And for once, I really mean it.

* * *

I return to the newspaper office just in time to typeset the articles Mr. Westchester has written about the strike. "There's not a mine making money out there today," he says. His eyes gleam behind his glasses. "They're bringing in three more mine inspectors to look over every operation. The men will only go back to work when they're convinced it's safe."

I smile, happy that the men are finally taking action. "How long will that take?" I picture all those mines sitting idle. "The owners and leasers must be losing their minds."

"And rightly so, but it's not that bad. Some will be back to business tomorrow. The rest by the end of the week."

"And the union?"

"Splintered. Some of the men are working with a couple organizers from Chicago." He squints at his notes. "A new group called the IWW—the Industrial Workers of the World."

"Maybe they'll be a more honest lot."

Mr. Jeffries and Mr. Westchester exchange a knowing look. "I guess we'll see."

Before I can ask more questions, the telegraph boy runs in,

card in hand. "Should I wait for a response?" he asks as Mr. Jeffries shoves some change into his hand.

"No, no." Mr. Jeffries waves him away as he reads. "Stop printing that!" he roars. He rushes back to his desk. "They caught him. He made it to Bishop, but someone at the hotel recognized him."

He clears his throat and reads from the telegram. "Hiram L. Granger was taken into police custody at 4:38 p.m. Charged with felony theft, trespassing, negligence, and involuntary manslaughter for the events at the Goliath mine. Manslaughter charges to be added in regard to the Donovan killing."

"Manslaughter, not murder?" I can't help but think of Papa lying in the street. I run a hand through my unwashed hair. A moan escapes my throat.

Mr. Jeffries smile fades. "It's not time to fret yet." He tugs at his beard. "I will write to the attorney general. And I'll pen an editorial. We're far from beat." The skin around his eyes crinkles, and he smiles. "There's new evidence, and we have the power of the press as our weapon." He makes a sweeping gesture with his arms, taking in the whole office. "What's Mark Twain say? 'Right is right.'"

"...and 'wrong is wrong.'" I exhale for all I'm worth. Mr. Twain's advice has mostly worked so far. Who am I to doubt him now?

I hurry to set the type for the article Mr. Jeffries scribbles about Granger's arrest. "Is that all for today? I only ask because Clara is coming home and we wanted to have a bit of a celebration."

I turn and look at Mr. Jeffries and Mr. Westchester bent over their desks. The sight of them working so hard makes my chest feel light, but full at the same time. "Would you like to come—and Marta too, of course? It's not fancy, just supper and visiting, but I'd be real happy if you would join us."

Mr. Jeffries and Mr. Westchester look at each other.

"Well, umm…" Mr. Jeffries says.

Mr. Westchester scowls at him. "We'd be honored, Kit. An early night will be good for all of us."

Mr. Jeffries hurries to get Marta, while Mr. Westchester and I head to the bakery to buy a cake to take as a surprise.

As we all walk toward the cabin, Mr. Jeffries outlines ideas for future articles. "Mark my words, the boom is only beginning. Goldfield will be bigger than Tonopah in no time. Bigger than Reno even."

The door bursts open before I can even touch it. "Come in! Come in!" Clara urges, pulling us inside. The cabin has been scrubbed top to bottom, and the table is set with actual china. "We had help." Clara grins, nodding at the woman sitting on a stool in the corner.

"Aunt Minerva!" A slow grin spreads across my face.

Aunt Minerva smiles, and for a moment she looks just like Mother. "Don't forget Sophie and Casey," she says, indicating the women standing next to her.

Leslie, Arnie, and Clara join hands and begin singing, "For she's a jolly good fellow…" Mr. Westchester, Mr. Jeffries, Marta, Casey, and Sophie join in, the whole lot of them sounding an awful lot like the Ladies' Aid Society. Aunt Minerva doesn't sing, but she does smile through the whole thing, so that's almost as good.

I wipe the tears from my eyes as Clara pulls me into a hug. "I thought this was a party for you," I whisper as I hug her back, hard. I swear I feel a teardrop hit the top of my head.

She clears her throat. "Let's eat. Everyone sit."

We all gather around the table. The talk is lively, and the food is good. Even the sight of Arnie and Leslie holding hands and laughing doesn't quell the warm feeling that wraps itself around my chest.

Memories of dinners like this—of Mother and Papa joking and laughing—come to mind, and for once they don't make me sad, at least not too sad. "Mother would have liked this," I whisper to Aunt Minerva.

Tears spring into Aunt Minerva's eyes. She reaches out and tucks a strand of hair behind my ear. "She'd be very proud of you, Katherine. You're becoming quite the lady."

I blush. Maybe I am. Maybe not exactly in the way Mother intended, but maybe in all the ways that count.

Before she leaves, Aunt Minerva reminds me of her new house in Tonopah. "Building should be complete middle of August. I'd really like it if you and Clara came to live with me." She smiles at Clara, who takes her hand. Then she presses a wrapped package into my lap. "For inspiration," she says with a wink. "Open it later."

That evening, after everyone has left and Clara and Leslie have gone to bed, I open Aunt Minerva's package. It's a book titled *Around the World in Seventy-Two Days*. I open the cover and read the inscription.

> To my niece, Katherine. May you continue to use your
> pen for good—and may Miss Bly inspire not only
> your writing, but your life. Always remember, even la-
> dies can have adventures. All you need is a good dress,

a sturdy pair of shoes, and a firm resolve, and you will
do well.
With love,
Your Aunt Minerva

I hug the book to my chest. Then I pull my keepsake box out from under my bed. I take my time, going through it piece by piece. I find a picture of Mother taken long ago on her wedding day and another of Papa standing in front of his store in Baltimore. I tuck both inside my copy of *The Adventures of Huckleberry Finn* and place it inside the box, along with the newspapers detailing the events of the last few days. Then I slide the whole thing back under my cot.

I open the book Aunt Minerva gave me and spend the night reading about Nellie Bly's proposal to travel all the way around the world by herself. I can't help but wonder what Mother would think of a lady like that.

Chapter Thirty-Four

Mark Twain wrote, "Average men don't like trouble and danger," and I reckon that's the truth. I know it was true for Papa at least. And for Tom and Jesse who ran from trouble faster than Tom Sawyer himself. But Mr. Twain didn't say anything about the average woman.

Come to think of it, few folks famous for either writing or talking mention women at all—average or not. I wonder why that is.

I ponder the thought as I take in the scene in front of me. It's been over a month since the mine collapse and Mr. Granger's arrest, and, for the most part, life in Goldfield has returned to normal. The mines are up and running again, and business is booming. The corner of Main Street and Ramsey Avenue is teeming with people stirring up dust and milling about the street and sidewalks. The first train from Tonopah is scheduled to arrive tomorrow, and the town is abuzz with preparations for the Railroad Days celebration. Tulle and colorful banners line Main Street in anticipation of the big event, and the women of the Ladies' Aid Society already have a stage set up and are practicing their songs—out of tune as ever—may God or Mr. Hessel's barbershop quartet save us. Newsboys hand out flyers announcing prize fights and drilling contests and even a tug-of-war, and stores up and down the block advertise candied apples and popcorn balls and some sugary concoction called fairy floss that I can hardly wait to try.

I tuck the book Aunt Minerva left me in my dress pocket and adjust my newsboy hat to what I hope is a rakish angle. I pull my notebook and pencil out of another pocket and commence recording the scene in front of me. I'm nearly done describing the boy-size man riding a unicycle and juggling beer bottles when a blur of skirts catches my eye. Miss Sheldon hurries across the crowded street, darting around a mule team and two motorbikes whose riders are circling each other, chests puffed out, fists raised to strike.

She catches me watching her and falters for a minute, but quickly regains her composure and swoops past me. She would have made it into Exploration Mercantile without speaking to me at all—and truth be told she nearly did—if only she had been the slightest bit faster or if her fine skirt had been a tiniest bit shorter. But the skirt is long and elegant and trails behind her like a cloud, swooping over dirt and sidewalk, until the delicate lace catches on a nail sticking up on one of the steps, and brings her swooping to a sudden and bucking halt.

"Good morning, Miss Sheldon." I bend down and untangle the lace from the nail.

"Katherine." She smooths out her skirt, checking for a tear. "Barbaric town. I'm looking forward to leaving on the first train."

"You may have to wait for the second." I tap the notebook in my hand. "The first ride is reserved for dignitaries and the like."

Miss Sheldon sniffs. "The second then."

I consider doing the polite thing and saying I'm sorry to see her go and that I wish her good luck in her endeavors, whatever they might be. I really do chew on the idea for a second or two. I even try two or three ways to phrase it in my head, but, as Huck Finn says, "You can't pray a lie." I don't think you can wish one either—at least not convincingly and certainly not with a clear heart. "Perhaps life will be more to your liking elsewhere," I say, pleased with both my word choice and my clear conscience.

"Perhaps." She frowns like she's not fully convinced of the possibility herself. She hesitates, waiting for the stock boy to open the door for her, then enters the mercantile quickly without a backward glance.

I roll my eyes, but I can't help noticing that all the swoop has gone out of her step.

A sinking feeling crashes into my stomach, settling there. I actually feel sorry for Miss Sheldon. I may even miss her when school starts up again next week. The thought makes me laugh an inside-your-chest kind of laugh. Maybe it wouldn't kill me to wish her good luck after all. Heck, maybe it would even do me some good. I'm fairly certain Mother would agree with that sentiment. I can practically see her nodding as I stick my head into Exploration Mercantile and peer through the semidarkness. Before I can change my mind, I call out, "Good luck, Miss Sheldon. I really did learn a lot from you."

She turns. Her blue eyes shine as she stomps over to the door and hisses, "Clearly I did not teach you nearly enough. Yelling across a room like a wild person." She clucks her tongue and glares at me. "Will you never learn to act like a lady, Katherine?" She turns on her heel and flounces back inside.

I snort back a laugh. "Good luck and good riddance, ma'am."

I tip my hat in a jaunty wave, catching the eye of the shopkeeper, who ducks his head and struggles not to laugh.

I grip my own skirt in my hand and stride across the dusty street. The men have either finished their fight or abandoned it before the fisticuffs began, because traffic is moving briskly once again. Miss Sheldon has given me an idea.

I run across town, dodging workmen and slipping by women and children on their way to help with the festivities. I run all the way to the newly built train station. The clean pine boards and crisp black paint are so fresh, so full of promise and industry, that I pause for a long moment to admire it. "Progress." I say the word right out loud, startling the ticket agent and the half-asleep dog sprawled across the bench.

I study the handwritten schedule tacked to the wall. My heart speeds up as I consider my options. "One ticket, please. Round trip." I set my money on the counter. "Tonopah and back."

"First one's full up—unless you're someone important." The agent squints across the counter. "You someone important?"

I push my hat out of my eyes and smile. "Kit Donovan, world-class reporter and adventurer extraordinaire." I hold out a hand for him to shake.

The ticket agent blushes and takes my hand. "Pleasure, miss." He slides a ticket across the counter. "Enjoy your trip."

I peek at the slip of paper. It takes every ounce of self-discipline I possess not to squeal with joy. A first-run ticket on the new train! I pull out my book and tuck the ticket carefully inside. Once I'm certain it's safe, I skip away from the counter.

I sit on the bench. On my right, a finely dressed man reads a newspaper. On my left, a dog rolls on his back and drools. I smile a howdy at them both and take out my notebook. For once, I'm happy to blend in with the crowd.

I find a clean page and compose one final promise. September 13, 1905. *I, Kit Donovan, vow to live up to the moniker "world-class reporter and adventurer extraordinaire." Perhaps I will even become a lady in the process.* I smile at the thought—and part of me is nearly certain that somewhere Mother is smiling too.

I look around the train station, smelling the mixture of fresh-cut pine and crushed sage and admiring the way the tracks glint in the midmorning sun. I squint at the ribbon of gleaming metal running out into the wide and empty desert. It almost looks like a streak of gold in a quartz vein. I turn back to my notebook and scribble the thought before it skitters out of my head and is lost in the wind.

Heck, even Nellie Bly had to start somewhere—and Goldfield, Nevada, is as fine a place as any. I laugh as the man beside me lights up a cigar and the cur jumps off the bench with a groan. Well, maybe it's not exactly fine. At least not yet. It's still full of dogs and dirt and a despicable person or two. But, as Mother once said, it does have potential. And, who knows, maybe I do too.

Author's Note

One of the great joys of writing is getting to immerse yourself in times and places vastly different from your own. I've been lucky enough to spend the last few years of my life walking in two worlds. While most of me has been here, living my life in a small Oregon town, a part of me has been walking the streets of 1905 Goldfield, Nevada, with Kit. A turn-of-the-century boomtown is an interesting place to reside—full of strange events and fascinating people. Though Kit, her family, Arnie, Clara, Mr. Jeffries, Marta, and the Grangers are fictional, I included some real-life people who came through Goldfield in this novel and tried to stay as near to the truth (as I understood it) as possible.

Goldfield is an actual town in South Central Nevada. Gold was first discovered there as early as 1900 or 1901 by a Shoshone man named Tom Fisherman. In 1902, two young men, Harry Stimler and William Marsh, located the first claim, and a boomtown was born. Like most gold rush towns, Goldfield started out as a camp. People lived in tents and hastily built cabins. Because lumber was scarce, people used whatever they could find to build houses—including barrels, bottles, and even a boulder that had been hollowed out. As more gold was discovered and the camp grew into an actual town, people began to use more substantial materials—building houses, hotels, offices, stores, churches, and saloons out of lumber, brick, and stone. By 1907, Goldfield had reached a population of over 20,000 people and was the largest city in Nevada. You can still visit Goldfield today and see many of the old buildings (including a haunted hotel) and the cemetery (where one man is buried after dying from eating paste). You can even attend their annual Goldfield Days celebration.

Western Shoshone men, women, and children—like the character of Arnie—lived in and around Goldfield in 1905. The rush of prospectors looking to strike it rich pushed many of the Shoshone people to the edge of the mostly white town. Though a couple of Shoshone men like Tom Fisherman and Harry Stimler are remembered for the parts they played in putting Goldfield on the map, the Shoshone people received little of the wealth and prosperity the goldfields produced.

Virgil Earp, the lawman made famous by the legendary gunfight at the O.K. Corral in Tombstone, Arizona, came to Goldfield in 1904. He worked as a deputy sheriff there until he died of pneumonia in October 1905.

Jackson "Diamondfield Jack" Davis was a gunman and prospector in Goldfield. He established many mining camps in Nevada, including one he named after himself—Diamondfield. He probably never stole a hiding place from a young girl during a shoot-out.

Doc Adkins made many memorable plays throughout his baseball career, but it was his work as a pitcher for the Baltimore Orioles that Kit would have been thinking of when she threw that rock at Leslie.

Cozad's Dog, Pony, Monkey, and Goat Circus did indeed come to Goldfield in 1905. The animals performed tricks as well as dramas and comedies, and there really were three hundred Shetland ponies giving free rides to the children that day.

Father Dermondy was the Irish priest of Goldfield's Sacred Heart Catholic Church. Much loved, Father Dermondy was known for his good will and charity to everyone in town.

President Teddy Roosevelt's children did indeed have a badger named Josiah as part of their White House menagerie that also included a lizard named Bill, a pig named Maude, and a bear named Jonathan Edward—as well as a host of other animals both large and small.

A leaking gas stove in the Bon Ton Millinery is believed to be the cause of the fire that swept through Goldfield on July 8, 1905. The city was nearly lost when the water pressure dropped, until Bert Ulmer of the Little Hub Saloon thought to use beer to protect his building from the flames. The idea caught on, and soon townspeople and firefighters were rolling out kegs of beer from local saloons to stop the fire. And, yes, the parrot Mr. Jeffries mentions does exist in newspaper reports of the fire. The parrot is reported to have been rescued by his owner only to have flown back to his cage in the burning building—calling out "Fire! Fire!" until he died.

The Mizpah Hotel is an actual hotel in Tonopah, Nevada, and it's still in business. You can stay in one of their forty-eight rooms and even see the beautiful elevator that caught Kit's eye in the story. The Mizpah didn't open until 1907, but it was one of the finest luxury hotels in Nevada, so I couldn't resist taking some authorial license with the dates. It just seemed like the perfect place for Kit to run into Aunt Minerva.

In September 1905 Goldfield celebrated the long-awaited arrival of the first train on the new Tonopah and Goldfield Railroad. Townspeople marked the occasion with great fanfare, including games, food, and even a visit from the governor of Nevada, John Sparks. I'm pretty sure there was fairy floss too.

Acknowledgments

As Old Joe Smiley said, "It's amazing what can be done when folks pull together." Writing and publishing a book is one of those things that takes a community, and I am forever grateful for mine.

Big thanks—

To agent extraordinaire, Kerry Sparks. Signing with you felt like winning the lottery. I could not ask for a better partner and guide on this publishing journey. Your sense of humor and rock-star business sense are hugely appreciated. The fact that you're an Oregon girl is just icing on the cake.

To my lovely editor, Kristin, and everyone at Albert Whitman & Company. You've made my first publishing experience a true joy. Thanks so much for your kind insight and real enthusiasm for Kit and her story.

To the wonderful people at Fishtrap. Your fellowship came at a perfect time in my writing life. You gave me the boost I needed to write this novel and introduced me to an incredible writing community. I'm forever in your debt.

To Oregon Literary Arts. Your 2013 fellowship made all the difference. You confirmed my belief in this story and the financial assistance helped me create a publishable novel. I'm so incredibly grateful.

To my critique group, Ruth, Judy, and Katrina. Your wise comments, generous support, and beautiful stories fill my well each week. Thanks so much for reading work that's never quite ready and sharing the hardships and the joys of this business.

To Drew and Deborah. Writing can be a solitary venture. Our

email and Skype chats about words, books, and life sustain me more than you know.

To Christina. Thanks for reading Kit's story. It's such a treat to share this writing life with a friend I've had since childhood. Go Raiders.

To Allison. Thank you for your unwavering interest in this book. You are a beautiful friend.

To SCBWI Oregon. Thanks for organizing such a vibrant and welcoming writing community.

To Lorin and Brenda and everyone else at BONI 2013. Your thoughtful critique helped shape Kit's story into the book that you see today. I couldn't be more grateful.

To my Class of 2k17 debut group. It's been a pleasure to get to hang out with such a talented, smart, and kind group of writers. You've made being a new author a fun adventure.

To the nameless man at the rock shop in Goldfield. You gave me my first glimpse at Goldfield's fascinating history. Our quick conversation changed my life. Thank you.

To Virginia, whose impromptu tour of Goldfield was priceless. Thanks for jumping in the car with a couple of strangers and giving us such a wonderful history lesson.

To the great folks at the Central Nevada Museum and the Tonopah Historic Mining Park. Thanks for answering all my questions, opening up the archives, and generally helping a writer out. Your exhibits sparked my imagination and gave me the details I needed to hook this story together.

To the many teachers and librarians who put books into my eager hands all those years ago. Your hard work didn't go unnoticed.

To my students. Thank you for inspiring me every day.

To my mom. You've taught me so much about strength and perseverance. I tried my best to give some of that toughness to Kit.

Finally, to John. You've supported me, studied with me, listened to me, and wandered many dirt roads and historic cemeteries with me. I could not have done this without you.